Saved By His Submissive

The W.I.L.D. Boys of Special Forces

Book 1

By Angel Payne

5-30-15

Jill!!
← How awesome
to see you, sweet
woman!! Thank
you for being my New
York guiding light!
Angel :)

Saved By His Submissive
Copyright © 2013 Angel Payne Writes, LLC
Second edition © 2014 Angel Payne Writes, LLC

All Rights Reserved
ISBN: 978-0-9888701-2-3

Published by Angel Payne Writes, LLC

Edited By:
Jacy Mackin
Tracy Roelle
Meredith Bowery

Cover Art
Rachel Rivera – Parajunkee Design
www.parajunkee.net

Dedication
Nobody does it better…my Sir, you are my hero, always.

Acknowledgements
Shayla: Again I find myself deeply, profoundly grateful for you.
Your continued belief in me is such a gift. Thank you.

Lexi: You're just a damn genius, and don't deny it. I'm so excited
for our new friendship.

Dee: Your gorgeous artistry brought Garrett to life with such
delicious decadence!
Thank you for one of my favorite covers ever…EVER! On to Zeke!
You ready, woman?

Special Thanks to the Angel's Wings: the best damn street team a
dork like me could ask for!
You guys literally ARE wings, lifting me up so many times when
I've needed it,
and I love every single one of you.

Very special thanks to the men and women of our armed forces.
You are ALL special, each and every day.

A portion of the profits from this book will be donated to the
following fine organizations.
Please support them:
Wounded Warrior Project
Special Operations Warrior Foundation
DAV Homeless Veterans Initiative

Chapter One

Heaven. He had to have died at last, and somehow—*God only knew how*—ended up beyond the pearly gates.

Garrett Hawkins didn't bother questioning the admission details beyond that. No sense in tempting Saint Peter, or whoever the fuck was standing watch today, into checking notes and realizing a mistake had been made. Wouldn't do the guy any good. At this point, Garrett wasn't past blowing the balls off anyone who told him he had to leave.

The deal was, Heaven was nothing like the scene they'd taught him in summer Bible school. No sugar-spun clouds. No bad haircuts. Not a single angel with a half-tuned harp.

Heaven was silk sheets, his tongue on the inside of Sage Weston's left thigh—and her answering sigh because of it.

"Garrett! Damn it! Higher. Please…higher!"

He chuckled and sank a soft bite into her tawny flesh. "Is that any way to talk in Heaven, sugar? Quiet. You're gonna get us tossed out."

He spoke the last of it as he crossed to her other thigh, making sure his mouth brushed over her glistening, spread pussy in the process. Christ, how he wanted to stop there, and he thought about it as he watched new drops of arousal on her sweet pink folds, but there would be time to return for all that sweet ambrosia and then some. In Heaven, they finally had all the time they needed.

A shiver claimed the new skin that he began to suckle and lick. "Sergeant Hawkins, you're making me insane!"

"I hope so."

"Ohhhh! Bastard!"

"Mmmm. You taste like cream and honey."

"*Garrett!*"

He sighed and laughed again. "So impatient. So greedy." He trailed his lips toward her knee, inciting another protesting moan from the silk ribbons of her lips.

"Impatient? You've been teasing me like this forever!"

"And isn't it fun?"

"I hate you."

"No you don't."

"I'm leaving."

"No you aren't."

He was about to taunt the inside of her ankle when she really did yank it away from him. He raised his head in question, only to have the back of it bonked by her other foot as she swung that over the edge of the bed as well. "Sage! Hey!"

"Don't pull petulant on me, Garrett Hawkins. I invented it, and I do it way better than you."

He almost smiled. She'd been a ball of sass and fire since they'd met at that dive bar in Tacoma, and he loved her a little more every time she rekindled the attitude. It also made up his mind about the next words out of his mouth, issued as a deep and heated growl.

"You're not going anywhere, Ms. Weston."

Her eyes widened, ablaze with bright peridot shock. She pushed out her chin and tacked on a smirk. "Is that so, Sergeant?" She stepped into a little white thong trimmed in sexy-as-hell pink lace then tugged on a white tank over the bra he hadn't gotten the chance to get off yet. "Why don't you watch me?"

He laughed, though the sound was made of anger, not mirth. Thanks to the countless sessions with Shrink Sally, as he'd affectionately come to call the poor woman assigned to "fix" him a year ago, he also recognized that the rage was directed at the guy in the mirror across the room, not the woman in front of him. That only tripled the resolve for his next action.

Without giving her any warning, Garrett hooked two fingers into the lace at her hip and pulled hard. The surge of her body returning to his side matched the rush of joy in his blood and the roar of arousal in his cock. This was where she belonged. This was so fucking right.

With a grunt, he twisted the panties tighter. The fabric gave way in his grip. It fell away, exposing her incredible golden hips. Sage let a gape fly at him, though he took that from her too, ramming their lips together while he pulled her

2

and flattened her to the bed again.

"I've got a better idea," he growled, rolling his hips so she felt every pounding inch of his erection. "Why don't *you* watch *me,* sugar?"

She did just that, lashes jerked wide from those brilliant green eyes, as he jammed both her arms over her head then lashed them together using one of the bungee cords off his mission pack. For a second, he wondered why his pack made it to Heaven with him, but he was too grateful to question the issue for long. It was just as weird that her old bed had made it too, a wrought-iron thing he'd never liked much, thanks to its headboard full of fancy curlicues that tangled with each other like a damn tumbleweed. But right now, he was really grateful for the thing. The two bungee hooks fit perfectly around a couple of whorls in the headboard.

With a frustrated whimper, Sage wrenched her arms. "Wh-what are you doing?" She craned her neck, exposing the nervous drum of her carotid. "Garrett, why—"

"I told you." He stated it with steeled calm. "I'm not letting you leave. It was a mistake to do that the first time. It was a mistake not to go after you. So now I'm keeping you right here, safe with me. Just trust me, my heart. You're going to be very happy." Without preamble, he tore her tank top down the middle now. "And very satisfied."

Her breath caught on a sexy-as-hell hitch. "My hero." The sigh changed her voice, too. Her tone transformed from incensed to breathless, but climbed into a strained cry when he took care of her front bra clasp with one deft snap. "Oh…mmmm!" She moaned then arched into the fingers he trailed around her dark berry nipples, pushing her puckered fruit up at him. He gave into the craving to sample one with deeper intent, pinching the nub and then pulling. Hard.

"Shit! Ohhh Garrett!"

Damn. Her startled cry made him want to try it on the other nipple, and he did. Both her areolas were red and irritated now, their tiny bumps standing in attention around the distended peaks at their center.

To his perplexity—to his shame—he got painfully hard.

3

That didn't stop him from getting greedy. With both of his hands on her tits now, he couldn't resist tugging on both her beautiful nipples at the same time.

"Damn it!" she screamed. "Garrett, th-that hurts! Oh, God! Oh...mmmmm..."

She fell into an enraptured moan as he made up for the man-pig behavior, soothing each breast with long, tender licks. That wasn't a huge help to his aching body. His cock had gotten more hard and hot, throbbing between their stomachs. He shifted a little so he could dip his hand between her thighs, intending to continue his gratitude by giving her pussy a nice little rubdown—but what he discovered had him grinning in delighted shock. Her tunnel was gushing, warm, and creamy for him. She took one finger, then two, then three, her walls secreting more tangy juices all over his skin. Her arousal revved his mouth again. He pulled his tongue back from her nipple and bit into the stiff nub.

Her whole body bucked off the mattress. "Garrett! Hell! Why are you doing that?"

"Because you like it." He said it to her ear as he worked a fourth finger into her. With one of his thighs, he shoved hard on the knee he'd just been worshipping, opening her legs wider for him. "Because the pain makes you wet for me."

He dragged his mouth against hers again, but this time she didn't let him into her wet heat. She opened her lips only enough to get her teeth into his bottom lip.

"Damn you to Hades." She whispered it with her teeth still anchored in his flesh. He yanked back, licking at the flesh she'd torn open, though he did it on a dark smile.

"Too late, sugar. I think my passport's already got that stamp."

She looked adorable as she rolled her eyes. "Which is why you're in Heaven with me?"

Before he answered that, he did kiss her. He did it thoroughly and desperately, possessing her tongue in bold sweeps, permanently tangling his essence with hers.

"We've always lived on borrowed time, my heart. We both know it." He gripped her leg, hooking her knee around his shoulder. "Which is why I'm going to fuck you hard now. Which is why you're going to let me. Which is why you're going to love it."

Her eyes shimmered with tears. Her lips lifted in a misty smile. "Okay."

His penis surged against his fingers as he guided himself to her tight, moist entrance. "Tell me you want it."

"I want it, baby." Her obedience didn't land him in Heaven again. It made his whole heart and soul turn into paradise. "I want your hot cock, Garrett. Please. Now. Deep inside me."

"Yeah." He swirled the searing pre-cum around his bulging head, then pushed himself into the first inch of her channel. "Oh yeah, sugar."

"Garrett." Her strident gasp filled him. "Garrett...Garrett..."

"Soon, my heart. Soon."

"Garrett! Fuck, man. Open the door!"

What the hell?

His fiancé suddenly sounded like his best friend. Correction: his demanding, door-pounding, subtle-as-a-linebacker, *ex* best friend.

"Hawkins! Get your ass out of bed and answer the door!"

Garrett's eyes flew open. He squeezed them shut again. "No." His voice was a croak, absorbed by the grimy walls of the room in this no-name Bangkok hotel he'd checked into last night. He looked down, trying to piece together this new truth. The pre-cum was real. One of his hands was still wet with the stuff. His fingers were also really wrapped around his aching boner, as he lay beneath a mound of cheap, cloying sheets.

Sage was nowhere to be found.

Of course not.

Because she was dead. For a year, two months, sixteen days, and almost twenty-four hours now.

The knives of grief, all ten million of them, re-buried in his chest. As he gulped through the resulting dearth of air, he raised his clean hand to his chest, scrabbling for his dog tags.

More accurately, he searched for the gold band that hung on the chain between them.

Though his head ordered him not to do it, he slipped his ring finger back through the band. For one wonderful, extra moment, the knives went away, and he relived the day he and Sage had picked out the jewelry…the day when he'd thought it would soon become a part of his wardrobe for good.

He remembered every detail of how beautiful she'd looked. It had been a brilliant late spring day. Her hair was a cascade of light brown sugar that earned her his favorite nickname, falling against the freckled shoulders that peeked from her pink sundress. But her smile…ah, he remembered that the best. Her lips had glistened with her joyous tears, and quavered with her soft whisper.

I can't wait until you get to wear it for good. I can't wait until you're all mine.

A month later, he'd gotten the phone call from Heidi Weston that upended his world forever. The woman who was preparing to become his mother in-law stammered that he needed to come over right away. He'd actually packed a bag, thinking Sage had been hurt, maybe badly, judging by the sound of Heidi's voice. He was prepared to stay long enough to get as much info as he could about her condition, then head for the base to force himself onto whatever flight was headed anywhere near Botswana. When he'd walked in to see the CNO and the Chaplain sitting there, each holding the hand of a sobbing Heidi, his knees hit the floor along with his pack. Only half their words reached his brain through his roaring senses. *Tribal warfare…region unexpectedly unstable…van sidetracked off the main road…likely rebels…found burned out…nothing but ashes found…*

He swallowed hard, and pulled his finger back out of the ring. As expected, his brain crowed while his heart screamed on the torture rack of memory. He waited, breathing hard, for the agony to end. He begged the wounds to bleed hard and fast, letting the anger get here and turn the pain into a scab. After that, he'd be able to move again. To function again.

"Hawk! Damn you, man!"

6

Anger moved in on the grief. Thank fuck. Fortunately, nothing got him more pissed off than Zeke's mommy hen act. After rolling from the bed, he tugged on his briefs then stumbled across the room. The dirty light and traffic sounds beyond the thin shutters told him it was about midday. Or maybe his growling stomach did.

"Okay, why are your panties in a wad?" He glanced at Zeke after opening the door, the last of his grogginess obliterated by the neon Hawaiian print of his friend's tacky tourist ensemble. Z's khaki shorts were clearly on his timber log legs for one purpose: covering his sorry ass. Like anyone would notice the damn thing after getting blinded by the lime green and banana yellow shirt. "Don't tell me you're bored, with all of Bangkok out there for the taking. We don't roll on this mission until nightfall. That gives you at least five hours to work your flogging arm and your kinky cock through a lot of cheap tail, my friend. I'll bet the girls at Club Subjugate are missing you something fierce, Sir Zekie."

"Sir Zekie. Aw. That's cute, honey." The guy busted into the room, kicking the door shut behind him. Zeke's six-foot-six frame was only a couple of inches taller than Garrett's, but the man's mountainous build intensified the effect of his stature, especially in this room designed for people half his size. "As much as Chelsea and Chyna like my side-by-side spanking special, shit like that gets redundant by myself. You tried the fun-filled dungeon field trip once. Think you want to sign up this time?"

Garrett snorted and flopped on the bed again. His friend wasted his breath with the memory. Yeah, he'd gone. Yeah, he'd tried it. Z had gotten him in a weak spot around the six-month mark after Sage's death. He'd been desperate to forget the pain for a while, hoping "the magic of BDSM," as Z called it, would help. More urgently, he'd been hoping to figure out the kinky-minded demon that crawled in the back of his imagination since—

Well, he knew since when. And that secret would go with him to his grave. An occasion, God willing, that would come sooner than later.

7

Needless to say, he'd scratched the itch just fine that night. Or as truth would have it, hadn't scratched. That part of things wasn't such a state secret, which justified the response he tossed at his friend.

"You really think that offer's relevant?"

Z shrugged. "Lots of water has passed under your bridge, dude. Maybe commanding a sweet little subbie will fire your rockets this time around."

"No," Garrett snapped, "it won't."

"Right. Because you'd rather stay here and just beat off after your wet dreams about Sage."

"Fuck off."

"It's been over a year, Hawk."

"Fuck *off.*"

"Fine." Z pulled the faded Yankees cap off his head, revealing the miniature broadcasting station literally sewn inside it, before scrubbing a hand through his thick dark brown hair. "Turns out free time just got drastically cut, anyhow. That's why I'm here collecting your sorry ass."

He'd just cracked open a lukewarm soda and was about to take his first guzzle. He stopped the can halfway to his lips and shot a quizzical look across the room. "What do you mean, 'cut?'"

Zeke dropped into the room's sole chair and shrugged. "CENTCOMM received a line of new intel. Seems we're gonna be more effective going in to rescue these girls as the bad-ass, uniformed machines we've been trained to be, instead of a bunch of American dorkgasms looking for some girl-next-door type pussy." He stretched his tree trunk legs out, crossing them at the ankle on the foot of the bed. "So as soon as you get your ass dressed, we're buggin' back to the embassy. They're gonna let us change, and get haircuts and shaves." He scratched the scruff on his jaw. "Thank all that's holy."

Garrett cracked a dry smirk. "You sure it's just not because you blew our cover with that shirt? Maybe somebody with half a brain looked at you, and realized no normal person, even a dorkgasm, would willingly dress in that."

Z looked at his get-up with a frown. "What's wrong

with the shirt?"

"Oh c'mon. It's hideous. It's not yours, is it? Central gave it to you, right?"

"Yeah, uhhh, right."

Zeke followed up his hasty answer by cracking one of the shutters and feigning interest in the activity outside. Garrett rose, shoved into jeans and a plain white T-shirt, and listened to the scene that his friend beheld. Scooters zoomed, taxi drivers argued, bicycle bells dinged, and food sizzled. All in all, it was a typical day in Bangkok: probably the same kind of day that ten American aid workers had been enjoying just six weeks ago, before they were scheduled to board a plane for their mission in Myanmar.

The five men and five women had never arrived for their flight. Two days later, the men had been returned unharmed, spelling out the abductors' purpose with more clarity than a Soi Cowboy tittie bar sign. Undercover CIA agents had been rapidly inserted on the case, and sure enough, after ample questions were asked and money tossed around, they were invited in on the newest trend for discerning American businessmen looking for a good time in East Asia: American girls who would do everything a native girl would, at exactly the same price.

Tonight, the assholes running the racket were going to find a new surprise waiting for their sorry dicks. Garrett's blood surged with the anticipation of delivering that surprise. He hoisted his pack, slipped into his "lazy American tourist" loafers then cocked his head at Zeke.

"You gonna sit there moping because I called your shirt a fashion disaster? Come on, Fashion Sparkle Barbie. Let's depart this fair establishment."

To his perplexity, Zeke didn't budge. He closed the shutter with unnerving calm. "Just another sec, Hawk."

The gnat of suspicion in his senses morphed into a mosquito. "What is it?"

"Sit down. There's one more thing we gotta discuss."

The mosquito started biting. "No," Garrett snapped, "there isn't."

9

Without looking back at Z, he went for the door. He had his hand on the knob before his friend's rejoinder hit the air.

"You don't get to load up for the op unless we drill down on this."

Garrett watched his fingers go white around the knob. Officially he and Zeke were equal rank, but his friend's tone clearly pulled a top dog on him. That only meant one thing.

"Franzen put you up to this, didn't he?"

Z lowered his legs then balanced his elbows on his knees. When he lifted his head, deep assessment defined his stare. Garrett almost rolled his eyes in return, but he caught sight of himself in the dusty mirror over the bureau. His hair, a nice gold when it was clean but the color of a worn dishrag now, was as rumpled and long as Zeke's dark brown waves. His eyes also looked like rags, blue ones that'd been used on muddy boots. His skin was sallow. He hadn't slept well since—well, in over a year—and it showed in every wrinkled, grungy inch of him.

He scowled. If he was Franz, he'd likely have a few concerns about adding his name to the mission roster too. It didn't matter that he'd proved himself on over three dozen ops in the last year. He knew the concern was for *this* trip. He didn't have to be told why. But he'd put up with the formality anyway.

"Yeah, okay," Zeke conceded. "The Captain and I had a brief talk about your involvement on this one. You're a key piece of the team, Hawk. We could really use you. Even though you look like crap, your reflexes are still the best on the squad. You're able to make smart snap judgments even if the shit gets thick and the op goes sideways."

Garrett dropped his pack and leaned against the door. "Are you planning that much on this one taking a detour?"

"No. Hell, no." Like the protest about the shirt, his friend's answer flew out suspiciously fast. "It's just—we're gonna be deep in the forest on this one, G. I wouldn't be surprised if we come across fucking Jurassic Park or something."

"You know Jurassic Park is technically off the coast of Costa Rica and not Thailand, right?"

"It's sick that you know that."

"It's pathetic that you don't read."

His buddy's stubbled chin gave way to a grin. "And it's nice to see you getting pissy about something." In a murmur, he added, "Maybe there's hope for your humanity after all, Hawkins."

"Shut up and get to your point."

Zeke let the smile fall. "Okey dokey, Prince Charming." He rose and crossed his arms. "To be frank, the Captain and I are concerned about your focus on this one."

A needle of irritation joined the knives in his chest. "That's never been an issue before."

"We've never been called to retrieve hostages before."

Garrett snorted. "Yeah, what about that? The Rangers and Delta getting their nails done or something?"

"You think I know or care? The op is what it is. More importantly, the hostages are what they are. American women, many with fair hair and eyes." Z leaned forward, intensifying his gaze. "I need to know you can keep the emo lock box down on this, G. Complete objectivity. These girls will be terrified and traumatized, but our main objective is to get them to safety using any means necessary. The conditions will be shitty and the time frame will be worse. I need to know you can do that. I need to *know* you're gonna maintain your edge."

Garrett pushed off the door in order to take a determined stance. He bolted his stare into Zeke's now, unwavering in his purpose, unblinking in his concentration.

"You think I'm gonna go cookie crumbs on you because some girl *looks* like her?" He shot out a bitter laugh. "You think that alone would do it? You really don't remember what Sage and I had, do you?"

"Why do I need to? You're doing the job to stellar perfection for me and half the world."

"And?"

Zeke's eyes slid shut and his mouth tightened, his version of contrition for the accusing words. "You haven't let

11

go of her. You still got that goddamn ring hiding between your tags, which should be secured to your bootlaces, assface, *not* your sorry neck. I can write you up faster than—"

Garrett cut him off with a derisive laugh. "Oh, that would be entertaining."

"Listen, moron. I've got genuine concerns here, Garrett."

"Got it, Oprah. Can I get you a tampon for that now?"

Zeke closed the space between them in one wide step. His jaw went harder beneath his stubble. "What you can do, damn it, is look me in the eye and swear to me that you're squared with the personal shit and are solid to go on this op."

Garrett notched back his shoulders and set his own jaw. He confronted the stare of his friend again. He'd seen those hazels oiled with booze, bleary with exhaustion, afire with adrenalin and likely a thousand other things. But this was one look he always treated with respect. The stare of the guy who would be at his side out there in Jurassic Land, holding the gun that could save Garrett's life. He'd be counting on Garrett to do the exact same.

"I'm solid," he said. "And you know I'd tell you otherwise, Z." The last shrouds of his dream fell away from his mind, dissolved by the salvation of mental mission prep. "Let me help you get these dick lickers."

Zeke didn't answer at first. He subjected Garrett to another long minute of silent scrutiny. That was all right. Garrett had been through it before, could deal with it. What he couldn't handle were the daggers that Z tried to add to the others in his chest, the blades that tried to gouge the others out.

That wasn't going to happen. Not today, not tonight, not any time soon. The knives were his. The pain was his. And as long as both were still there, he still had some part of her with him.

Finally, Zeke cracked a lopsided grin and chuckled. "All right, you charmer. Let's get the hell out of here. You need a shower, dude. Bad."

"Says the chump who smells like ass."

Zeke knuckled him in the shoulder. "You sure you got

everything in that pack? Did you get your Jane Austen novel off the back of the toilet?"

"I've got your Jane Austen at the end of my dick."

"Hawkins, your dick is probably blue as your balls by now." Z snapped his fingers. "Hey! Maybe that's where you should secure your tags, yeah?"

He rolled his eyes before scooping up his pack again, and discreetly adjusting the body parts his friend had just insulted with screaming accuracy. His cock was still doing its best to relax, and his balls throbbed in frustration, sending shots of erotic what-the-fucks at him. They were supposed to be enjoying some post jack-off serenity right now, and the bastards were hitting the target damn well at reminding him of that every two seconds.

Get used to it, guys. He sent the dismal promise as he and Zeke made their way out into the sultry Bangkok afternoon. *Life isn't going to change anytime soon.*

Angel Payne

<u>Chapter Two</u>

Day 433

The paper's running low. Soon it will be gone. I'm not sure how I'll hang on after that, without the words to write each day…the few seconds that I have to look at them and remember that I'm real. That somewhere in the world, you're *real, and what we had was real. I think they might be moving us again today. I don't know what will happen, but I think we'll be sold again or killed. This time, I'm praying for the strength to leave this packet behind—and in doing so, to leave part of my heart behind with it. These pages will tell you everything. They'll explain where we've been and who's held us, and maybe help you guys catch the assholes. I have to believe that someone will find this. I have to believe that they'll get it to you somehow, and that you'll read it all, and know I never stopped loving you. I never—*

"Sage! Put it away!"

Rayna's hoarse whisper resounded through the cave, or whatever this place was, that the two of them had been transferred to and kept for the last two weeks. Sage didn't waste time minding her friend. She slipped the note into the hidden pocket of her small pack as her friend turned to keep watch again, flipping her russet ponytail against her thin shoulders and peering through the barbed wire wall that functioned as the front of their cell.

She and Rayna had stayed free for over a year because they'd depended on each other's strengths, like her crossbow aim and Rayna's wolf-perfect hearing, along with a hell of a lot of luck. The skills were all still there. It was the luck that had run out. They'd finally been recaptured, drugged, and taken God-only-knew where. This definitely wasn't Africa anymore. It was moist. *Really* moist. Not as wet as home, but few places were as damp as the American Northwest.

She closed her eyes for a precious moment, conjuring every detail she could remember of the condo that had been she

15

and Garrett's home in the three months before she'd left for Africa. The giant pillows in front of the fireplace. The cathedral roofs that turned the rain into music. The lake outside the windows, and the egrets that dipped gracefully over the water each morning.

The same way Sergeant Garrett Hawkins had swooped into her life and captured her heart.

"Hellooo, bitches!"

In the space of those two shrill words, her memories were blasted apart again.

Reality reigned once more in the form of the four black-clad gunmen Rayna had heard on approach. They were followed by the source of the greeting, their leader: a coffee-skinned grease ball who referred to himself as "King." Sage had fast concluded nothing good was due to them because of that, and she'd been right. At first, the man had referred to them both simply as "the investments," leading to the conclusion that the men who'd recaptured them in Africa were simply middlemen, and King was the bigger player in this picture. Those were the days he'd held them in the warehouse, when somber East Asian women were brought in to wash and style their hair, paint their nails, shave their legs…and other body parts. Outfits were brought in to size on them, if the scraps of fabric could be called that. The treatment had left nothing to their imaginations about the fate for which they were being prepared.

One night, the "spa treatment" had gone differently. The women brought in for them snapped on surgical gloves as King selected body jewelry from a bed of jewels. When they pinned Rayna down, forced her legs open, and pierced her with brute force and an ugly needle, she'd screamed—and Sage had snapped. She'd managed to scatter the jewels, take down two henchmen with head butts to their balls, and get the "therapist" away from Rayna before a hard whack to the back of her head had turned the world dark.

She had no idea how long she'd been out, but she'd woken up here in the cave, expecting to see diamonds taunting from between her own thighs. Instead King himself was positioned there, pinning her legs with his knees as he wrenched at his fly. She'd taken a couple of steady breaths. On the third, she'd reared up enough to squeeze his sorry balls with all the strength in her arms. The action earned her a mixed bag of results. Good news? King got nowhere near her again. Not-so-good news? Her hands didn't feel like crushing anything after they spent three days shackled to the walls. It was amazing how the pounds came pouring off a girl during a multi-day forced fast. Gee, the spa that thought of everything.

After that, she and Rayna were no longer the "investments." They were the bitches.

King's grin slanted higher as he approached the cell. "Have you rested well, bitches?" He cocked his head, looking from her to Rayna and back. "Hmm. Seems so. But do the flowers ever look soiled from the beautiful land of Seattle? I think not. This is a good thing. Tonight is going to be big for you. *And* me!"

A scythe of terror slashed her gut. "Big" could only mean one thing. They would no longer be under King's thumb. That didn't mean the next thumb would be any better. Sage focused on the asshole's leering yellow teeth, along with a fantasy of whacking them all from his mouth, to control herself from glancing at Rayna. The effort failed. It was impossible not to catch Ray in her peripheral, due to the trembles that now commanded every inch of her friend. They both knew the order King was going to issue next.

"The redhead goes first." Two of the guards moved at once. After releasing the steel gate, they secured Rayna with beefy hands around her shoulders. One of them pulled her wrists together then bound them with the *thwick* of a zip tie. When Rayna let out a pained whimper, Sage surged to her knees, a welcome rush of fury replacing her fear.

"Hurt her and you'll answer to me, shitheads."

King rolled his eyes and lifted his hand in a dismissive arc. The other two goons swept into the cell, then shoved her against the wall. One of them stuffed a rag into her mouth. He fastened it in place with a couple of zip ties around her head. He followed by securing her wrists in the same condition as

Rayna's. The other guard hauled her to her feet by pulling on her ass.

As all this happened, Rayna got pulled out of the cell. King stepped over to greet her by raising a hand to her quivering chin, and using the other to pet her long copper hair.

"Eyes of a wildcat and hair of fire," he murmured. "And yet, you have always been the sweeter of my two special candies." He used his grip on her chin to lift her face, leaning close as if to kiss her despite the grimace Rayna didn't hide. "I wonder if your slit is fiery as your hair, my lovely."

He finished by licking the seam of Rayna's mouth, making her jerk and whimper against his grip. Sage lunged against her captors, letting out a useless scream against her gag. King chuckled as the guards wrestled her into submission. Because her limbs were constrained, her lungs took over the task of hanging on to the rage. She sucked in huge breaths through her nose, since breathing through her mouth was *not* an option right now. The rag was drenched in a cocktail of tobacco, dirt, marijuana, and sweat, making her want to vomit the weak soup and cold chicken legs they'd been fed earlier.

As it had so many times in the last two weeks, her mind pulled from her body and almost hovered, watching all of this like some horrible scene in a movie that gave her an excuse to go for more popcorn. This wasn't real. This couldn't be her life. She kept waiting for the shivers to stop, for the dread to go away. She stared at the cave's cold black stones, yearning for the moment they peeled back to reveal bright stage lights and a director in those funny riding pants, laughing and telling her the scene was a wrap, and she could go home now...

But that wasn't where she was going. Nor Rayna. Within a few hours, she suspected hell would be a pleasant alternative to her fate. As she finally let herself look over at Rayna, she forced herself to take in every strong feature of the woman who'd been her best friend, her only friend, for the last year. After tonight, she'd never see Rayna again.

Within the next year, she'd be forced to forget who she was, as well.

"I'm too sexy for my shirt, so sexy it hu-hu-hurts—"

King answered his phone before the thing could play another note of the nauseating song. Instead of a greeting, the man only grunted into the phone. "What? Already?" he finally said. "So be it, then. Make everything ready. We are bringing the additional sluts now." He shook his head and re-pocketed the phone. "It seems our buyers are here a bit early, bitches. There will be no time to pretty you up, but I am not concerned." He turned to Sage and ran an oily finger beneath her shirt, over her nipple. "If our guests want to see what they are paying for, we'll just let them look."

A snarl clawed up Sage's throat as she charged again at the pig, hoping to get in a solid head butt. King swerved, but not fast enough to avoid a spray of her spit, courtesy of the gag. An animalistic sound surged out of the bastard as he glared at the white blobs on his hand and arm. He shook the spit off before raising his hand again, to sweep a brutal backhand into her face. Sage heard the thud of his heavy topaz ring as it connected to her cheek bone, but the sound was eclipsed by the clanging pain throughout her head.

"Sage!" The shriek was Rayna's, sounding weirdly muffled as she got pushed in front of her friend. The guards led them down a semi-underground passageway. Though the block rocks of the cave still surrounded them, the walls on their left gave way every five or six feet to bunches of thick tropical foliage. After they'd walked a minute or so, Sage glimpsed lights through the trees. She made out the shadows of low-lying buildings and picked up on the labored sound of clunky compact car engines. Bar glasses clinked somewhere, and an old Bon Jovi song blared from tired speakers. They were in a small village, though they weren't exactly led into the middle of town square. Across a small clearing lay a dome-shaped Quonset hut. Dim lights burned from the high windows.

She and Rayna were led past more guards then trundled inside through a back door. The room they entered was small and musty, walled-off from the rest of the hut by corrugated aluminum walls. A few strings of old Christmas lights and a half-dozen kerosene lamps were the only light sources in the space, which didn't help her disorientation as one the guards spun her around and told her to sit. Not that he waited for her obedience anyhow. After throwing her to the hard-packed dirt floor, he grabbed Rayna and hurled her down too. Without their arms to fling out for balance, they both landed in painful heaps, their knees and shoulders taking the brunt of their falls. For a few seconds, Sage even forgot the throbbing in her face from King's blow.

"Careful, you idiots!" Watching King direct his masochism on someone else, as he stepped over and cuffed both guards on the sides of their heads, was satisfying in a sick way. "We're not renting those two tonight. Sales will be final on them. The blond is already scuffed up, so take care."

Sage watched in grim triumph as the two men glared at King's back. She wished one of them would point out that it was him who "scuffed" her up in the first place, but they both pulled the wuss card and held their cowardly tongues.

Thanks to the prolonged pressure of the gag, her own tongue ached, but she forgot the agony the next second. A shaking cry whipped her attention back down and to the side. She joined Rayna in returning the stares of five women who were caked in gaudy cosmetics, raw fear, and little else. One of the girls, a strawberry blond in a low-cut red leather mini dress and matching boots, scooted toward Sage.

"Dear merciful Lord. You've got a shiner the size of Kalamazoo, girlfriend. And that rag must be wretched. Let me—"

"No." Rayna grabbed the woman's wrist. Red Mini's heart was in the right place in wanting to dislodge the gag from Sage, but Rayna set the woman straight in a somber tone. "The bastard is using it as punishment. Take it off, and he'll give her worse."

"Who is he?" A curvy chestnut brunette trembled hard as she curled against the curve of the wall. King's magical makeover team had dressed her in a black tube top and a cheetah print skirt that wasn't much bigger. "Wh-what's going on?" Tears coursed down her face, taking trails of her makeup with them. "Why is this happening? We came here to help people! We were on our way to Myanmar. We just wanted to serve. Now wh-what's going to happen to us?"

"He said 'renting.'" The matter-of-fact statement was given by a woman in a royal blue version of Red Mini's outfit. Aside from the dresses, the women were literally twins. "I think we can draw the logical conclusions from that term."

"Oh my God!" The brunette sobbed harder. "I—I can't! I can't!"

Another woman, black-haired and in a lemon yellow halter with pink shortie-shorts, crawled over to her. "Yes you can, Mandy. Listen to me. You do whatever it takes to survive, you hear me? Just do whatever they say. Don't make them upset."

"You d-don't understand," the brunette rasped back. "I'm—I'm a—virgin."

One of the guards sidled in closer. "In that case, *waan jai*, maybe I'll bid on you myself."

"Hell yeah, baby." His friend cracked an oily grin. "Teo will be good to you, honey. He's popped the plug on three virgins this year alone."

The first guard shrugged. "Eh, it's almost getting boring, ya know?" He slid a sideways glance down at Sage. "If I was making the big *baht,* I'd wanna buy something like that to take home and tie up for myself." After looking to make sure King was still in the other section of the hut, he grabbed Sage's hair and rammed her face against his crotch. "I have a million ideas for how to break a tiger like you, gorgeous. Again and again and again…"

Sage instinctively tried to yank away, but she was crouched, bound, and about half the henchman's size. Teo grunted and kept her locked against his burgeoning bulge, rolling her nose along the khaki fabric that smelled like sweat and urine. Okay, this was *not* where a single one of her bondage fantasies had ever led.

Think of home. Think of home. He'll get bored in a minute, and stop. Think of—

"Oh yeah, baby. You're a sweet little *e-raan.* Nice little slut. Open your mouth for me. Suck those balls right through my pants. Yeaaahhh…"

21

Behind her, Rayna remained thankfully silent, but the other five women let out gasps of horror and protest. Sage knew they meant well, but the louder they sobbed, the harder the bastard toyed with her. She reached inside, frantically scrounging for her mental disconnect button.

Think of Garrett. Think of home. Think of the egrets on the water.

Who the hell was she kidding?

She'd never see home again.

Once King had haggled the highest price for her, life as Sage Weston wouldn't exist any longer. She'd have a new name, if her owner decided to call her anything at all. The tracks of her life would be erased by the ocean of anonymity. Of slavery.

She and Rayna had discussed this a thousand times over the last two weeks, yet she realized some fortress in her brain had been holding back the reality of it. This helpless, humiliating instant blew those walls to dust. In the wake of the explosion, her mind screamed in grief and her heart floundered in despair. The effort of both sapped the strength from her body. She was a shell, numb and senseless. When the other guards hissed that King was on approach again and Teo tossed her back to the ground, she barely felt the impact.

The curious thing was, King's "approach" now seemed more the charge of a crazed rodeo bull. His features matched the mien, his mouth bared in a grimace, the whites of his eyes like crazed flashlights.

"The auction is off," he snapped. "Get the bitches out of here."

"Off?" Teo's buddy didn't have such a snarky tone now.

"Take all of them back to the cave," King fired as if the guy hadn't spoken, "then wait for my instructions. *Reaw-khao!* Hurry!"

"The cave?" echoed another henchman. "*All* of them?"

King rammed the heel of his palm up that guy's nose. "Imbecile! Isn't that what I just said?"

The soldier didn't get a chance to check his bloody

nose. Before King was done with the reprimand, violent shouts erupted outside the hut. A door was bashed in somewhere. Then another.

"Get them *out of here*!" King dictated. "No bitches in the buildings. They cannot be found. Hide them. Now!"

Teo and his friends started hauling them to their feet. "You heard him, sluts. Move."

Sage and Rayna struggled to get each other upright again. "What's going on?" her friend rasped. Sage shook her head in a wordless *I don't know.* Her pounding heartbeat shoved frantic wheezes out her nose. Adrenaline shot up her blood with alternating pellets of heat and cold. Mixed feelings assaulted as she and Rayna stumbled behind the other women. They wouldn't be sold tonight, but that didn't mean the danger was over.

The next second, they were slammed back to the dirt. Before Sage could stop her body's momentum, her head slammed to the floor. A curtain of silver spots crashed over her vision, yanked by pulleys that screamed in terror. No, wait. The screams were human. They belonged to the Miniskirt Twins and Virgin Girl, accompanied by the women's frenzied retreat away from the door, barreling into Sage and Rayna as they did. Their cries mixed with more voices from outside the hut, seeming to come from the direction of the village. They all sounded male, and really pissed off.

The women around her shrieked again. The reason for their panic was explosively clear. Just beyond the portal, there were blasts of rifle fire and explosives. The air filled with thick smoke and acrid gunpowder.

The henchmen bellowed curses in three languages as they dropped the women in the middle of the room then ran for cover behind steel crates. Virgin Girl shrieked and sobbed, piercing deeper pain into Sage's head. She blinked and tried to focus, but the world erupted in flashing lights and wild, confusing shadows. She half-expected the Bon Jovi tune to get switched to a GaGa dance beat. Welcome to Club Violence and Terror. She volunteered her brain as the spinning mirror ball.

"Stop," she begged, her senses revolting against the

23

sensory assault. "Oh God, please stop!"

Miraculously, the world obeyed.

Suddenly as it had started, the rifle fire went silent. Aside from the soft sobs of the women heaped on top of her, she couldn't hear a thing. A gust of balmy wind blew over the clearing outside, rustling the tall grasses. Bon Jovi had become Linkin Park. The song was beautiful and passionate, ripping the air like an insane middle finger thrust at the violence that had just occurred.

"*No matter how far we've come, I can't wait to see tomorrow...*"

One of the soldiers dared a harsh whisper. "Teo! You alive, *peuang?*"

"Yeah."

"What the fuck, man?"

"I dunno. But this is bullshit. I didn't sign up for this. Let's get the hell—"

"*Freeze,* assholes."

The interjection was low, lethal, and pure liquid steel— yet it could've been another rifle shot for the shock it blazed into Sage. Maybe that was it. Maybe somebody really had taken more shots, and she'd been hit this time. She was dead and finally in Heaven. Yes. That had to be the explanation, because she couldn't allow herself to believe the truth of it. She *wouldn't* allow herself to believe. Dreams didn't just come true like this, especially in her life.

"Drop your weapons, boys. Slow and gentle. You know the routine, don't you? Lie flat on the ground with your hands where I can see them. Perfect. Now aren't you two prettier'n a couple of hogs all fat and ready for the fair?"

In the end, it wasn't all the words that finally convinced her. It wasn't even the pig joke, which was so "him," as well. It was his laugh. That little soft, dry chuckle that she couldn't ever remember right, even in her most vivid dreams. Oh God, that laugh. *Yes.* This really was happening.

Garrett.

She tried to get out some semblance of it our around the gag, but her heartbeat was a dervish of delirium. She struggled

24

just to get air in, meaning she started inhaling the dirt floor. The stink of it was a horrid contrast to the sheer beauty of hearing his voice again. Tears seeped, turning her cheeks into mud baths. Her brain raced. Her senses swam.

Desperately, she tried again. "G-Gahh—"

"Nice work, Hawk Man." The soldier who spoke loomed in the doorway before entering, his huge strides eating up the space. A smile tugged at Sage's lips. Zeke. The Army had kept the A-Team together.

"Well, you didn't bring me along for my pretty face." This time, no laugh punctuated his dark tone. She watched him swing a leg over Teo, then wrench the henchman's wrists back and fasten them in heavy plastic cuffs. His movements were precise and clean, even angry, which was oddly comforting to her right now. "I'll take these fuckers outside. You see to the women."

"Nnnaaaaa!"

Great. The moment she'd been dreaming of for over four hundred days, and she sounded like a freaking Muppet. Frustration and desperation turned her into a wriggling ball as she tried to right herself and get to her feet. He couldn't leave again! She couldn't let him! The terror was illogical, she knew, but she couldn't stop its visceral hold on her mind any more than she could hold back a monsoon. "Nnaaaa," she cried again. "Gaaaawwwet!"

"Hey." A pair of hands, reassuring as the voice, descended on her shoulders. Sage recognized Zeke's hulking form immediately. He crouched beside her, trying to help her up. "Hey hon, easy, easy. You're safe now, okay? We're gonna get you to safety. I'm with the United States Army. My name is Sergeant Zeke Hayes, and—"

"Yeah, uh know!"

For a long second, the burly man looked like a six year-old who'd just de-masked Spiderman. "Holy…shit! Holy—" He scrubbed a hand down his face before breaking into a full bellow. "Hawk! Get back in here. *Now.*"

Angel Payne

Chapter Three

Okay, so Zeke had been right in grilling him before the mission. It was a little harder to keep his head in the game on this one, especially as they'd arrived and surrounded the hut— especially because he knew what they'd find inside. Or at least prayed they'd find.

Turned out their timing was better than perfect. They'd gotten here in time, and the women were safe. That didn't mean he had to stick around and help Zeke with the head count. He was glad to be out of that cramped room, with all of those women crying in relief—and ripping his gut out in the process.

But now the asshat wanted him back in there? Zeke had to know this wasn't the easiest fucking thing for him. Which meant that whatever the reason for the callback, the beer tab was on Z tonight.

"This'd better be good," he growled, stomping back into the Quonset hut. "Your panties have been twisted more times today than—"

A fist in his gut would've been less painful. And joyful. And terrible. And incredible.

Zeke had just helped the woman to her feet, though it was doubtful she'd continue standing on them. She looked weak as a fawn and shaky as a newborn colt.

She also looked exactly like Sage.

He gulped painfully as he glared at Zeke. His "friend" didn't even bother to look back. Z was too busy cutting free the zip ties that had cut purple welts into her wrists. When the woman winced from the fresh flow of blood to her hands, the cavity in his chest filled with pain too.

Forget the beer tab. Zeke was going to pay for his whole three-day bender after this. He didn't bother asking the guy what kind of a sick joke he thought he was pulling, because Zeke knew—*knew*—that some pots didn't get stirred. So if that wasn't his friend's purpose, what was?

27

Zeke gently helped the woman lift her head. They'd zip-tied a filthy rag into her mouth, and his friend started exploring how to best cut that free as well.

After two seconds, Garrett barely noticed the thing.

She looked past it, directly at him. No. She looked *into* him, just as she always could. Just as she always *would.* She cut him open from sternum to scrotum, filling every vital organ in his body with life again, blinding him with that brilliant green light that had haunted his dreams and been a relentless ghost in his soul.

She was a ghost no more.

Shit. Holy, heavenly shit.

He didn't remember how his legs carried him, or how many steps he took. It only mattered that he yanked the knife out of Z's hand, palming it himself. He had to be the one who set her free. He needed to be the one who saw her face when the last disgusting piece of her captivity got peeled back.

He cut the tie with a savage jerk. She reacted with a little cry, but he knew he hadn't hurt her. The sound was one of need. Of release. Of love.

When he pulled the rag free from her face, tears ran through the dirt underneath. In wordless wonder, he cupped both sides of her jaw and kissed each tear until he got to her lips. She sighed against his mouth, opening to him, inching her shaking arms around his neck.

"My heart," he said against her lips.

"My hero," she whispered back.

Garrett stiffened and swallowed. The words entered his gut and twisted it like scarab beetles. Hero? Right. Some champion he was, buying the story from the CNO hook, line, and fucking sinker. No skeletons in the van merely meant the rebels had moved the bodies as some kind of a sick fuck-you to God only knew who. There was no sense in jeopardizing extra American lives to look for two charred corpses. The region was unstable and unsafe now.

Goddamnit, he'd believed every line they fed him. He'd settled for saying goodbye to her photo on a tripod as they tossed flower petals off a cutter in the Sound, instead of demanding they all look harder, deeper, further for her.

Never again. He vowed it now with every cell in his being. He'd never again give up on her. The angels had given her back to him, and he sure as fuck wasn't blowing the chance. He'd never again let her go, and he'd never again rest before knowing she was safe, secure, completely protected.

He began making good on that oath that moment, clutching her close and claiming her mouth with a kiss so deep and consuming, they both dragged air in harsh, heavy breaths afterwards.

He kept her pressed against him, still barely comprehending that her heart beat beneath his and her arms actually trembled against his neck, before he murmured, "Welcome back, Sage Weston."

Sage pulled back a little. She tilted her face up at him, her chapped lips tremulous with the question that tumbled off them. "Welcome back...to what?"

"To life, sugar." He brushed her lips softly with his own again. "To life."

* * * *

Several hours later, he watched another degree of that life dance across her features as she laughed into his cell phone. She held the phone on the side of her face that hadn't turned five shades of blue yet, causing Garrett to Zen-breathe his way out of another surge of fury. She'd shrugged off the injuries, unwilling to tell him how they'd gotten there, telling him that she'd shared all during Franzen's debrief and didn't want to go through it again with him.

Garrett told himself to be patient. Less than forty-eight hours ago, he'd woken up in a grimy hotel room about to masturbate with her wraith. Now, ensconced safely in the US Embassy's guest quarters, he was about to climb into bed with her very warm, very alive self. *Be grateful, you nut sack. And patient. Very patient. That includes what's about to go down here. You have no idea what she's been through. She may not want your dark blue balls all up in her business yet, got it?*

He turned from her, trying to focus on something less arousing than the sight of her in his old Pike Place Market T-shirt and a pair of utilitarian white panties. The task was *not* easy. The combo was sexy as fuck, no matter how basic its inspiration. She had nothing with her when they'd gotten here, and had been too tired and hungry—and full of her usual impatience—to wait for clothes to be scrounged up, other than the underwear. He'd assured the Embassy staff they could wait for a while, concerned only with Sage's plea to be somewhere quiet and alone with him. The fact that she still needed him, at least emotionally, had nearly given him wings up the stairs behind her.

The second they arrived in the room, she'd rushed for the shower, spending the next twenty minutes moaning in ecstasy beneath the hot spray. Garrett had paced the bedroom, fighting an erection that could've pounded enough nails to raise a barn. He was still in full steel-stomping mode now.

Concentrate on something else.

He looked out the window at the courtyard that grew brighter with the peachy shades of dawn. A grim smile took over his lips. It was a good day already. King and all his henchmen were behind bars. The Thai police had gladly turned the assholes over, and now they'd face international repercussions for what they'd done to Sage, Rayna, and the five aid workers.

The shitty thing was, men like him were like cockroaches. Kill one and the whole intrusion got stirred. He had no doubt that other SOF teams would be called here soon to try and quash more of the monsters.

Sage's throaty laugh was a welcome step into his thoughts. He turned and visually feasted on her again. She was propped against the wall with his phone against her ear, her legs stretched out and crossed at the ankle. The muscles in her calves and thighs were prominent, but all the curves that'd invaded his imagination for the last twelve months were still there…barely. She'd lost a lot of weight. There were old scratches on her ankles, indicative of heavy hiking through thick brush. He gazed at the pronounced muscles in her arms, too. Every inch of her body that he could see was clear evidence of what she'd survived in the last year.

What *had* she survived?

Patience, damn it. This isn't an op you can control. You can't just kick in the doors of her psyche and demand answers like she's a friendly informant.

"I'd better get off the line, Mom. They haven't fully finished debriefing us, but if one more CIA suit knocks at my door right now, I'll strangle him with his tie. Yes, I'll call as soon as we get back stateside." She bit her lip, and swiped at the tears that escaped anyway. "Yep, he's right here. I love you too."

She clicked the call off and extended the phone to him with a watery smile.

"Is she doing okay?" Garrett asked.

Sage nodded. "Yeah. Just stunned, I guess." She shook her head, bemusement touching her features. "Suppose I'll get that reaction from a lot of people."

He put the phone down on the utilitarian bureau, then scooted around to the foot of the bed. After he sat down, he braced his elbows on his knees. "Yeah," he said quietly. "You should prepare yourself."

About a minute passed. It felt like an hour. He tilted his head in order to steal peeks at her, watching her shred her bottom lip as she stared at the far wall. He could practically see the thoughts tumbling through her head, a mental gymnastics team on crack. It was just as hard to follow in terms of what she was thinking.

Patience.

"Did you...have a service?" she finally asked.

During the drive in from the jungle, he'd tried to explain what he'd said about welcoming her back to life. He'd followed it with the flyover version of what had happened after she and Rayna had disappeared. He'd tried to smooth over the rougher parts, as semi-impossible as that was. There was no way of sugar coating the visit from the CNO, the papers Heidi had been asked to sign, the medals that were promised, the condolences imparted. He'd told her about the Army's certainty they weren't still alive, and the dictate from sources much higher than him that a search wasn't feasible, hopeful, or

31

possible.

To his perplexity, Sage had merely nodded and said they'd done the right thing. When Garrett questioned that ludicrous shit, she'd turned and gazed out into the night, her eyes matching the darkness, turning into deep forests he'd never seen there before.

What the hell had happened to her in the last twelve months?

He forced the thought into a side pocket of his mind. He was damn determined to get an answer to that, but right now, she needed hers more.

"Yeah," he murmured, "we had a service. We did it on a Navy cutter, out on the Sound." He lifted one side of his mouth. "You would've liked it, sugar. Except for the being dead part, of course." When she returned his smile with a tentative smirk of her own, all his ribs turned into mush, baring his heart to the warmth of her regard. It gave him the courage to continue. "We tossed yellow and pink roses onto the water, along with your—well, what they assumed were your ashes. And we served grilled cheddar cheese sandwiches while listening to classic disco."

She laughed again. "You're right. I would've loved it. Except for the being dead stuff."

He joined her in a chuckle, but it was all he could manage before his next words came out, shaking as they did. "Damn it, Sage. I'm so glad you're not."

The air thickened back into awkwardness again. He kept his stare threaded into the thin bed blanket, suddenly unable to meet her gaze.

"Are you?"

It was only two words, but they asked so much more. He knew it, and he knew she did too. She inched one foot toward him then nudged him with her big toe. "Then why don't you show me?"

He curled his hand around her foot. The sensation of touching her, really touching her, and of caressing her warm, soft skin…it turned the crumbles of his ribs into dust, and dissolved his senses into a chaos of confusion, need, heat.

"Garrett." Now she leaned over, and grabbed his wrist in one of her tiny but iron-strong hands. "Please. I need this. I need…"

She drew his hand up to her cheek.

"I need you."

He took a shaking breath as she leaned her face into his palm. Then another as she turned and kissed his wrist. God*damn,* her lips were so warm and soft and succulent. *Don't think about that. Think about the Mariners chances for the Playoffs this year. Or getting the oil changed on the truck when you get home. Or—*

Shit.

She pulled his middle finger down. Wrapped her mouth around it. Her gaze, now green and clear as Spring itself again, opened to him in blatant need.

He was done with breathing. With patience. With the goddamn Mariners. With anything else except needing her in return.

"Oh, fuck me, sugar."

He groaned it as he surged at her. He ground their bodies together, mashing his mouth onto hers. When he pulled up to give them both a gasp of air, she curled a breathtaking smile up at him.

"Isn't that my line, soldier?"

He didn't have the self-control to return her grin. His blood, until now barely banked, burst into a bonfire, raced through his system then gathered force inside his balls. He didn't waste a single moment to let her know it, either. Shoving her thighs wide with his knees, he fit the khaki-clad ridge between his legs against the cotton-covered groove of her own, and rocked with slow, teasing thrusts until Sage's mouth parted on high, breathy cries. He stared in fascination at the locked edges of her teeth beneath. Damn, he'd forgotten how breathtaking her mouth was.

He lifted a finger to her lower lip and pressed down. "Open up," he said with guttural demand. "I'm going to taste you, Sage."

With a gorgeous mewl, she complied. He rose up,

33

bracketing her jaw with one hand, holding her still for his descent. He dove in, ramming his tongue deep, exploring the cavern of her mouth with two overriding intents. The first? To claim her again, to fill her with the taste and heat and feel of him alone. The second? To make sure she knew exactly what he was going to do to her body next.

Beneath him, she didn't just open up. She blossomed. Incredible sighs erupted up her throat and soaked him with her essence in return. The feel of her hands on his back, jerking up his T-shirt to drag their way up his back, made him vibrate with a million electric tremors of arousal.

"Garrett!" Her plea was strident and sweet in his ear. "Oh, please!"

He ran a hand downward, tucking it beneath the band of the panties, his lust roaring hotter when her body drenched his fingers in creamy heat. He couldn't control himself from going further, inching a finger up her secret channel. They moaned together when her vagina clamped on him like a long-lost lover, sweet and tight in its desperate bliss.

Damn. What was it going to be like when he slid his cock into her?

He couldn't wait to find out.

His breath came in harsh spurts as he shoved the panties down to her thighs. In seconds, he returned his fingers to the curls a few inches higher, spreading her again, coaxing the ridge of flesh where she was most sensitive, stroking her desire into a blaze to match his.

"My heart," he murmured against her lips.

"My hero." She gasped and arched into his fingers, stunning in her hot, panting desire.

He hovered his face an inch above hers, breathing in the sweet natural essence of her, a mix of spring mist, wildflowers, and complete woman. "Now I know why I couldn't let go. Everyone told me to move on, but I told them all to fuck off. I refused. Part of me knew. And now," —he sank his lips deep into hers— "I'm not ever going to let you go again."

"I love you, Garrett."

She smiled again at him, her eyes dreamy. Her lips

were stung from his kisses, her face aglow in the radiance of expecting him to return the words. His heart rang with them, and his soul clamored with the need to bellow them from the fucking rooftops if he had to…but in the pit of his throat, the consonants were a gob of mud, the vowels were a tangle of nails. Even thinking of dissolving the mess made him shake with pain and loss.

What the hell is wrong with you?

That was the ten million dollar question, wasn't it? His lack of an answer was agony. He'd dreamed of seeing her like this again, open and ready and beautiful for him. He'd clung to this memory for what felt like forever.

This memory.

This memory.

Holy fuck. This was how she'd looked the night before she left for Botswana. The night he'd lost her forever.

"Garrett?"

He dropped his head, breathing hard. He couldn't take her this way. Not like this.

He craved the Sage who'd shared his dream this morning. The squirming, writhing Sage…in his captivity, under his control. Holy God, he needed her.

"Garrett? Baby?"

He lifted his face again, curling a slow grin at her as he did. "I'm here, sugar." With slow, gentle circles, he started another kiss. As he skated a hand up beneath her shirt, he tilted his head and trailed tiny bites on her lips. She rolled her mouth against his, trying to give back as good as he gave, but he stopped her, increasing his pressure, always bringing her under his rule again—until with a frustrated cry, she nipped at him and captured his upper lip with a giggle of triumph.

Garrett growled low, raised his hand to her erect nipple, and tugged it hard.

"Ahhh! Garrett, what the—"

Before she could finish, he'd lifted her shirt all the way off, hurled it to the floor, and returned his mouth to the peak he'd just pinched, licking the irritated skin with the flat of his tongue.

"Oh." It left her on a startled breath. The sound turned into another tiny keen when he pulled again at that distended nub, using his teeth this time. She tunneled both her hands into his hair, digging at his scalp with her nails. "Ohhh! Shit!"

She began to writhe now. And God help him, his dick throbbed harder.

She gasped as he took both her hands and pinned them over her head. He snarled low, yanking down his fly with his other hand.

She twisted and trembled. He grunted and gritted his jaw. His pre-cum alone was a geyser. Looking at her like this, completely his, tamed for him at last, had his cock screaming to seal his claim on her.

"Kick the underwear free." He gave her the order on a harsh, hot rush of sound. "Then you'll spread wide for me, sugar. I'm gonna claim every inch of you, Sage. Every fucking inch."

He watched her breath hitch once, then speed up into a wild gallop beneath her trembling breasts. "I love you," she said again. "I need you. Please, Ga—"

"Hush." It left him on a monotone, which was an odd contrast to his curt, commanding actions. The second she got the panties free, he pushed back one leg then the other, letting out a hungry rumble at the sight of her spread and glistening pussy. When he reached and plunged two fingers into her quivering entrance, Sage screamed and then, remarkably, laughed.

"Oh, Garrett! God, yes!"

He lunged over her then, drilling a stare of dark intent into her. Laughing wasn't part of this. She'd laughed the night before she'd left him. She'd laughed as she'd orgasmed that night, drowning him in her joy and her love and her beauty...right before she'd left him. She'd laughed, filling the condo with it so that the memories of it haunted him for that horrid, dismal week before he was able to get back into the mission rotation on the squad. No. Laughing wouldn't be a part of things tonight.

"I said *hush*."

That was when he flipped her over and brought his hand down on her ass in a resounding *smack.*

Angel Payne

Chapter Four

Wow.

Sage blinked, unsure if she'd actually just experienced…well…*that.* Had he really just spanked her? Had he really just done it as the back-up to an *order* he'd given her?

If she were honest, it wasn't outside the realm of possibility. Garrett had burst into her life by defending her honor, fists first, at Opal's Tavern on that unforgettable June night. He'd sealed the deal just three weeks later, making her body feel like the meteor shower overhead, over and over again. Joe and Hannah Hawkins might as well have given their son the middle name of Firestorm instead of Flynn.

So yeah, it didn't take a rocket scientist to put the man's intensity together with all the newer things she'd seen in him over the last four hours. Cobalt smoke hovered at the corners of his gaze, which had once been the pure blue of a summer sky. Tense lines now embedded themselves at the corners of his mouth. Nothing casual remained in how he moved. Every action was sharp, full of purpose and battle-honed balance.

Sage had noticed it all, and understood. She'd seen it all, and accepted it. His grief for her had gouged a chunk of his soul. He hadn't filled that hole with anything easy or forgiving, especially for himself.

Now they were just dealing with a few readjustment issues.

To the tune of two more sharp slaps on her backside.

They hurt. Oh damn, how they hurt. For a second, she thought about breaking free and scrambling away. But the next second, something deep inside her body was startled awake. Something illicit, decadent, and until this moment, very secret. She'd thought these dark desires had been banished from her body, long-forgotten before the year in Botswana, and certainly long before she'd met Garrett. For a few brief months, during those carefree months right before boot camp, she let the fantasies romp free in her imagination, playing there with illicit fantasies of letting a man bind her, control her, use her solely for his pleasure. But beyond getting her hands on a good vibrator and a few mouth-watering novels, she'd never done anything about them...

Certainly nothing like this.

And ohhhh, how this felt...exhilarating. Heart-stopping. Like she was alive again. Like she was desired again.

Again. Please do it again.

Oh, God! Okay, her logic was still around here somewhere, right? Clearly, they needed to talk about this, to figure it out, to set up some—what did the novels call them?—limits. Right. Limits were good to discuss when a guy decided to pull down your panties, flip you over then smack his palm on your bare ass.

But she didn't move. She didn't make a sound. That shadowy instinct coaxed her to stay motionless, full of trepidation and anticipation, despite this new wilderness of emotional ground for them. It had been a long year for him, too—and eagerness filled her to know more about these new parts of the man who'd snatched her from the jungle, who'd brought her back to life. She wanted to know it all...especially now.

She breathed deep. Again. She waited, listening to Garrett's rough exhalations above her. The husky releases were choppy, hesitant...distant. Though the heat of his massive body still hovered over her, she shivered as if he'd left the room.

She continued waiting. It was one of the hardest things she'd done. His silence tormented her. His grip tightened around her wrists. With his other hand, he claimed her spine from nape to ass with a possessive, clawing sweep. A deep moan stole its way up her throat.

"Ssshhh."

He followed the track of his hand with his mouth, nipping her in tiny but savage bites. Her moan pitched into a little yelp.

"Ssshhh."

He dipped his touch between her thighs. With just a small grunt of warning, he pinched her sensitive folds.

40

"Ohhhh!"

He didn't shush her this time. With one deft move, he turned her over again. Without skipping a beat, he flattened his hand into a paddle and swatted what he'd just pinched.

Wow. And *whoa.*

"Garrett! What the—*shit!*"

Her exclamation coincided with the discipline he kept delivering to her mound. Shock ripped through her. And on its heels, self-reprimand. She was just the one asking for more, right? For the chance to finally let her wicked desires flare into delicious flames? Had she meant it, even if her imagination never included this?

Her mind had a tougher time answering that when her body weighed in on the issue. Every nerve ending sizzled like exposed electric lines. The most intense heat came right from the tissues he'd enflamed. Her pussy pulsed with awareness, and her entire vagina trembled and dripped anew. It stole her breath, spiraled her senses, pulled out her deepest sighs. Every swat Garrett gave seemed to unlock something inside her, something amazing. The ugly pain of the last year got slowly replaced by an exquisite pain that set her senses free, that told her body it was all right to feel this way again.

She sighed with the sheer radiance of it, raising her hips, silently begging him for more. She opened her eyes, needing to watch him as he did this, needing to know that this was really what he wanted too…

She blinked in surprise. The view wasn't what she expected. Garrett's teeth were locked beneath his slightly-parted lips. His jaw was granite hard, and his gaze was the same color and texture. Nothing about him conveyed pleasure or joy. It almost looked like—

Like he wasn't enjoying this at all.

"Garrett?"

Damn, she wished she could touch him. She needed to soothe the hard lines from his face, to feel his pulse, to try and understand where his thoughts hovered. But she could only watch in mute frustration as his gaze roamed the length of her body again, his expression still impenetrable.

41

A strange emotion drenched her. She didn't recognize it at first, but the truth set in, shitty and awful. She was ashamed. Drowning in the stuff. Her body didn't have the soft, womanly physique Garrett had adored. Her arms and legs were defined by the muscles she'd been utilizing nonstop for a year, but other parts of her were skeletal. Her breasts were at least two cup sizes smaller. Her hip and collar bones jutted from her skin. Her hair had thinned, even her fingernails were brittle. The erection that jutted from Garrett's fly was for the body he *thought* he'd be getting again: the curves and skin of the woman he'd claimed beneath the stars two years ago.

That woman didn't exist anymore. Not physically, certainly not mentally. The only thing she remained sure of was her heart—and its love for a man who now stared at her like a pathetic charity case.

Sage gulped. Damn it, she'd sworn she wouldn't cry again. She'd shed enough tears on him during the journey back here, and again during her epic-length shower, to have used up her allotment for the next two months. But the stinging bastards came anyway, dumping out her eyes, tracking down her cheeks. Like an idiot, she didn't hide them from Garrett, either. Sure, because her blubbering was going to magically flip his desire switch again, right?

To make matters worse, she sniffed with the grace of an elephant. She longed to roll the hell back over—until, for one beautiful moment, Garrett looked at her again. Really looked. Her breath hitched. Her stomach somersaulted in a familiar way. A tentative smile tempted her lips. For that amazing moment, he was back. He was hers. The brilliant blue of his eyes swept her away to days of laughter, warmth, sun and love.

He blinked—and just like that, the dark smoke returned to his stare. He was lost again behind a curtain of the stuff, his features coated again in anger, vacillation, and confusion, before he released her with a rough grunt.

"I can't do this." He dropped his head, as if the action were helping him make a choice, before he bolted from the bed. "I—I'm sorry. I can't."

"It's all right." Sage hiked onto her elbows, watching

him pace the room as if looking for something. "Maybe we can just talk about—"

"No." He stuffed himself back into his pants then zipped up. "No talking. Not about this."

She shook her head, feeling like he'd given her a book with the middle fifty pages ripped out. "Not about *what*?"

"Sage." He came back over, sitting next to her again. Though the smoke still clung to his eyes, Sage felt the pressure broiling in him. In the lines embedded at his temples and around his mouth, she saw the pain of unshared memories, the tension of unspoken words. "I'm messed up, okay?"

She reached for his hand. "Welcome to the club. My brain probably looks like a mine field after how the intel analysts tromped through it today—and I'd much prefer your boots over theirs." After she twisted their fingers together, she went on, "There'll be things for us to hash out on both sides of this, okay? So, fine. Let's get started."

His stare combed over her face from top to bottom, again giving her a split second of pure magic, before he dove back behind that wretched smokescreen. "You didn't sign up for *this* mess, baby."

"The hell I didn't. *Damn it*, Garrett. The day I took that engagement ring from you was the day I agreed to all your sloppy shit, too. So don't give me this crap." She gripped his hand tighter. "Let. Me. In."

He expelled a heavy breath before pulling her knuckles to his lips. Sage winced. His Prince Charming move would've had her crawling over into his lap, if she didn't see that dark haze of control dominating every corner of his gaze, infiltrating every taut muscle of his posture. Oh, yeah. She was still locked out.

She could almost dictate what he was going to say next. "I'll be back soon."

He set down her hands.

He turned and covered the space to the door in two strides. He shoved into his boots without lacing up. Before Sage could find the strength to scream at him, he'd slipped out. His steps echoed heavily in the hall before fading completely.

The room went cold. And airless. And unbearable.

She forced herself to move. "Come on, Sage," she whispered furiously. "You've done this before. You've taken steps when you didn't think you could. You've moved when you thought it was impossible."

That was because you always thought of Garrett in order to do it.

Ignoring the desperate cry in her throat, she reached for his T-shirt again. With shaky fingers, she pulled it over her head. The damn thing was inside out, but she didn't care. She picked up the grungy capris she'd been wearing when they got here, and forced her trembling legs into them.

Keep moving. Just do it.

She couldn't stay in this room. Not with his scent lingering in the air, with the sheets beneath her still warm where they'd laid together, maybe for the last time. *Probably* for the last time?

She needed air. Space. Sanity. A lobotomy.

On unsteady steps, she made her way out into the hall. But she hesitated outside the door. Where the hell did she go? *Could she go?* They were in the personal residence wing of the embassy, so sounds reverberated at her much like a hotel. Pots clanked in a kitchen. A vacuum cleaner revved down a distant hall. A couple of women chatted excitedly at each other in Thai. A group of kids bounced around a ball of some sort. Life was going on, but the concept seemed unreal. She stood in place, wondering where she fit into it all now…realizing that the picture felt all wrong without Garrett in it.

He would come back. Of course he would. He was *Garrett.* He always came back.

They were assurances based on a man she knew a year ago.

She folded her arms in, trying to gain warmth from the assurance, but she couldn't stop shivering.

A breeze kicked down the hallway, carrying the smells of plumeria, coconut, orchids, and pad thai. She turned that direction and walked out onto a veranda that overlooked a sunken courtyard. The area was like something out of an exotic movie. Flowers in bright pots opened up to the early morning light. In the center of the courtyard, large copper dragons overlooked a small lawn where red and yellow birds hopped. Somebody hummed a soft tune. The wind stirred again, promising a balmy and perfect day.

She took it all in, trying to summon gratitude for the splendor around her, for the very fact she was alive. But she couldn't change her emotional forecast. The radar clearly showed "mortified" with a ninety percent chance of "forever heartbroken."

Again not knowing where to turn, she opted for the breezeway to the right. Her luck continued its snarky trend when she came across a couple sitting together on a stone bench in a pretty alcove, though they may as well have been on the moon for all they noticed their surroundings. The bubble of new attraction glowed around them like shooting stars on full strength. Like she couldn't have her nose shoved more into the shit of things with Garrett, she couldn't help noticing the man was roughly the size of Half Dome, and the woman's hair was the color of a late summer sunset.

Hell. Zeke and Rayna.

"Shit," she whispered. "Sorry."

"Sage? Hey, wait!" Rayna's voice echoed along the tiles with a mix of surprise and concern. "Sweetie, what're you doing—" Her friend stopped when she caught up. "Holy crap. Honey, what happened?"

"Nothing. Sorry I interrupted. I'll just—"

Her resolve melted as soon as Rayna put an arm around her shoulder. She turned into the only person who really knew her now. Finally, the tears of frustration and anger flowed all over again.

Angel Payne

Chapter Five

"Where the hell have you been?"

Garrett leveled the question at Zeke after turning a corner outside the cafeteria and nearly colliding with the guy. His friend's gaze showed more copper than green right now, which meant Z was royally irked about something. Great, fucking great. Garrett sure as hell wasn't thinking clearly, and when that happened, he could usually count on his friend to do the job for them both.

"Well," Zeke grumbled, "now that you've taken the words out of my mouth..."

"What the hell does that mean?"

Zeke swung a nervous glance around the corridor. The regular embassy workers were starting to arrive for work, bustling into the cafeteria for their morning coffee and conversation, jostling too close for comfort. His friend gripped his shoulder and dragged him out the door. Once they were there, Z's irritation flared across the rest of his face.

"It means that I was playing out the we're-the-besties bonding bit with Rayna, and it was rolling toward an all-systems-go when your fiancé busted in and started the waterworks like she'd watched *The Notebook* ten times."

Garrett's gut coiled. "Shit."

What had he expected? That Sage would simply roll over and go to sleep after he left? That she'd be totally fine about getting naked, hot, and bothered for him, before he bolted the door spouting lines so tortured, they'd be cut footage from even the sappy-ass film Z had invoked?

"'Shit' is right," his friend snapped. "What the hell's going on?"

He turned and jammed his toe at the ground. Answering that was nowhere near an option right now. You didn't explain umpteen kinds of fucked-up during an early morning stroll, even if the listening ear belonged to your best friend. In this case, especially because of that. Zeke was the unspoken leader

47

of the squad's Whips and Chains society. The honor was perfect for his friend, who'd gotten his first tattoo at ten and collared his first submissive at twenty. No way in hell did Z understand why Garrett struggled with this crap, nor was Garrett inclined to unlock the box on that story.

That night, exactly between his thirteenth and fourteenth birthdays, was best forgotten—though his goddamn psyche didn't always pay attention to what was "best," did it? So much had changed in that hour when he'd snuck out of the house to go visit Uncle Wyatt, and had come home with a different view of the world. *Very* different. Well, at least of what it was possible to do with a woman. At that time, half his world view was obsessed with that, anyway.

Shame bombed him. He'd gone through the twelve years since that summer with a bullet in his psychological chamber aimed at Wyatt—and maybe at Josie too—as he not-so-subtly blamed them for the scene he'd secretly witnessed in the barn that night. Though Josie hadn't been totally naked yet, he'd known she soon would be. He'd also known that the uncle he'd worshipped his whole life, who'd inspired his dream of going Special Ops one day, had returned from Afghanistan a changed man in many ways—but most disturbingly, in *this* way. The conflict was grueling to resolve, especially as Garrett's own alternative tastes began to creep in on him.

He'd fast learned "those tendencies" weren't talked about in a place like Adel, Iowa. Hell, they weren't talked about anywhere. Even Zeke hadn't said a word to him until Sage was gone and they'd had a two-week dry spell for missions, turning Garrett into a wall-climbing nuisance of unspent energy. Z finally came clean about himself, becoming Garrett's tour guide down the dark halls of Club Subjugate, opening up a world that was more surreal and amazing than fucking Oz.

Zeke had made it all seem okay. When *he* practiced the dynamic. But when it came time for Garrett to demand the safe word and wield the flogger, it had been a different story. His mind, reeling with Sage's image, had hurled such a thick stew of guilt, confusion, and castigation, he'd only been able to wash out the taste by drinking himself into a stupor. Z had never judged his decision, the same way Garrett never held Z's choices against him. He'd left Subjugate, putting that shit behind him for good. Been there, tried that. The Dominant itch was scratched for good.

Or so he'd thought.

His face was stamped on the idiot coin for good now, wasn't it?

"Fuck."

No. You're not an idiot. You're a moron. You had the woman of your soul on a golden platter, but you picked today to revisit this shit? She wanted you inside her. She spoke words you'd been dreaming of for a goddamn year. Instead, you forced her down. Spanked her. Not just on her glorious ass, either. You smacked her on the most sensitive part of her body. You made her cry, and not in the oh-my-girlie-stars-that-was-amazing kind of way.

And just thinking about it again gave him an erection that put the flagpole across the courtyard to shame.

"I can't think straight." He said it past clenched teeth.

"No shit," Zeke replied. "You wanna talk?"

"No." He pivoted around. "No, goddamnit, I don't want to talk. I just need to get out of here. Now."

"You got it." The guy shoved away from the pillar that his shoulders rivaled for stone-hard texture. "Let me go grab the keys to the jeep."

"Rayna will stay with her, right? I don't want her to be alone, but—" *I need to bug out of here. Before this perverted monkey on my back eats me alive.*

"Of course she will, Hawk," his friend assured. "I'll check them both, then we'll bug."

* * * *

Fifteen minutes later, the aplomb in Zeke's bold features officially gave way to amazement. Not that Garrett could see all of his friend's face, since the interior of the hotel's lobby was engulfed in perpetual twilight, and they'd just walked in from a brilliant summer morning.

But sometimes, the tilt of a guy's head said it all. That

and one line blurted in total incredulity.

"What. The. Fuck?"

Garrett said nothing as he turned to follow the concierge who'd come to greet them, a tiny woman with straight black bangs, a practiced smile and enormous fake tits. She led them to one of many sumptuous sitting rooms lining the lobby then motioned for them to sit in big leather chairs. One wall was consumed by an expensive-looking portrait of an exotic naked beauty holding decorated fans over her body in all the right places. A backlit bar gleamed in the corner, and the air smelled like eucalyptus and mango. Aside from the artwork and the "hostess with the mostest" popping open a couple of beers for them, the place could've been a classy Hilton from back home.

"The wait will not be long," said the woman as she served their brews. Her English was a soft combination of proper British and come-fuck-me seduction. "Are these acceptable accommodations for you in the meantime?"

"Yes." Garrett gave her an obligatory smile. "Thank you."

Zeke swung another stunned glance at their surroundings. "I thought you just wanted to go get hammered."

Garrett nodded at the guy's bottle. "Go for it. I'm sure there's more where that came from."

A small pressure on his thigh drew his gaze lower. He watched the hostess's red-polished fingernail trail an inch closer toward his cock, nearing its one-hour mark of flagpole status thanks to Sage's first kiss. "You're a beautiful man," she murmured, licking her bottom lip. "You're certain there's nothing else I can...blow your way for comfort?"

Garrett caught her wrist as she touched his fly. "Thank you for the compliment, but I've already told you what I need."

"You sure as hell did that," Z added. Once more, he shook his head as if trying to wake up from a weird dream.

The woman pulled her hand back with demure grace. "Of course," she murmured. "You will not be disappointed with the companion we've selected, Sergeant Hawkins. Gia's tastes are compatible with your request. She's looking forward to—"

"I don't need to know her name," Garrett interjected tightly. "I don't *want* to know her name."

The woman nodded with a soft smile. She returned to the lobby without another word. Garrett looked back down at his beer, waiting for the inevitable snort from Z. Half a second later, the guy delivered on the expectation.

"Okay, asshat, I'm officially out of rounds to fire at your gray matter. I learned how to add up people before I could add two and two, but right now, I'm tossing in the towel on making any sense of you."

"Never recalled asking that from you." Garrett chugged half the beer while staring at his boot, now crossed against his opposite knee. He hoped Z would leave it at that. No such luck.

"All right. *You* indulge *me* for a second, because I need to get this shit straight. The woman who's been fueling your wet dreams for the last year has now pulled the miracle move of the century and come back from the dead. You were finally alone with her, the perfect chance to get some true-to-life action for those sorry nuts of yours, yet you're here, about to do the nutcracker dance with a total stranger?"

His friend's words did nothing for the muck ball in his gut. *Like I don't know all that already, Z? Like I don't know what a feast Freud would have with my psyche right now? They're called demons, my friend, and I need to purge them on someone besides the woman I plan to marry.*

Outwardly, he scowled at his beer label and muttered, "It's complicated."

"Shit howdy, Corncob Bob, ya think so?"

Garrett slammed his foot down. "Look, dickwad, this is partly *your* fault."

Zeke's posture shot straight up. "What the hell? My fault?"

"If you hadn't dragged my ass to Subjugate that night and—"

Fuck. His mouth had sprinted ahead of his brain. Way ahead. He realized it the same second Zeke did. His friend's eyebrows shot nearly to his hairline.

51

"Okay." Z drew each syllable out with knowing emphasis. "The puzzle pieces are starting to fit a little better. So this is about that wicked Dominant you keep denying, huh?"

The stomach sludge roiled with new fury, forcing him to his feet. He grabbed his bottle as he went, hurling it into the trash behind the bar, filling the little room with the crash of shattering glass. "I don't have a fucking 'Dominant' side. And I'm not denying anything!"

He didn't look back at Zeke as he wheeled and went back to prowl the main room again. With impeccable timing, the hostess reappeared and motioned him forward. Thank fuck.

"Yeah," Zeke called after him, "And I'm the Prince of Persia."

Garrett thought of flipping him off, but the urge got mentally back-burnered as he focused on the next hour in store for him—and the bigger challenge of not feeling like a total bastard for it. But he had to figure out this crap inside himself for good. Wait. Screw the "figuring out" part. The demons weren't getting a friendly chit-chat today. Guys like Zeke were comfortable with their demons. He wasn't one of those guys. He needed to dynamite this shit back to the darkness from where it came—and no way in hell was Sage getting anywhere near the blast zone.

The hostess led him up a gold, spiral staircase that ended at the hotel's third floor. He followed her down a hall with purple velvet wallpaper, softly lit by frosted glass sconces. All the doors were closed. He couldn't hear a sound, except the tinny house sound system pushing out an aria being sung in one of the European romance languages. Irony deserved a fist bump for that one.

Finally, the woman stopped and pushed open a door with another serene smile. She motioned him into the room like a game show model showing off a new car. Garrett dipped his head, hoping he looked a gentleman despite feeling everything but, before stepping through.

Before she shut the door with a quiet click, his dick surged in heightened agony.

The scene was exactly what he'd asked for. The woman kneeling on the four-poster bed had her head slightly bowed, long honey-colored hair falling over her face. She was nude and blindfolded. Her hands rested against green satin sheets. Fuck, the sheets were a great touch. He and Sage had green satin sheets at home. The color nearly matched her magical, beautiful eyes…

His cock jumped again, and he grunted from the pressure. The woman reacted with a little shiver. Again, so damn perfect. He approached the bed, stirring the shadows thrown by the candles ignited then positioned on shelves around the room. The only other light in the chamber came from two small gooseneck lamps. One was aimed right at her. The other was bent toward a small table loaded with sinful sexual discipline toys.

He watched her pretty white teeth sneak out and bite her lower lip. "Oh, yeah," he rasped. How did she know just how to do it? He closed his eyes, sucked in a rough breath, and let his imagination fall deeper into the fantasy. Giving in to the illusion was the only way his conscience could deal with this.

He tugged off his boots and shucked his shirt. The woman—*his* woman, he silently prompted again—surrendered to another shiver. Her areolas tightened and darkened around her pinpointed nipples. Beneath those erect peaks, her lungs hitched on uneven breaths.

Her nervousness clutched at him. It drew him to crawl onto the mattress and kneel in front of her. He stroked her soft, quivering mouth with the pads of his fingers. As if knowing what he needed, she parted her lips and raised her face.

"Tell me you want this," he murmured. "*All* of it. You'll get paid either way, beautiful, but I need to know you've been told what I need here…what we're going to do."

A sweet, sensual sigh escaped her. "Yes," she whispered. "Please Sir…I want this."

He descended his fingers to the place where her jaw joined her throat. "You're certain? You've been told exactly what I want? You'll completely surrender to me. Your body will be mine. Every move you make, every drop of your arousal, every sigh and scream you give, will be mine to call, and to command."

He felt a whimper vibrate in her larynx. She nodded softly, but said nothing.

"Speak it," he dictated. "Tell me again."

"Yes." The word was barely a breath. "Yes...please...yes."

A responding groan thundered through Garrett, He dipped his head, devouring her mouth in a deep kiss. He rolled their tongues and meshed their breaths while she tunneled both hands to his neck and scratched dual tracks down to his collar bones. The rasps of pain were also perfect. If she needed this half as bad as he, then his control would be an easier burden to bear.

Without breaking the embrace, he forced her wrists to the small of her back and held them there. The motions flattened their bodies to each other. His beautiful girl moaned, opening her mouth wider for him. Garrett growled. Oh hell fucking *yes,* this was good. The dream was getting better by the second.

When the kiss ended, he tugged his eyes open to drink in the sight of her bruised lips, the supplicating tilt of her face, the ripples of fear in her forehead as she wondered what he'd do next. Garrett raised his free hand to trace the edge of her blindfold with his fingers.

"Your safe word is 'truth.'" He issued the order in a coarse rasp. "Repeat it to me, beautiful."

A pretty smile lifted her mouth. She looked almost like a little girl about to get a trip to the candy store. With the exception that she was naked, blindfolded, and about to be helplessly bound beneath him.

"Truth." She rendered the compliance with breathy ease.

He rewarded her with another long, wet kiss. During it, he shifted both hands to her breasts. He cupped and squeezed the taut swells, rejoicing as her nipples went hard against his fingers. "I've missed these," he said, dragging his thumbnails across the erect tips. "Have they missed me, too?"

"Yes."

He answered her whisper with a pleased growl. "Very nice, sugar. Now give it up a little louder."

A heady rush of adrenalin hit him along with the dual twists he gave to her hard peaks. She arched against him, her head jackknifing back, her body tense.

"Ohhhh!" she shrieked. "Mmmm, yes!"

"Good girl," Garrett murmured. "That's my good, gorgeous girl." He stroked her reddened nipples, easing her pain, adoring her more for her obedience. She leaned toward him, seeking him out with her hands, which shook in her blind quest for connection to him.

When her fingers hit the defined ridges of his abdomen, she emitted a gasp of delight. Her pleasure doubled his, but the craving took over again, the demand his system issued for complete power over hers. He slammed his hands atop hers. She didn't resist his grip. With a grunt, he pressed her fingers down, forming them tight around the throbbing ridge in his khakis.

"If you want to touch me, fine—but you touch what I tell you to. Right now, that means my cock. Stroke it like you want it, sugar."

"Yes," she said with a readiness equal to her obedience. Her hands groped his sacs, and pulled his khakis tight around his stalk. Garrett endured that for about thirty seconds before unzipping and bursting free into her eager fingers.

"Fuck." The word spilled out as she grazed his balls with her nails, before stroking his length with perfect pressure. His head fell back. "Holy fuck, Sage! Where'd you learn to do that?"

She purred softly against his chest as she rounded the hot bulb of his cock head, her fingers teasing, squeezing, caressing. "You're beautiful, Sir. So wet already..."

His senses careened. Wait. Why did she sound so different? Why did she seem so certain of what she was doing? So...practiced? What the hell? Dear God, what had she been forced to do during that year of her disappearance, surviving however she could, saying whatever she had to? She sounded

like she blended right in around here. No. *Hell, no.*
Unacceptable.

He had to bring her back to him, damn it, and keep her
here—this time for good.

"I didn't ask for those words, did I, sugar?" He issued it
with low but fierce force, pushing her hands away.

She dropped her head and fell back. "I am sorry, Sir."

While she spoke the contrition, Garrett left the bed and
kicked out of his pants. "Don't be sorry with your words. Be
sorry with your body." As he pivoted and considered the rack
of toys, he instructed, "We've discussed the rules, haven't we?
You're mine tonight. *Completely.* You belong only to me, and
you *will* obey me, Sage."

He heard her breath catch. "Y-yes, Sir."

"Now, you'll lay down for your punishment like a good
girl. Your lesson is going to be five swats on your spread
pussy. My discipline will continue when I fuck the rest of your
lesson into you."

He heard her breath catch again, though she said
nothing else. With measured movements, she moved into place
for him. The sound of her limbs sliding against the sheets,
eager and acquiescent for him, made his cock swell more. The
damn thing was at a parallel angle to the floor. He tried his best
to ignore the torment while he considered the choices on the
rack, but gave up the effort when his gaze settled on a riding
crop that had a custom feature. The leather tongue at the end of
the rod had been slit and inset with a handful of longer leather
strips, turning the instrument into a mini flogger too. With a
swift flick, he tested the toy on his thigh. The swatter delivered
a good sting, though the sensation came in two waves, drawing
out the heat of the impact. Interesting—and intoxicating. He'd
make her scream *and* squirm with this.

"Perfect," he murmured. "*Perfect,*" he repeated, after
turning to the woman who lay there for him. With her golden
hair spread against the satin and her body bare except for the
blindfold, she was an image of trembling readiness. He was
ready, too. No turning back. He would claim her, consume her,
conquer her—and never again would he go through the agony

of having to let her go again.

With that resolve, he paced to the side of the bed. Attached to a leather tether was one of the padded wrist cuffs he'd requested. With rapid flicks, he opened the buckle then tilted his head toward the woman. *His* woman. *Always.*

"Arm." He said it with steady calm, knowing the directive would be heeded. Sure enough, though goose bumps sprouted on her skin, she extended her wrist for the bondage.

After he cinched in her other wrist, he moved to the end of the bed. When he clutched one of her ankles and dragged it out toward its own cuff, the woman finally broke into a whimper. He went still.

"Problem, sugar?"

Her throat undulated with a deep gulp. "No, Sir." Her murmur carried an edge of fear, though he looked at her nipples turn darker and tighter. Telltale dew drops appeared on the well-trimmed mound between her legs. Two streams of such different intent, flowing through her body. So mesmerizing. So fascinating. And arousing as hell. Nevertheless, he didn't move his hand from its firm grip around her ankle.

"Do you still trust me, beautiful?"

The query made her shoulders drop and her torso writhe in a sexy melting motion. "Yes, Sir." Her acquiescence came before a dreamlike sigh. Garrett needed no further encouragement. The fantasy was flowing perfectly.

"You know we have to do this." His tone was gentle but his hold commanding as he fastened her ankle inside its cuff. She writhed and shifted through more of the melting thing as he pulled out her other leg, opening her body completely for him. "You know what I need to do here." The clink of the second buckle coincided with another rush of shimmering cream to her pouting pussy lips. "You know this is necessary. I can't fuck you if I can't keep you safe, if I don't know you won't disappear again. If I'm not sure—"

You won't die again.

He banished the terror with a determined grunt. She wasn't going to die. She was here, buckled down for him, so wet and ready for him. Yes. *Yes.*

As he ran his hand up her thigh, he confirmed it. "You want me to fuck you, don't you, Sage?"

She wriggled again and moaned. "Oh please...yes!"

Her mouth stayed parted after that, pulling in deep gulps of air to fill her chest, which pumped in frenetic proof of her mounting need. Her fingers pulled at the leather tethers above the wrist restraints. Her legs shook as she tested the limits of the ankle cuffs. Her hips flexed and her ass bunched, joining in an effort to thrust her sex higher for his view. Garrett took his own turn to pause and gulp. She was a mixture of such striking textures. While her muscles flexed in taut frustration, the tender petals of her core bade him closer...closer still...

With that thought spurring him, Garrett mounted the bed, into the open V between her legs. He rose high on his knees, using the vantage point to drag his stare over every inch of her again. Wherever his gaze touched, he let the crop follow. It wasn't long before he dragged the leather fronds over the erect ridge of flesh nestled in the center of her glistening sex. She gasped and threw back her head as he swiped her pussy again. More goose bumps dotted her thighs and arms.

"Now," he stated, "I want you to tell me how much you want me again—and how you'll gladly pay the price for my cock."

Her entire frame succumbed to another shiver. But she wet her lips and stammered, "Yes, Sir. I do want your hard cock. And I will pay the price for it."

"Good girl." He gave her the praise just before his first *whap* on the middle of her spread, rosy folds. She yelped from the spank but bit it short the next second, her chin set with the resignation that more were to follow.

"Again," Garrett ordered, sliding the crop along the inside of her left thigh. "Say it again."

"I want you, Sir."

"Perfect." He brought the flogger down on her mound more gently the second time, making her twist her hips with breathtaking abandon. "You have three more swats to go, sugar. After I give each one, I want you to tell me exactly what

58

you want." As he finished that, he flung the flogger down again.

"Ohhh! Y-yes! Please, Sir. I want your cock, Sir."

Thwack.

"You want what?"

"You! Your cock!"

Thwack.

"Ooohhhh!"

Garrett didn't let her come down from the adrenalin. He landed the fifth strike in the middle of her sob, yanking her cry into a scream and coaxing new juices across her reddened, sensitive blossom. To make the sight more incredible, the insides of her thighs quivered, shimmering with her aroused perspiration.

Holy hell. She was spectacular. His cock reared on him in fury. He couldn't wait to detonate with her. His body already felt like a state fair fireworks finale. For the first time since he was a teenager, he didn't know if he could contain his orgasm long enough to get inside her. On a ragged breath, he ground his jaw. He *had* to make it.

She gasped, and he marveled at the sight of her pulse beating in her neck. He tossed the crop aside in order to lean over and slide two fingers along that hammering artery. Her heartbeat sped up at his contact. Incredible heat surged through him. *Goddamn.* This was what pure power felt like. No wonder the high could corrupt some men. He didn't feel corrupted. He was floored. Humbled. Grateful.

"Mine," he whispered before replacing his fingers with his lips. "You're mine, Sage, and I'm never letting you go again."

Her throat constricted, as if choking off a tight sound, maybe even a sob. "You...have such a vast heart." She choked it as if realizing it for the first time.

Garrett reared his head back and gazed at her. "No," he ordered. "No more sadness. We've both had too much sadness!"

"Yes, Sir. I am sorry, Sir."

He stroked her cheek with his thumb. "Then what is

59

it?" He pressed tighter against her, forcing his cock to flatten along her stomach and not seek her hot core. He lifted his hand to her blindfold. "Damn it Sage, no secrets! There's nothing between us anymore, do you un—"

His voice clutched as he ripped the blindfold off.

And reality crashed back in.

The woman tethered under him blinked against the light with huge, black-lashed, velvet-dark eyes. Not brilliant green. Lush brown.

His stunned grunt filled the space between them. He delved his hand into her dark blond hair, and twisted hard. She winced as hair pins dragged out with the wig he pulled free. The woman's natural chestnut waves tumbled free.

"Shit."

The sound came from him, though nothing about the croak felt familiar or real. But it sure as hell didn't belong to this poor confused call girl, who'd been through enough of a head-fuck today, thanks to him.

Oh yeah, the crap soup brains belonged solidly on his shoulders. He couldn't keep the mess to himself anymore, either. *Yeah, way to pull down the impressive stats, Hawk. A four-mile radius in three hours, yielding two terrified women and one cock that can still drill through the side of a tank.*

And zero points in the decent human being department.

"Sir? Are you all right?"

Her gentle whisper unraveled his soul by several more miles. The woman was pinned beneath him on a bed to which he'd tethered her—and *she* was trying to comfort *him*?

"Shit," he repeated. After hurling the wig and blindfold aside, he shoved the crop to the floor with his knee as he slid off of her. In a haze of heavy silence, he moved around the bed to set her free from the cuffs.

The woman slowly pulled her legs back together. Garrett sat back on the edge of the bed. After a few long moments, he reached for her ankles and started rubbing the circulation back into them. "Better?" he said, attempting a kind smile.

She returned a quiet smile. "For me? Yes." She tucked

her legs beneath her as she came close and curled to his side. She let her hand continue down, swirling around the continuing persecution of his erection. "But for you? No." Her hold tightened. "Let Gia help you, soldier." She swung over to straddle his lap. "I really do want to help…"

Garrett braced light hands to her rib cage. "I know you do, sweetie. Thank you, but…no. You're beautiful, but—"

Gia stopped him with a finger against his lips. "It's ay-okay, sugar." She giggled after deliberately throwing the endearment back at him. "I understand." She gave him one more fast kiss before scooting off his knees. "I hope things will work out for you and your Sage."

He fought to summon a smile at that. Instead, he scrubbed his stubble and chose another battle, the one to silence his brain's teasing sing-song of *nooot fuck-ing liiikely, nooot fuck-ing liiikely…*

With a weighted sigh, he scooped up his clothes. The brunette's satin robe hung against the back of the bedroom door. As he helped her into it, he asked, "Gia, you got a shower around here?"

"Sure thing. But I'm telling you right now honey, the 'hot' don't work so good."

He snorted. "Right now, I'm not interested in the 'hot.'"

Angel Payne

Chapter Six

Sage gave as many details as she could to Rayna, though she deliberately glossed over the grittier stuff. Hell, how did one talk to their friend, even after what they'd been through together, about feeling the way she did from Garrett's behavior? *Hey, Ray, I know you were pinned in that cave and had your body altered against your will, but can I tell you about how wet I got when my fiancé held me down and smacked my pussy? Did I mention how it made me think of nothing but begging him to tie me up, to drive into me until I couldn't think anymore?*

Of course, that turned things weird when she got to the part about Garrett's invasion-of-the-body-snatchers exit. Luckily, Rayna wasn't able to ask too many questions by that point, because Sage turned back into a mess of sobs again. True to form, her friend held her through every tear. It was easy to feel the trembles in Ray's own frame too. Both of them needed only one hand to count how many times they'd allowed themselves emotions like this during those months when survival was more important than feelings, when breaking down simply hadn't been an option. Maybe they needed to make up for lost time now.

Lost time.

The words jolted her like sunlight breaking through clouds.

Lost time.

She gasped from the revelation. Damn it, why hadn't she seen it? Garrett had gone through a year of hell, too. He'd endured her funeral, for God's sake. While she'd assumed he was alive—no, somehow she'd *known* it—and clutched to the hope of that to keep herself going every day, he'd been learning to live without her. No wonder he'd gawked at her like she was a zombie. Maybe to him, she still was.

Oddly, that thought gave her a surge of hope as Rayna walked her back to the room. It was almost lunch time, but she

63

declined her friend's invitation to the cafeteria. Her eyes were swollen from crying and heavy as bricks with exhaustion. The second her head hit the pillow, she plummeted into sleep.

Though a bomb could've hit the embassy and not roused her, she felt Garrett's presence the second he got back. Her eyes flew open. Her senses were instantly alert to his every sound, not that he made a lot of those. She listened to the rasps of his boot laces, the clunks of the dog tags he'd tied to them, the thuds of the shoes hitting the floor. After a few seconds, she expected to hear the sough of his pants coming off. He always stripped them off after his boots. At least a year ago, he did. And hell, did she love it.

Against the backs of her eyelids, she hit the play button on a beautiful scene of him peeling off his bottoms after a day at the base. She stood at the door like she always did, openly ogling as his powerful thighs and calves got bared then breaking into a grin as he'd turn, his erection a bold silhouette against his briefs. Many times, he'd follow that by crooking his finger, beckoning her to come to him. Or sometimes he'd pace over and get her for himself, blue flames filling his gaze as he exposed his intent for her evening's "appetizer."

A light touch at her forehead jerked her from the fantasy.

She popped open her eyes. Garrett was just a breath away, on his haunches, gazing at her. His hand hovered near her temple, his fingers wrapped in a strand of her hair.

Wow. He'd gotten really good at the sneaky thing. Fantasy or not, he hadn't made a single noise in crossing the whole room.

After getting over her initial shock, she gazed at him. The sight of him was heaven.

Then hell.

"Hey." His rasp matched his appearance. Rough. Tangled. Tired. And more than a little guilty. That remorse seemed to deepen, digging into the creases at the corners of his eyes, as he watched her reaction. Clearly, he recognized that she caught every tiny sign of what he'd been doing in the last two hours. The kiss stings on his lips. The fingernail tracks on his neck. The lingering reek of cheap perfume on his skin, despite the fresh tang soap from a recent shower.

She rolled onto her back and squeezed her eyes shut. Like that was going to cut out the humiliation and agony. Nausea assaulted her thankfully empty stomach. And yeah, the darkness made everything worse. Much worse. Her stupid imagination was stuck on the freeze-frame of him from the bedroom back home, beckoning to her. Still wanting her.

She shook her head, emitting a bitter laugh. The embassy honchos who'd greeted them had talked about medals waiting stateside for her and Rayna. She had a good idea of what they could put on hers. *For bravery, valor, persistence of will, and enduring a fatal strike to her heart* after *her rescue, the country thanks Sergeant Weston for keeping her stupidity at bay long enough not to embarrass us all…*

"I'm such an idiot." She slammed the heels of her hands against her eyes.

"Sage."

"No. Don't. Please don't, Garrett. Can't you leave me with a shred of dignity here?"

"*Sage.*"

"I get it, okay? My body isn't what it once was. I don't fire your chamber anymore. Done. Let's move on."

"Sage, damn it!" The bed sagged with his weight. He leaned over her. Hell, even in her fury, her body woke up to his nearness, his heat, that intangible, spiritual zipper that refastened every cell inside her to him again. She really hated that connection right now, especially as he grated, "It's not what you think, okay?"

She spat out another angry laugh. "Seriously? You're going with that one? I've been on the run in Africa for the last year and that's old even for me, buddy."

He pressed closer. "I'm sorry that you think—"

"Shit. *That* one, too?"

"Are you going to listen to me?"

"No," she snapped, "because there's nothing for you to say. There's nothing you have to explain, all right? You thought I was dead. You moved on. I understand. So at least you tried, and thank you, but—"

Suddenly, he'd plunged his hand into her hair, clawing her scalp, forcing her head toward him. His stare was waiting for hers with such enflamed intensity, she felt sucked into an incinerator.

"The *fuck* I moved on!" It seethed from his locked teeth. He dragged a trembling thumb across her cheek. "My life stopped the second I walked into your parents' living room and saw the chaplain sitting there." He stopped, his chest pressing against the confines of his T-shirt with his hard breaths. "I couldn't move, Sage. I *didn't* move." He shook his head. "I could only move again when the rage set in. It sucked, but at least it filled the goddamn crater inside, after they told me you were—" He cleared his throat with a ragged cough. "After they told me you were gone. But at least I could function again. At least I could think again—if that's what you could call it.

"I started with Franz first. Yeah, I woke up my commanding officer in the middle of the night at his house, demanding that we scramble a team and head for Botswana to try and find you. Maybe I knew even then that you really weren't dead. I just felt like we had to try." He dropped his hand, pulling hers into it. "He let me bawl like an infant on his couch, but he still told me no. All those fuckers shut me down at every turn."

"Shit." As it came out beneath her breath, fresh tears brimmed. She wrapped her other hand over his, loving him with new depths of her soul. "Baby, I'm sorry."

He lifted his face again, his lips twitching as if a smile brewed there. It never materialized. The cobalt smoke had returned to his gaze, thicker than Sage had ever seen it. "Well, I wasn't sorry." He said it with leaden determination. "I left sorry behind when I left Franz's house that night. Something took the place of it, for good."

"Something like what?" she asked softly.

He stiffened. "I don't know." His lips compressed. In the silence of his contemplation, a breeze fluttered the curtains across the room, throwing a shaft of afternoon sun at him. For a moment, the anguish of his face was edged with light. The glow kissed the moisture at the ends of his hair and fringed his tawny lashes. The sight made her want to stop time, though her soul filled with crushing sorrow. Even the light from the galaxy's most powerful fireball couldn't penetrate the shadows in his eyes.

And she doubted she ever could again, either.

"Sage, it was something…dark, okay? Something hard and savage and vicious." He jutted his jaw, and his free hand fisted tight. "But it kept me going, at least. It kept me alive."

She looked away, trying to let his words sink in completely. Something on the nightstand glinted in the late afternoon sunlight. It hadn't been there when she'd taken a drink of water before falling asleep. Somehow, she knew what it was before she reached for it. The gold band felt as meaningful and magical as the day they'd picked it up from the jeweler. She held up the ring at an angle in order to check the inside. As she hoped, the inscription was there. She read it through a haze of tears.

My Hero.

Even engraved on the inside of his wedding ring, the words had always been a lighthearted tease between them, a fun reminder of what he'd done to get her attention that first night in Tacoma. Okay, "fun" probably wasn't the best phrasing on that. He'd come out of the brawl with the assholes with a busted lip, a black eye and nasty cuts on his knuckles, though the bawling-out she gave him in the tavern's kitchen afterward was certainly as painful. At the end of the night, they'd exchanged phone numbers. Along with his digits, he'd written: *Garrett Hawkins: Your on-call hero.*

She'd given him the words just ten hours ago, in the middle of King's Quonset hut. When she had, the meaning of the syllables changed forever. They weren't just stamped on her heart. They were branded in her soul.

"Whatever that force was," she murmured to him now, "I'm thankful for it."

Garrett pushed her hand away before heaving to his feet again. "No," he snapped. "Not whatever it *was.* That's what I'm trying to tell you, Sage. This shit, it hasn't left me. Finding you didn't dynamite my mental warehouse on it." He'd gotten to the window. With a violent *whoosh,* he shoved aside the drapes and locked his hands against both sides of the frame. "If anything, it's worse. After you—well, after you were gone, I used it like coffee, just to get up in the morning. After I returned to action, it helped shut off everything except for the missions." He grunted, and his shoulders slumped. "Fuck. Franz was never happier. I turned into a perfect machine, became his number one go-to guy besides Z. We were pretty much the dynamic duo of the First SF Group, turnin' and burnin' the bad guys as fast as we could find them."

Sage turned to look more directly at him. "So you concentrated on doing your job better. And it sounds like you did."

He didn't return her scrutiny. In his profile, she watched a hundred feelings launch emotional grenades at each other before they all exploded through his fist. A few splinters flew off the wood of the window frame before he said anything again.

"Do you understand what I'm saying? I concentrated on getting revenge for *your* life by taking as many as I legally could." He rotated his head back toward her. His lips were a tormented twist, his nostrils puffed like a bull with his hard breaths. "My soul took a swan dive into despair, and I dragged as many others into the ocean as I could. And now, even though you're back, I can't figure out how to climb out." He shoved back from the window. "Shit!"

Sage scrambled across the bed but stopped when her surge made him jerk back. "It's okay." Fresh tears stung her dry lips. "I understand. It's okay. Let me help."

"You *can't* help!" The boom of it visibly shook the thin curtains. "Don't you fucking see? I tried it, Sage. Just getting near you—I tried. I wanted to just love you, and I ended up—" He searched the room, his gaze desperate and agonized. "I ended up doing what I did."

Sage sat back on her heels. "Oh, hell. Do you think I'm nine, Garrett? I guarantee you, I'm not. And I'm very aware of what it was."

"That doesn't change—"

"Sexual domination."

She couldn't think of any other way to get through to him. From the jump of his brows and the tighter tension in his body, it looked like she'd succeeded. With the subtlety of a sledge hammer.

"Look," she stammered on, twisting her hands in her lap, "I know we've never discussed it before, but—"

"Damn straight we've never discussed it." He stomped back to the window.

"Maybe we should."

"Maybe we shouldn't." His shoulders tested the limits of his T-shirt again. "Maybe we absolutely won't."

"Why?"

"Because I'm not that guy, okay?"

She lifted a tiny smile. "Maybe now you are. Hmm. *Sir Garrett.* It has a nice—"

"Stop." He spun back toward her. Despair no longer filled his stare. In every inch of his eyes was the deep, unblinking blue of a very pissed-off animal. "There's nothing remotely nice about it. Don't say it again. *Ever.*"

She spread her hands, supplicating to him. "Garrett—"

"I'm not doing this, Sage. Not now, and not with you. That part of me *isn't* for you."

She rose to her knees. Fine. He wanted to play king of the damn jungle? She could do jungle. She had been for a year. "Not good enough, Sergeant. *Why,* damn it?"

His glower intensified. "Are you fucking kidding me? Fine. Because I happen to love you, remember? Men don't do shit like that to the women they love!"

"Even if the woman likes it?"

He halted as if he'd walked into a sword. His eyebrows plummeted. The anger and confusion on his face declared war on each other. "I'm throwing the bullshit flag on your ass, Sage Weston. No sane woman can actually admit to—"

"What?" The sword had climbed into his gaze and she met it head-on, molding it into the steel resolution beneath her own posture. "To what, Garrett? To letting you take charge of

69

me? To letting you command me, control me and—gasp!—be stronger than me, after I endured a whole damn year of having to do that for myself every damn day?" When he did nothing but park himself into a stubborn pose, she thrust her chin out in rebellious fury. "Yeah, I guess that makes me insane."

A minute of thick silence passed. Neither of them moved. At last, Garrett closed the two steps back to the bed. He paused another moment, before sitting again. Sage kept still, consciously ordering herself not to dive for his lap, curl herself around him, and not move for hours. Couldn't he feel it too? Couldn't he sense how much she needed him? Could he really have stopped caring completely?

The question finished invading her mind about the moment he reached for her hands again.

"Sage, my heart…we could've gone into that shithole last night, found bags of diamonds, and I'd have been less knocked on my ass. You are the gift I never expected to find again. This…you, here…it's the fulfillment of my craziest, wildest dreams. And yet I got you back here, and I treated you like—" Beneath his breath, he gave himself a filthy verbal flogging. "Don't you understand?" he finally growled. "Damn it, you should be wrapped in satin, and sleeping on fine linen, and treated like a queen. And all you've gotten is—"

"No." She smashed her hand over his mouth. "I should be wrapped in *you.* Sleeping next to *you.*" When his throat constricted on a swallow, the backs of her eyes pricked yet again. When would these stupid tears stop? "You obstinate dork. I don't want to be your stupid queen under glass, okay? I just want…"

"I know." He said it after pulling her hand away, though he kept her fingers curled inside his. "And I'm here." He pulled her knuckles against his lips. "I'm right here, and I'm not going anywhere. You have me here, Sage. Always."

He released her hand. But the look on his face made Sage push it right back, looping her grip around his neck. She twisted her fingers into his hair, a silent command to keep his gaze locked on her. To the man's credit, he endured her scrutiny. He smiled, if that's what the look could be called.

Both edges of his mouth wavered as if stabbed into place by dull thumbtacks. It reminded her of the event posters in the mess back on base. Lame messages proclaimed in half-peeling tempura paint.

Her stomach coiled into a tighter knot. Dread needled her whole body.

Damn it. *Damn it.* Yep, lame message was definitely the case this time.

"I have you," she echoed, "always. But…not in *all* ways." When Garrett rushed his stare back toward the window, she persisted, "I'm right, aren't I?"

"Sage." He sighed heavily. "This isn't up for discussion."

"Of course it isn't. You've already made up your own ass-backward mind, haven't you? You still think you're going to turn into some kind of sadistic beast and hurt me, so you're just not going to let me in. You're still going to slink off into your shadows, and fuck another by-the-hour tart because you think I can't handle your damn 'shadows.'"

He whipped his stare back. It had morphed into a glare. "This is for the better."

"Really?" she flung back. "This *what,* Garrett? Tell me, what the hell am I to you now?" She grabbed his ring again then held it up between them. "Is this going to just become an expensive little amulet?"

A pulse rammed in his jaw. "That's not fair."

"That's truth! This ring is supposed to stand for sharing our lives, Garrett. For sharing, not for running from each other!"

The accusation ignited him. *Thank God.* He surged toward her, his face ferocious. Weirdly, his rage thrilled her. At least she could still get to him. There was hope.

"So what now?" She knew it was a push. But desperate times called for having girl balls. "Well, Garrett? Do you have the answer for *this* one? What do we do? Do we define what we have left over? What am I going to be now? Your roommate? Your responsibility? Your precious 'mission package?' Do I get to be 'turned over' once we're back, so I'm

71

not your damn concern anymore?"

He yanked back with a violent jerk. His whole body coiled. There was no way she couldn't feel it. His thick thighs shook the bed as he prepared his body to act on the bail-out his mind had clearly commanded. Sage's body went taut, preparing for the Arctic cold that would take over as soon as he bolted.

But he didn't leave. As he'd truly promised, he stayed. He lifted his hand to engulf hers, surrounding her fingers plus the ring inside a grip that bordered on crushing. The sight of him consumed Sage's senses with equal effect. She was swept away anew by his rugged beauty, suffocated in the fire of his powerful, unmerciful focus.

"You're mine."

The words rumbled from the depths of his chest. She was left with no doubt about their intent. They were vows, not just syllables.

"You're *mine,* Sage. Call in any deity or god or spirit you want; I'll swear by their names and all their fucking saints and angels, too. As far as I'm concerned, it took them all working together to bring you back to me, anyway."

She parted her lips, wanting to say something but choked by a maddening desire to kiss *and* wring his neck at once. He didn't make things easier by sliding to the floor next to her, taking a knee as he continued gripping her hand. "You're not a gift I'm going to waste. I swear by this ring and everything it still means to me, you will be safe. I'll protect you from any animal, asshole, criminal, or deviant who thinks they can lay so much as a fingernail of harm against you. And yeah," –he finally rose to his feet, let her go, and crossed back to the window— "that includes protecting you from me too."

Sage didn't shift. At last, she let out a hard sigh. The hard hunch of his shoulders told her he was ready to keep sparring with her, but what good was it going to do? The damn bear had made up his mind and taken his position. If the poles of the whole damn earth flipped and told him that position wasn't right any more, he'd fight to the death for it. Fate had stripped him of getting to do it for over a year, and now the man wasn't just making up for lost time, but doubling his efforts. To him, the stance made sense—because to him, her number one enemy was only a breath away. His own.

Fine. If that's the way he wanted to look at things, that's what she'd work with.

All she had to do now was give him bigger enemies to fight.

You want to keep me safe, Sergeant Hawkins? That's just peachy by me, baby. Let's rumble.

Angel Payne

Chapter Seven

Ironically, perhaps even thankfully, the embassy made the decision to send Sage and Rayna home on a commercial flight instead of a military transport. The news came down early the next morning, and Garrett was packed and ready to head to Suvarnabhumi Airport by three that afternoon.

On one hand, he was glad they'd be enjoying the marathon-length journey in civilian comfort. On the much larger other hand, he already sensed that Sage wasn't going to let him relax during the next twenty-four hours. She boarded the van with a serene smile and a graceful glide that didn't match the fuming woman who'd turned her back on him in bed last night, unwilling to hear his explanation about had happened—more accurately, *hadn't* happened—at the hotel. Thinking back on all that now only reconfirmed his suspicion. Sometime between giving him that cold shoulder and this afternoon's warm smile, she'd hatched a plan of some kind—and something told him he wasn't going to be happy he couldn't pound a few irritated fists into the fuselage of a pretty 747.

The departure from protocol was explained as necessary due to the media frenzy that had developed stateside for the girls' story. Every major news station wanted their shot of the "miracle nurses' return to the living," and the Army, knowing a prize PR op when they had one, sure as hell wanted to supply it. The circus began even at Suvarnabhumi, with CNN, Fox News, BBC and a few of the other major networks on hand, cameras and microphones recording every step they took to the plane. Garrett, Zeke and six other guys from the squad were there, dutifully surrounding Sage and Rayna in a sea of US Army dress blue, as they'd been instructed.

Orders or not, Garrett didn't leave Sage's side, not even when she stopped to buy flowers from local children, or when she veered off their path to take up CNN's offer for a wave to her mom on their live feed. When she paused *again* and said she needed to use the bathroom, he didn't break stride, forcing her along by the crook of her elbow.

"We're twenty yards from the plane," he said into her ear from locked teeth. "You'll get your chance there."

With a deft wrench, she broke free from him. She tilted her head, eyes flashing like a confident little cat. Garrett knew that look. It always made him yearn to slam her into a wall and fuck the breath out of her. Not a damn thing had changed.

"I have to pee *now,* Sergeant Hawkins. If you're worried about 'protecting' me in the ladies toilet, you're more than welcome to join me."

For a second, he thought of calling her bluff. But the next moment, he looked down at his dress blues, followed by a glance at the news crews. The last thing he needed was some cameraman revved on three Red Bulls, catching a secret shot of him pulling a pissing match with their "darling" of the moment. He bit out the *f* word beneath his breath, let her go, and leaned against the wall. She smiled and sashayed into the bathroom.

She had him by the balls, and they both knew it.

Three hours later, the scheming little minx didn't seem inclined to loosen that grip any time soon. Shockingly, Garrett hadn't punched any holes into the 747 yet—though that trend might change any second now.

The temptation pressed harder as her husky laugh broke the air again, a response to another joke cracked by Ethan Archer. He'd always liked Ethan, one of their hardest-working squad members despite being male model pretty, until about an hour ago. The young corporal was pulling out all the stops on his I'm-so-modest-and-you're-so-cute act, and Sage was doing very little to slow him down. It had gotten worse over the last ten minutes, when a pocket of turbulence caused some of Sage's bottled water to dump on Archer's thigh. The sight of her wiping off the spill in a fretful frenzy had Garrett clutching for his seatbelt release.

That was it. Her stranglehold on his family jewels stopped *now.* She'd be spending the rest of the flight next to him, where he could keep an eye on her saucy, conniving little backside until Mount Rainier circled into view.

As he rose, Archer did too. When the corporal turned, looking for the nearest head, at least three women lifted their heads in open appreciation. Garrett chuffed. *Come to papa, Dolce and Gabbana,*

Archer easily observed that the nearest toilet was two rows behind Garrett's location. The corporal scowled. He knew a showdown with Garrett was inevitable in this direction, but if he bee-lined for the head at the front of the plane, it was a blatant pussy move.

Archer turned toward the rear toilet. Garrett made his way to the little service galley past its door.

"Hawk." Archer gave him a tight smile. The guy was pretty but not stupid. He had to know what was coming.

"Hey, Runway." Garrett deliberately used the guy's nickname, which had been bestowed by the squad due to Ethan's centerfold-ready looks. Though Ethan earned it in a more legitimate sense by taking down a drug lord's helo with a ground rocket six months ago, it was clear at which context Garrett aimed with the label right now. Archer's wince confirmed he knew it too.

"Is something up?" the corporal asked.

Garrett leaned against the bathroom door, deliberately ignoring the question. "You and Sergeant Weston seem to be having fun."

To his credit, Archer planted his stance and squared his shoulders. "Seems like she's needing a little fun."

"Yeah, well…playtime's over."

"She told me you two are taking a break. She also told me it was your choice."

Garrett grunted. Two days ago, he'd been gasping against a hundred daggers of grief in his chest. Archer's words dumped a gallon of acid onto the leftover scabs. The shit overflowed and stung his retort. "Yeah, that's probably what she said. That doesn't mean she's ready for a goddamn romp on the mattress, man."

Archer ticked a brow. "Who says I want to 'romp?'"

Acid, say hello to Mr. Matchstick. "I know what you

want to do, asshole." Garrett grabbed the corporal by the V of his shirt. "I know you're deeper into that kinky tie-me-up shit than Zeke, and that you're already thinking of strapping her down in some deviant dungeon and—"

"The proper term is BDSM, Sergeant." For some reason, the guy's composed comeback was more censuring than a cuss-ridden rant. "And, when power is properly exchanged by a willing submissive and a loving Dominant, the results can transform people. It even heals them from things, such as being on the run and fearing for their life every day for a year."

"Thanks for the gung-ho on that, Corporal." He didn't relent on his hold. "Now keep it the hell away from Sergeant Weston."

Archer returned a careful nod. "Respectfully speaking, it seems Sage is capable of making that decision for herself."

"As you brilliantly mentioned two seconds ago, Sage just spent a year running in the wilds of Africa then the jungles of Thailand, not sure who to trust or where to go. I don't think she knows what she wants for breakfast tomorrow morning."

"Ah, but you do. And now that you're 'taking a break' from each other, you know that even better." The guy tilted his head with that unnerving Zen-like concentration. "Respectfully speaking, of course."

It was official. Garrett now wanted to put his fist into Archer's perfect face more than the plane's wall. He could practically feel Shrink Sally popping up on his shoulder, pen tapping her chin, gently discussing crap like misplaced aggression and sideways control issues. He gave the doc a hard mental shove. After her specter did a header into the box of snack pretzels, he refocused on Runway.

"You want to bring respect into this?" he snarled. "Good. Go ahead. Respect her—from as far the fuck away from her as you can get." He unfurled his hand from the guy's shirt. With less decorum, he jerked open the bathroom's door. "After you're done fixing your makeup in there, plant your ass in my old seat. I'll watch over Sergeant Weston from here on in."

"Yes Sir."

He ignored the little lip twitch Archer added to that, knowing it would take his ire to places it shouldn't be. Not that it wasn't there already. Not that deep inside, he didn't admit that every note of the guy's subtext hit the nail on its damn head. Not that he didn't know he was using protectiveness as an excuse for every emotion he had and every asshole move he made—a pair of lists that seemed to be swelling by the hour.

Sage's perturbed sigh broadcasted that fact to him as he claimed the seat next to her. But when he twined his hand into hers, she didn't resist. He waited a minute. Tightened his hold. She shifted a little but didn't pull away.

He turned and narrowed his eyes at her in curiosity. She kept her eyes fixed on the in-flight movie, her brows quirking at the action on the screen. "I had no idea Stallone could still run that fast."

He snorted. "Some things haven't changed."

She leaned her head back. "I guess not."

He looked down. "Hands," he murmured. "Not elbows."

The corners of her mouth quirked. He was talking about their hold on each other. Usually they twisted themselves together all the way to their elbows. It was a tiny detail she probably thought he'd forgotten.

"I remember." He said it into her ear. "I remember everything, Sage." He drew back a little before going on, "I also remember this usually meant I was deep in the doghouse."

Her lips lifted a little higher. "You have a good memory, Sergeant Hawkins."

Garrett glowered. "Fine. I was an ass to Archer. I'll apologize."

"I'll give you that," she countered. "You *were* a butthead to Ethan." Her gaze didn't waver from the small village getting blown up on the overhead screens. Garrett watched the orange and yellow colors reflected in her eyes, though he seriously wondered how many of those fireballs were due to the movie. "But that's not why you're in the doghouse, and you know it."

He forced a deep breath in and back out. "Were you listening when Zeke talked to you, Sage? Didn't he explain—"

"Yes," she snapped, "he did. I got the whole Zeke Hayes special rundown, okay? You didn't go through with it. Fine. I heard him, loud and clear."

His gut twisted. "But you don't believe him."

"No, that's not—Oh, God!" She huffed, sounding exasperated. "I believe him, Garrett. I do."

He wondered why his intestines still felt like goddamn knots. "All right. So…what is it?"

She finally jerked her face at him. "What is it?" A snort burst out of her. "Are you honestly asking me that?" She looked nearly ready to punch him. Garrett wished she would have. He wished for anything other than the tears that pooled in her eyes instead. They didn't just turn her gaze the color of Kryptonite. Her pain *was* that shitty stuff for him. "You went there in the first place, Garrett." She pulled in a shaky sigh. "It was a crappy thing to do."

He didn't say anything for a long moment. In that silence, he lifted his free hand to thumb away her tears from her cheeks. After that, he gave her a quiet nod. "You're right. And I'm sorry." Before he continued, he nudged her face up so their stares were entwined again. "But I'm not sorry for why I did it. I meant what I said last night, Sage. I'm going to protect you, if I have to protect you from me."

She struggled to shake her head. Her face told him she didn't understand, but he knew what filled the gaze he gave her in return. Knew it in every corner of his soul, every beat of his heart. He'd only have a few more moments to convey it to her, courtesy of the dress blues rules they were already shattering, but if he got ten violations slammed at him, it'd be worth it. For a year, he'd dreamed of this. For every dream orgasm he'd had with her, there were ten fantasies of this. Of having her near, holding her safe, flooding her with a stare full of his love…

He'd walk through a thousand more slimy jungles for this. He'd throw down his life for this.

If he lost her again, he'd want to be dead, anyway.

* * * *

In true Pacific Northwest style, the Seattle-Tacoma weather gods broke out one of their best downpours in honor of the girls' homecoming. It was another lucky twist of fate, because when Heidi was finally reunited with her daughter and the TV cameras zoomed in for their close-ups of the mother and daughter sobbing on each other, nobody paid attention to one Sergeant Hawkins behind them discreetly wiping "rain" off his own face. Rayna had a similar reunion with her brothers, who could easily fill out most of an epic movie cast even with two of their seven out on deployments. Zeke kept careful watch nearby, until something outside the terminal window caused a thunderhead to cross his face that made the clouds outside look like cartoons.

After making sure a Sea-Tac security officer was instructed not to take his eyes off Sage, Garrett snuck behind the camera crews and stepped next to his friend. "Dude, you look like you saw the spawn of Hell himself."

Zeke's lip curled with rancor. "I did."

"What're you—"

His friend cut him short with a rough grunt and a curt nod. Garrett followed the trajectory of that move, looking outside. Their plane had taxied to a gate at the end of the terminal, adjacent to what looked like the airport's main security operations. Considering who they'd just shuttled home, the move wasn't surprising. His scrutiny took in a one-story building with a mess of communication equipment on its roof, with a swarm of people in dark blue uniforms both inside and out. There were four standard-issue police cars present, flanking a black van that looked anything but standard. Because it wasn't.

Standing in the rain outside that van, his wrists and legs chained and his elbows bracketed by two FBI suits, was the man he'd last seen kneeling in jungle grass, busted in the act of trying to broker women into slavery.

King.

If blood could really scream, Garrett was certain his did. Rage and disbelief took over a corner of his body. As if beckoned merely by the strength of that chaos, the asshole below raised his head for a moment. He turned up a slow grinn as soon as he spotted Garrett and Zeke. He took in their fury, and tongued his lips as if finishing off a juicy steak. "Evil" was too good a term for the bastard. So was "worm in the sewer of humanity."

Garrett barely controlled the craving to pound down the window. "What the *fuck* is he doing here?"

Zeke emitted another furious rumble. "I don't know. But I'm gonna damn-well find out."

"Good." It was agonizing to take in a breath. His hard nod came easier. "Good."

"I'll call you."

"You sure as hell will."

"Rayna and Sage don't get told. Not right now." His friend tensed, making his body seem like a mountain atop an earthquake. "Rayna's already battling some fucked-up nightmares. Lots of them."

Garrett felt his brows jerk up. "And you have firsthand knowledge of this already?" He shook his head. "Shit, dude."

"It's not like that, asshat." Zeke backhanded his chest with brutal force. "I slept on the couch in her room, okay? She's been through hell. She hasn't had anyone to be strong for her. I just...needed to be there. It just needed to be me."

"Yeah." Garrett said it as he turned and looked back at the mob who still clamored near Sage, Rayna, and their families. "I get it, Z."

Hell, did he get it. Every muscle in his body went taut as Sage looked toward the position he'd been occupying, behind her right shoulder. When she discovered the Sea-Tac officer there instead, her gaze scoured the terminal in panic. Garrett stepped over, making sure he hit her line of sight. When she found him and visibly relaxed, it was the greatest high of his day. Screw that, of his year.

He fought the compulsion to finish off the deal by lunging for her, sweeping her into his arms, and dragging her home, safe against his side. Her grateful little smile didn't help his resistance. He settled for what he could do about things. He nodded back, and mouthed two words at her.

I'm here.

From the depths of his being, he swore to stay near. He promised it with the same solemnity he'd show if kneeling before her with a sword in his grip and a shield at his chest. She wasn't getting rid of him, no matter how many industrial-strength chains he'd just seen hanging on King's body. Knowing the bastard had been extradited back to the country would have been a game-changer alone on his promise. But the slime bag was in the same goddamn *city* as her now.

Sage laughed at something her mom said. Now that she felt safe again, she allowed herself to indulge in humor. Garrett savored the warmth that filled him with the sight, knowing he wouldn't get to relish it for long. Soon, she'd find a way to restart her rebel yell behavior toward him. Her attempt to unravel his thinking about "Sir Garrett" would take flight with some new inspiration, and he'd be tempted all over again to hogtie her simply for lack of other options.

Damn it.

He'd been hoping that the long journey from Thailand and the return back to familiar soil would be the magic erasers on his darker sexual urges. But just the flash of that image in his head, of tying Sage up until she was totally at his mercy…

Shit.

His cock surged in ways that weren't cool in the middle of a jammed airport terminal, with half the world watching on live feed. Thank God the crew from TMZ had skipped this particular news op. His hard-on was safe from their digital boner detectors for now.

And Sage still wasn't safe from him.

He redirected his thoughts toward just getting her home right now. Maybe in a few days, things would be different. Maybe after Zeke did some digging, and assured them both that King was bound for some high-security hellhole somewhere, he could relax and re-wire his head so it interfaced with his dick correctly again. The ways that Sage deserved. The normal ways.

Whatever the fuck "normal" was anymore.

* * * *

His ringing cell roused him from a dead sleep. That part was pretty normal.

When it did that at seven thirty in the morning, it wasn't normal.

Garrett gaped at the phone's screen, certain he hadn't read the time right. The last time he'd slept past five, let alone seven, had been in the days Sage made it worthwhile to sleep in. He hadn't set the alarm last night, certain he'd wake up just because the den couch was as comfortable to sleep on as a bed of nails. But sure enough, here he was, clicking the green button to blurt a greeting to Zeke.

"Hey."

"Hey, man." There was a discerning pause. "Whoa. Did I wake you up?"

"Don't worry about it. What'd you find out?"

He didn't elaborate further on the question. The bombshell of seeing King had jarred Zeke as deeply as him. Zeke had likely sparked up his street network the second they'd left the airport. Z knew the workings of the Seattle streets the same way Garrett knew every part of a corn thresher. He had to admit that at times, he couldn't believe he was best friends with an orphan from the darker corners of Pioneer Square, but right now, he'd never been more grateful Z had kept up with that underground network.

"Plenty," Zeke gave up in a growl, "and none of it's pretty."

"Hell."

"Yeah, that's what this is gonna feel like."

He got up and peeked around the corner into the bedroom. Not a sound or a movement came from the bed, piled with the poofy linens in dark green and cream that Sage picked out when they first bought the place. She was burrowed deep and sleeping soundly, and if she wanted to do so until next week, he was going to let her.

"All right," he said after returning to the den, "lay it on

me."

There was a weighted breath on the other end of the line. "His real name's not King. I know that doesn't surprise you. His sixteen different *other* names might, however."

"What the—" He let out a stunned whoosh. "Sixteen?"

"That's only where the numbers begin with this guy. Apparently, he's been at this shit for a while. He grew up in Vegas as Isaiah Irwin. He dropped out of school when he was fourteen, and started in the scene as a junior-level pimp. That's when he became "Ice" Irwin. When the big man there decided to offer franchise opportunities to his boys, setting each of them up in major cities across the country, Irwin was the Sea-Tac guy. He set up a very successful racket here, going high-end with his game. He catered to the tech corridor execs and the guys coming to visit them, strictly shit out of the Alexis, the Four Seasons, the Edgewater. Naturally, he had a different identity that he used with each hotel."

Garrett pounded a finger on his knee. "Slick asshole."

"No kidding. Well, everything was going along peachy, happy girls and happy clients, until Irwin, or whatever the hell he called himself by then, decided to set up a little side biz and not tell the boss about it."

"What kind of a side business?"

"He got a bunch of guys onto the base as contractors."

"*Our* base? Fort Lewis?"

"Affirmative. Now you know where I'm going with this one, yeah?"

He wouldn't be surprised if a megawatt light bulb of understanding appeared in the air over his head. "Holy shit. Was he tied into all those weapons that started disappearing off base a few years ago?"

"The ringleader. He set up a new identity for the racket; had the balls to name himself Rambo Righteous for it, if you can believe it."

"I'm learning to believe anything from this bozo right now."

"He ran the goods to the highest bidders in Afghanistan, Pakistan, Iran, you name it. Three guesses as to what city he used as home base, and the first two don't count."

"Bangkok, Thailand." Garrett said it before Z finished.

"Check," his friend replied. "But the reason we never caught him is because he got a line on someone greedy from inside the supply chain. He didn't need the base anymore, so he pulled his guys out before we nailed their asses. Another racket set up, another alias established."

"Of course," Garrett muttered. "And this time, he was Chuck fucking Norris."

Z gave him a dark chuckle for that before going on. "Once the bastard got integrated into Bangkok, the criminal world was his fucking oyster. Drugs, diamonds, even those ridiculous fake Rolexes."

"And human trafficking."

"Roger that. Loud and clear."

Garrett couldn't contain a long, enraged growl anymore. "He's the goddamn eBay of illegal and immoral."

"But the racket he ran with the highest debt to pay back is the firearms game. When you add his injured party to the mix, the United States government, you end up with an extradition back to the scene of the crime faster than you can say 'do me in the ass again please, warden.'"

Garrett dragged an ottoman over with his foot then hiked his heel on it. "I hope the bastard is squealing like a pig as we speak."

Zeke sent back an unsettled snarl to affirm the sentiment. "I hope the asshole isn't doing anything right now except brooding in solitary."

He waited for a deeper explanation of that. When Z didn't give anything up except heavy silence, Garrett pressed, "What do you mean?"

For another long moment, his friend still didn't talk. When he finally spoke, his voice dipped into a tone Garrett only heard on their messiest missions. "I mean that King's still connected all over the area, Hawk. Big time. He got enough flow to buy out the big man from Vegas about six months ago, and now he's *numero uno* daddy pimp in town. My guys on the street tell me that he's even sold a few of his girls here into the

Thailand stream."

Garrett kicked the ottoman. As the cushion slammed into the wall, he lurched to his feet. "What!"

"Yeah, he's a real beautiful specimen of humanity. Guess if he finds a girl who has no real family and can't be traced, she's invited to a yacht party on the harbor, which fast becomes a barge trip to Bangkok."

He began to pace. His fingers ached with their hard grip on the phone. "Z, if he's still got money all over town, even the prison walls won't stop him. FDC Sea-Tac might as well be the damn Four Seasons."

Zeke snorted. "You think that's a news flash to me, dude?" There was a pause and a rough scratching on the line, sounding a lot like his friend swallowed hard. "Hawk…he's already put out some lines on Sage and Rayna too."

"Fuck!"

"That's a good way of phrasing it." His friend emitted another rough breath. "And once he connects the dots from the girls back to the guys who led the mission that took him down…"

"Hell."

He didn't need Zeke to fill in the rest of that scenario for him. The statements they'd taken from Sage and Rayna, as well as the aid workers they'd rescued, painted a vivid enough picture of the man's disgusting depravity. Now that King was sitting on his ass at Sea-Tac FDC, he had lots of free time to scratch that sordid itch—with a revenge fantasy that started with recapturing Sage and Rayna.

"I've already taken this to Franzen," Zeke continued. "He'll be interfacing with the Feds on this, who will hopefully put a lockdown on who King gets to see and 'chat' with."

Garrett's heart took a swan dive into his gut. "But he wants us to bring the girls to the base, doesn't he?"

"Hell no! King—well, Rambo Righteous—had at least a dozen guys in on the weapons racket. They probably know the place better than we do." It sounded like Zeke got up himself. The drone of a distant television came over the line. "The girls go nowhere near the base. We're also on clamshell status on telling them anything. In case—" His friend coughed uncomfortably. "Well, in case they do get taken again, the less they know, the better."

Just hearing the words caused a haze of rage to sneak at the edges of Garrett's vision. It was a direct contrast to the scene he looked out on from the den window. The neighborhood sparkled in morning sun, and the snowy heights of Rainier were radiant in the post-storm gleam. None of it made a dent in his tension, or eased the lock of his teeth as he answered Z. "That is *not* going to happen."

"I happen to heartily agree, my friend." His friend's heavy footsteps sounded on the line. After that, a discernible flicking sound. A cigarette lighter. It wasn't surprising. Z only smoked when he was too tense to do anything else, and this situation likely qualified for that. "Hawk, I know this goes without saying, but it'll make me feel better. Don't take your eyes off Sage."

"Check the box already, man. I assume you've got the scope on Rayna?"

"I'm running a gauntlet of seven brothers to do that, but yes."

"Call me later."

"Check."

He hung up from Z, and with the phone still in hand, made his way back to the bedroom. Yeah, it had only been ten minutes since he'd last been in here, but this time, he needed to see her, to touch her. To assure himself, especially now, that the last three days hadn't been a dream he'd wake up from back in Bangkok, drenched in cold sweat and jamming his finger into a ring between his dog tags.

He stepped into the dim room, crossed to the bed, and took care to lower slowly to the mattress. He dipped the thing with his weight anyway, which gave him extra incentive to pull gently at the covers. He'd leave as soon as he saw the soft curtain of her hair and the soft contours of her face...

Which weren't there.

"Sage?"

He murmured it at first, certain she'd buried herself

really deep in the mountain of covers—which didn't move even after he jabbed at them.

"Sage."

He ordered it now, stripping the whisper from his voice as he swept the linens off the bed. The *empty* bed.

"Fuck! Sage!"

This was the part where he was supposed to wake up. This was the moment where he jolted out of the nightmare and faced the grief. But he didn't wake up. The bad dream and the shitty reality were one hideous thing now. She was really gone.

Angel Payne

Chapter Eight

Silence. Blessed, glorious silence.

Sage had swum the lake many times but never just enjoyed its serenity. She'd always been in too much of a hurry, plowing through the water in a hard breast stroke, revved by thoughts of what she had to do that day, of things she had to organize, of paperwork to complete and orders to carry out on base. The exercise had always been satisfying but never fulfilling, just another task to cross off the list.

She'd never simply turned over on her back like this and floated. She'd never let the sun warm her face, the breeze flow over her skin, or the water embrace her like a giant swath of liquid velvet…

"Sage!"

So much for metaphors about velvet. Garrett's bellow might as well have been a bear's claw ripping through that plush fabric.

She flipped over and gave him a little wave. At first, a smile brimmed to her lips despite his savage tone. Dear God, he was a magnificent sight, even far away on the shore. All those missions he talked about had bulked him in all the right places. His gray tank, emblazoned with ARMY in black letters, was tight against his broad chest. His baggy black shorts hung to the middle of his tree trunk thighs, leaving plenty for her to ogle below that. Even his calves bulged with muscle.

Her expression fell as he stomped into the water, sending a furious spray in his wake. Was he really coming in after her?

"Shit," she muttered, swimming to the dock. By the time she got there and climbed the ladder at the end, the boards were shaking. Garrett had launched onto them from his end and now marched toward her at a pace resonating somewhere between pissed drill officer and agitated Highlander. She picked up her towel with fingers that trembled despite the summer morning.

"Uh…hey." Maybe if she pretended he wasn't pulling a marauding gorilla act, so would he.

No such luck. He halted when getting about three feet from her, his glare as scorching as a blow torch. "What the hell are you doing?"

Sage couldn't help her sardonic glance. "The last time I checked, it was called swimming." She nodded at the lake. "This big body of water here? You can get in it and float around, and it feels really good. You should try—"

"Are you joking about this?" Forget the blowtorch. His stare went utterly black. The dark energy curled through him, tautening those muscles into an almost frightening sight. "Damn it, Sage! Do you know what I thought when—" He dragged a hand through his hair. "Did you even think to leave a note?"

Sage's confusion did a fast turn into irritation. It was a simple hop to reach full anger. "I swim a lot in the mornings, Garrett. Or at least I used to, in the days before I got up every day before sunlight so the rebels, the pirates, the insurgents and the slave traders wouldn't find me. This seemed like a nice way to get back into normalcy." She tugged the towel tighter before starting back up the dock. "Whatever the hell 'normal' is with you anymore."

"Wait!"

She didn't alter her stride. She couldn't—and wouldn't—handle his chest-beating bullshit another second. How had she considered this stuff even kind of cute during the trip home, when he'd called her on the flirting act with Ethan, pulling rank so he could sit with her instead? She'd outright adored him for it once they got to Sea-Tac and the waiting ocean of media, especially when a lot of the reporters followed them to dinner with Mom, Rayna, and her friend's small village of a family. Yes, she'd been grateful for his blistering glares and dictatorial orders then. They'd been *appropriate* then!

She looked down at the water and fumed deeper. There were still a few ripples left over from where she'd been lost in the first peaceful moment of the last four hundred thirty six days of her life. But they were fading fast. Way too fast.

"Sage. I said *wait.*"

She hated herself for stopping. The ire soaked the words she turned and spat at him. "Right. The same way you stopped and waited when walking out on me at the embassy?"

For a second, remorse flashed across his features. It got burned away the next second, as usual, by the overbearing jerk he pulled on more comfortably than those shorts. "*Damn it.* I've explained myself for that. I've eaten my hat with you for that. Don't go piecing that one together on me again, sugar."

Before she could help herself, she marched over and jammed a finger in his chest. "*Don't* 'sugar' me."

"Fine. But you won't leave the house again without telling me where you're going."

She jumped both her brows. "Excuse me?"

"You heard me, sug—" He jammed his lips together. "You heard me."

Those last three syllables made Sage's pulse freeze on a few beats. No, not the words. His inflection on them. Low. Anxious. Ominous. Sage raised her gaze and looked at him. *Really* looked. As she did, slivers of ice shot through her body. Holy crap. She'd been slammed so senseless by Garrett's fury, she didn't have time to breathe and remember one of the most basic psychology rules they were taught in Medical Department Basic. Anger was most often spawned by fear.

He wasn't mad at her. He was afraid for her. From the staunch set of his shoulders to the pulse hammering in his throat, the truth of it came into glaring focus. He was terrified.

Sage pulled her hand back, but didn't surrender her position. "What's going on, Garrett?" she asked softly. "What are you not telling me?"

He turned his gaze back to the shore. That didn't prevent her from watching more smoke drop over his eyes. "Just leave me a note the next time you go swimming."

She blinked. Well, hell. So much for the whole attempt at understanding the ogre. His fist of a tone became a punch to her gut, twisting around everything there in a mix of dread, fury and frustration.

"Fine," she spat back. "And I'll eat my damn cauliflower too. Thanks, dad."

It was more than a snarky comment, and they both knew it. The guy who'd contributed his sperm to create her hadn't been around for her since a drunken rant after her tenth birthday party. She'd been through enough therapy since then to realize she'd likely never speak the word "dad" with affection in this lifetime. Garrett loved her anyway. At least he used to. She wasn't so sure what he felt for her anymore.

Remarkably, her little bratty test made the slash of his mouth soften a little. He reached and palmed the back of her head, making her breath catch from the warmth it spread through her. When he pressed his lips to her forehead, she released the breath on a sappy sigh.

"You hate cauliflower," he whispered.

His steps back up the dock were wide, heavy, and resigned.

Sage yanked the towel tighter as she watched him eat up the distance with his strides, letting an equally long thread of bittersweet emotion wind around her heart. A little smile curled her lips. He really remembered…even all the little stuff. And his whisper, given with such tenderness, told her that more than a few sparks of his old self still burned inside his warrior's shell.

Those sparks gave her hope. Maybe, if those cinders were mixed with the smokescreen he'd billowed to keep the whole world out, they could kindle into something new, some*one* new. A Garrett who was burned yet better. Different but stronger.

A man who could handle the woman *she'd* become.

She realigned her stance and held her head high. Okay, there was hope. Yeah, it was going to take more bratty moves, more pissing him off, and a lot more of staying one step ahead of him, especially to find out what had caused that new fear in his stare and that new coil of tension in his shoulders. But the hope was here. The hope was real.

As she let it fill her heart, she smiled and murmured, "Yeah, dork. You hate cauliflower too." And as she followed him back up the dock, she deliberately set a slow, thoughtful pace. Plans like this took time and care, especially when it came to an attempt at changing the will of her intractable, adorable fiancé. And despite his every-move-you-make watchfulness, she found it funny that Garrett hadn't grabbed a huge clue about their new reality. The last year had molded *her* will into an entity as formidable as his. She would *not* fail this mission, even if she damn-near killed herself in the process.

Angel Payne

Chapter Nine

The woman was going to kill him.

If she didn't take out her own gorgeous ass first.

Garrett shook his head with those thoughts as he got to Gray Airfield and slammed his Sierra hybrid into park. Had it really been only seven days since they'd gotten back from Bangkok? It felt like eight decades.

If murder *was* her intent, she was hell-bent on robbing him of his sanity first. And no, it didn't matter that he'd deduced her little plan from the second she'd smiled coyly at Archer during the trip home. It was all pretty transparent, her grand scheme to keep him so busy "protecting her from *herself*" that he forgot his original monster act on her in Bangkok.

Right.

He would've laughed at the ludicrous track of her thinking if he weren't so hideously aware of the bigger threat that shadowed her each day. Zeke made that official less than ten hours after the first time he'd called. One line of text was all it took to turn Garrett's cautious trepidation into full-blown paranoia.

Bounty on S and R is at $50K each. Don't leave her side. I've got Rayna. ~Z~

Garrett had taken the charge as serious as a mission order from the guy. From that night on, he left the den couch and sleeping bagged it on the bedroom floor instead. His ass and the dock got to be good friends during Sage's morning swims. As for his chaperon duties during *any* of her off-condo excursions? There was actually an upside to that. He was developing some damn good skills for bodyguard work after he left Special Forces. He couldn't imagine any spoiled Seattle heiress or Hollywood starlet jacking his blood pressure the way Sage had the last week.

At first, her antics were mildly amusing. Day one, she'd announced she wanted a tattoo. Aside from helping her with the pain by getting her hammered at Scotch & Vine afterward, that went surprisingly well. Days two and three, she'd subjected him to nonstop trips to six different malls, where he contemplated a few water boarding sessions against holding her bags and following her through every store. Just when he thought the torment couldn't get worse, she announced she was going back to the custom lingerie boutique for a fitting on new bras. *It's okay,* she'd told the attendant, *he's my fiancé. He can watch.* When he'd been able to break away from the torment of watching someone else play with her breasts for half an hour, he impaled the minx with a glare that told her payback was a bitch—and somehow, he *would* make sure that was the case.

Day four didn't bring him the chance. Nor did day five. She'd learned there was a two-day emergency preparedness drill going on at Tacoma General, and she wanted to help by being a fake disaster victim on which the hospital's staff could practice. Garrett had grudgingly agreed to the choice, figuring King's street spies would never think to look for her under wound makeup at a major city medical center, though the drill wasn't the simple role play he'd expected, either. She'd "left out" the part that she'd be constantly sped into and out of the ER, jostled onto stretchers, dropped *from* stretchers, gotten her limbs twisted and banged in a variety of ways, and the rest of her body jabbed in ways that had Garrett rearing off the wall a few times to remind the bozos they were working on an actual person, not their personal version of Fix-Me Barbie.

He'd gone to bed that night in a fuming silence. His voice came back with thundering resonance the next morning. He'd been tugged awake by the sound of Sage talking on the phone, in the process of agreeing to a forty minute interview at the KOMO 4 station that afternoon. By the time he barreled downstairs, demanding she tell the fuckers no joy, she'd already confirmed the interview time and hung up. He picked up the headset to call the station back, but Sage stood there with folded arms and a tight glare, made worse by a backdrop of unshed tears.

The shitty thing was, he knew exactly what caused those tears. She didn't give a crap about the interview, but his unexplained tension was clearly eating at her. If he canceled the interview, she'd demand some answers, drill at him for explanations. That was so *not* going to happen—so the interview would.

He'd stormed back upstairs and called Zeke, who relayed that Rayna received the same call and had pulled the sulk on him, as well. They'd both shown up to the station and tried to comfort each other with the "let's hide the targets in plain sight" logic, but it didn't prevent the afternoon from being one of the longest of his life. While the girls had fun, and the phone lines were jammed with Seattlites clamoring to welcome their miracle nurses home, he and Z tried to keep vigil over the fifteen semi-secure entrances into the building. He remembered missions in Bumfuck, Egypt that had been less stressful.

Today's little "Sage adventure" was going to be worse. If he didn't kill her first.

He locked the truck with a flick of the fob over his shoulder. As he stuffed his keys into his backpack, his cell rang. When he saw it was Z, a fusion of dread and relief hit him. He could almost predict what Zeke's opening comment would be in response to the frantic text he'd fired off before driving here, but his chest already felt lighter knowing one other person on the planet understood the agony assaulting him right now.

He leaned against the outside wall of the hangar then pressed his wireless earpiece to answer the call on the third ring. Zeke's roar filled the line as soon as the line activated.

"Is she fucking nuts?"

Garrett grimaced as he glanced up. On the tarmac forty yards away, a DHC-6 Twin Otter was getting checked out, fueled up, and loaded. Several guys in nylon parachute suits strode out to the plane with pre-checked jump packs. "Apparently, that answer would be yes."

As he spoke, he swept his stare around the rest of the area. *Goddamnit.* The Fort Lewis airfield backed right up to several of the McChord Air Force Base tarmacs, making this area one giant snatch-and-go opportunity for any of King's minions who still knew the base and could get around the security gates in their sleep.

"How the hell did she slip out on you?"

"I took a shower," he responded. "So sue me." Hell, he felt like doing much worse than that to himself already. "I thought it was okay. I left her on the couch, half-dozing under a blanket and watching a *Friends* marathon."

Z made a gagging sound. "*Friends.* Shit."

"Uh, yeah. Needless to say, she knew I'd linger in the rain locker."

"And the second you were under the spray, she left." His friend blew out a harsh but sympathetic breath. "But she left a note too? I don't get it."

Even forming the answer to that made Garrett's gut feel like a chunk of the concrete under his boots. "The note told me nothing except she was safe and not to worry."

"Huh?"

"The first ten pages of the Airborne Jump School study guide, dropped in the middle of the driveway, told me something different."

His buddy chuffed. "Somebody was in a hurry to get into somebody else's car."

"Yep." He emphasized the last of it with a pop of fury.

"And something tells me you know who volunteered for shuttle service."

"Ditto on *that* affirmative." It was all he had to say. He knew Z would figure out the rest. He could practically hear the gears of the guy's mind at work over the phone.

"Yo, Hawk?"

"Yeah?"

"Don't kill Archer."

"Is that an absolute order?"

"He knows four languages, and he's one of the best heads on the team for negotiating."

"How nice. I don't negotiate."

"You don't say."

His friend's knowing mutter got phased out as Garrett activated the skills he *was* good at. Z often joked about it being good his family name invoked a bird that saw the world ten times sharper than a human, complete with invisible feathers that stood up when an enemy was near. That was the part that worried him now. His feathers were suddenly at full ceremony salute, as if something wasn't right about the air around here. About the people around here.

Keeping Z on the line, he tucked his head around the corner. After docking his sunglasses atop his head, he swept his gaze through every nook and crevice in the cavernous building. A crew was working on the Chinook chopper that served as the workhorse for the Reserve Aviation unit in supporting local ranger troops in search-and-rescue operations. Everyone seemed to know their role. Plenty of smack talk flew while an iPod screamed a Nine Inch Nails song. Nothing seemed out of the ordinary. In spite of the way NIN always relaxed him, a frustrated snort peeled loose from his throat.

Wait.

Bastard. There he was!

A machinist lingered near one of the work benches, only that was all he seemed to be doing. Garrett watched the guy rearrange a tray of wrenches three times in a row. The soldier's uniform looked three sizes too big, and his boots didn't match the regulation eight-inchers worn by the other techs. He was plenty alert, however. His constant glances around the area, made furtively from beneath his cap, were long enough to qualify as sneaky stares. Or outright infiltration.

The intuition became certainty when Garrett observed the biggest object of the guy's attention.

Sage stood just outside the hangar, laughing at another joke made by Ethan Archer.

Jealousy screamed at his brain for entrance, but Garrett shoved the feeling aside. There was no time to be chums with the hulking green emotional monster. Protecting Sage was more important than kicking someone's face in for charming her, though this didn't mean he deleted Archer off his To-Do list. Not by a screaming long shot.

"Zeke."

"What?"

His friend's voice, weighted with a quarry of stony meaning, conveyed that he'd heard the change in Garrett's tone. Not for the first time today, Garrett was deeply grateful that the man knew him so well.

"There's a face in this place that isn't saying Go Army to me, man."

"What *is* it saying?"

"All the King's men."

"Fuck. I had a feeling, when you didn't speak up for a few seconds…"

"Damn glad you're turning part hawk too."

"He's none of the minions we got in Thailand, though."

"He wouldn't be. Only King was extradited, and the bastard's in solitary now at FDC, thank fuck."

"Well, someone's still taking orders from him. Every instinct I've got doesn't trust this guy, especially the way he's sizing up Sage."

"Can you get a shot of the asshole's face on your cell?"

"Working on it." He scooted around the perimeter of the hangar, hanging in shadows whenever he could. "Stand by."

He caught a lucky break when one of the machinists called to the "soldier" from his perch on a ladder next to the copter's rear rotor. The tech needed a special wrench from the tray right in front of the guy. Sneaky Boy was forced to come out of his corner. As he lifted the tool to the tech, Garrett captured three decent shots of his features. Though the asshat didn't get the wardrobe right, he was spot-on with the guise from the neck up. He was clean-shaven, and beneath his work cap, his haircut looked like a flawless high-and-tight.

"Got 'em," Zeke confirmed less than two minutes later. "I'll see what I can find out."

"Thanks," Garrett answered. His gaze swung outside again. Sage was still there and laughing with Archer. Six other guys from the team ambled over to join them. She greeted them with that stunning, wide smile of hers, bouncing a little on her toes, adorable and impish even in her one-piece, yellow and black jump suit. Archer must've scrounged that up from somewhere as a cute little "gift," damn him.

She was beautiful. Golden. Glowing. Happy. She hadn't looked like that since the moment he'd cut off her gag in the jungle, half a world away. The realization twisted through him like a poison vine from that jungle, turning his heart just as deep and deadly a shade of green.

"What are you going to do now?" asked Z.

Garrett fought to cut back the vine. He battled hard, damn it. He told himself this wasn't the time or the place to be a mindless caveman.

None of that seemed to matter when he spat his response to Zeke.

"I'm going to negotiate."

He clicked the call off before his friend could utter a single swear word of repercussion.

Angel Payne

<u>Chapter Ten</u>

"Oh, hell."

Before she even turned, Sage sensed what Ethan's tight utterance referenced. More accurately, to *whom* it referred.

Just moments ago, she'd sensed a change in the air itself, a surge of strength that jolted the depths of her stomach and made her nerve endings burst open in awareness. When she'd gotten the same rush ten nights ago in Thailand, she'd written it off to her terror as well as the gun battle fireworks outside King's hut. No terror now. No guns going off now. There was only one common factor to both situations. One person. Only now, his entrance carried one distinct change.

Garrett was a more magnificent sight this time around.

She struggled to keep in mind that his conqueror's stride and his granite-hard glower were likely—probably—results of his wrath with her. Major failure on that front. All she could fixate on were how long his legs looked even in his baggy camouflage pants, and how incredible that black T-shirt defined the perfect male V of his torso. She didn't dare let her gaze travel along his biceps… Another major flop. God, how she looked, enduring another attack of oh-my-God-he-isn't-real because of it. And of course, Hades take him, he'd slipped on his all-man, battle-toughened work boots before chasing after her, too.

Yeah, chasing after you, remember? Not here to pick you up for lunch, not here to bring you some flowers. He looks like a gladiator, but he's pissed as a lion, girl—and his claws are aimed your *direction.*

She suddenly craved some cat scratch fever, lion style.

The sunlight hit the top of his head as he stepped clear of the hangar. His hair, still damp from his shower, literally glittered in the sunlight. Before he jerked his sunglasses back over his eyes, the blue flames in them licked out, incinerating what was left of her logic.

She was in deep shit. On a bunch of crazy levels.

She opened her mouth to say something but not a peep spilled out. She sure as hell wasn't going to feed his misplaced rage with an apology. They were barely still engaged, if that's what they were calling it anymore. But a "hey, how's it hangin'" sure wasn't going to help the situation, either.

Garrett took care of the dilemma for her. Sort of. From the inside of his jacket, he pulled out a sheaf of papers. "I think you dropped something."

Her heart thudded in her throat as he extended the pile. The Jump School insignia practically lifted off the page like a magical curse, searing into her conscious. "Thanks."

His only reply was to glance back into the hangar, as if he'd left something behind himself. Sage gulped and kicked the ground. Were they actually enduring something like awkward silence, when engines, trucks, and repair machines ripped up the air around them?

Ethan got noble about trying to smooth things out. "Sage, is everything okay?"

"Yeah."

"No." Garrett's interjection sounded like a simple comment on the weather, which meant the opposite. He added the hint of a smile as he added, "No, it's not, Corporal Archer, so I'll thank you to step the fuck back."

Ethan pivoted to Garrett and actually saluted him, which rammed Sage's heart to her stomach. Guys on a Special Forces team didn't have the time to stand on ceremony, and everyone here knew it. Ethan's move, while wrapped in the ribbons of military respect, might as well have been a knee in Garrett's crotch. No longer were they brothers at arms but subordinate and superior. It was a Special Forces version of the Unfriend button.

"With respect, Sergeant Hawkins, the training flight has been cleared."

"I'm aware of that, Harper," Garrett retorted. "I was the one who heard the Otter would be here for hiking season support and requested it for you guys. Or did you think I just tracked Sergeant Weston here with my keen spidey sense and a desire to mosey onto base for some tasty brunch in the mess?"

Sage empathized with the tension behind Ethan's silent glower. The guy dipped his head of thick chestnut hair, unable to argue with a word of Garrett's statement. The respect memo somehow hadn't gotten through to the smartass just behind him, though. Sage barely held back a groan as Tait Bommer, all mischievous eyes, silken smirk, and surfing idol looks, ambled into the conversation with a smooth chuckle.

"'Tasty brunch in the mess.' Ha; good one! Hey, we'll come join you, Hawk. I'll save some mud off my boots, and we can have it for dessert. It'll be better than the mush they're trying to pass off as pudding, and there's that cute little mashed potatoes server girl I've meaning to talk to again."

"Hey, Tait?" The query was issued by the next guy who came over, the dark-eyed counterpart to Bommer's beach god gilt. Kellan Rush was Tait's polar opposite in looks, temperament, and dating tastes, which made him T-Bomm's perfect flank, both on and off duty. "I'd suggest you shut up."

"Good suggestion." Garrett growled it as he tilted his head at her again. Sage still couldn't see his eyes behind the glasses, but she didn't need to. His scrutiny bathed her from head to toe in uncomfortable, incredible heat. "So you're still thinking of going airborne, huh?"

"Yeah." She lifted a tiny smile. So he also remembered the important things. He didn't look too comfortable about that fact right now, however. His mouth was taut, his face grim.

"You that hot to get to Fort Benning for sixteen weeks?"

He dug a toe at the ground. So did she. They'd always laughed about how they shared the habit, though she always nearly fell over when she did it in heels. Today, neither of them chuckled. Sage felt her smile faltering.

"Maybe I am."

She couldn't filter out the wistful threads in the assertion. Oh, screw wistful. Her tone planted itself right over the line into needy, and she didn't care. If she had to go invisible Whack-a-Mole hammer on his damn stubborn head, so be it. *You don't want me to go, Garrett? Then give me a reason to stay. Give me a reason to look at our home as something more than house arrest now!* "The airborne squads need medics right now." She nearly stammered it out, but the silence he left needed filling. Bad. "And…so…"

"So you found out about this little field trip," – he cocked a condemning brow at Ethan —"and got yourself added to the flight roster somehow, despite that on most of the paperwork, your ashes are still at the bottom of Puget Sound."

Sage jammed her toe down harder the next time and left it stuck that way. She was certain if she lifted it again, she'd drive it into Sergeant Hawkins' right shin. So much for trying to maintain her smile—or any shred of the fantasy she'd been entertaining about getting her hands underneath his T-shirt. "And *I* see your head is still wedged in the bottom of the funeral urn," she flung. As she forced herself to step closer to him, a now-familiar heat threatened the backs of her eyes. Damn it, was she now destined to cry every time they spent more than five minutes near each other? "I hope it's nice and dirty and dark down there too, you shithead."

"Sage!" Ethan's panicked burst layered atop the other guys' gasps. "Maybe a *little* restraint would be—"

"It's okay, Ethan. According to him, I'm still a ghost." She lifted her gaze, facing her reflection in those sun-drenched panels that sealed off his eyes from her. Guess he'd just pulled up a few of the extra barriers out of his heart for the job. The man had plenty of personal walls to go around these days. "So I could call him a paranoid, close-minded, overprotective bastard right now and still be perfectly fine."

She was more right about that than she wanted to be. Besides not reacting to her insult, Garrett didn't even seem to hear it. Instead, he jerked his head right then left, like a combat dog picking up a strong scent. "Fuck," he muttered, his gaze probing back into the hangar. "*Fuck.*" Hot on the heels of his cuss fest, his cell buzzed. He slammed a finger to his earpiece. "Talk to me, Z."

Boots crunched on the ground next to Sage. Ethan moved up again, his *GQ*-ready features compressing with a bloodhound concern of their own. "Guys." It was a reprimand at Tait and Kellan, who'd started exchanging Angry Birds strategies, complete with screeching sound effects. "Guys, stuff it!" He leaned closer to Garrett, listening carefully. As Sage watched his stance tighten, tiny hairs along her nape stood on end.

It was the same feeling she'd had after Garrett's gorilla tirade on the pier at home.

What the hell was going on?

She concentrated harder on Garrett too. For once, he wasn't paying attention to anything she did. If it were possible, the tower of his body coiled tighter. "Okay," he uttered. "Got it. Yeah man, of course I hear you. I've got three of them circling our position like buzzards, with a possible confirm on a fourth. We're goddamn candy on a playground out here. You said base police are alerted? Well, they aren't moving their asses fast enough. I *know*, Z. Shit, I hate it when I'm right about stuff like this."

"About stuff like what?" Sage wasn't able to constrain herself anymore. She moved up between him and Ethan.

"Check," Garrett muttered like she'd disappeared instead. "I'll keep you updated. Thanks, Z."

He ended the call with a hard exhalation. On the same breath, he dipped his head a little at Ethan. The pair of them had totally dropped their pissing match of five minutes ago, which would've made Sage proud if the motivation didn't seem so ominous.

"What's up?" Ethan asked.

Garrett nodded his head again, this time at the twin-engine plane on the runway. "How soon can the Otter leave?"

"As soon as we want it to."

"Good. That's good."

"Why?"

Garrett flicked a glance back at her again. Sage thought she'd fallen off his radar, but that action told her the situation was exactly the opposite. The prickles in her neck tumbled through her body. She squinted back toward the hangar but saw nothing different than the hustle and bustle of the work crews, just like before.

Her attention was yanked back by Garrett's hard pull on

her arm. "*Don't* look back there again."

"Why?"

He dropped her arm and raised his sunglasses. There wasn't a hint of smoke in his gaze this time. The fire in them had taken over, a searing cyan, clutching her heartbeat in its terrifying flames. He answered her query by giving her another order. "Stay."

Sage wasn't sure she could defy him if she wanted.

He pivoted to Ethan next, pulling the corporal several steps away. *Damn it.* She couldn't hear a word of what they were saying, and thanks to the training they'd had to make them lethal opponents in a poker match, she couldn't discern anything from their posture or frowns, either.

Finally, Ethan gave Garrett a brisk nod. "Got it, Hawk."

He came back toward her again on wide, determined strides.

"Ethan, what the hell is—"

"Not now." He issued it in a stern tone. His gaze swept the hangar and the tarmac now. Giving her a completely fake smile, he asked, "So you ready for an adventure?"

Sage blinked at him. "You mean we're still doing this?"

"Yes." That came from Garrett. His voice brooked less backtalk than Ethan's response. He scooped up one of her hands in a steel-reinforced hold, though he nodded toward Ethan. "You got the set-up, Archer. Tell the other guys I need hustle on this. I'll take Sage over like I'm giving her a last high-five for good luck."

"Right," Ethan returned. "I'll be out of my uniform by then."

"Excellent. We're about the same size. Should fit me no problem."

That caused Sage's confused gaze to flip even faster between the two of them. "Out of your uni—*huh?*"

The men were back to pretending she hadn't spoken. Ethan took off at a jog for the airplane. Tait, Kell and the other five jumpers were at his heels. On the flip end of behavior, Garrett adopted a casual stance that made her feel like they stood on a high school lunch patio instead of an Army base tarmac. He added to the impression by beaming a full grin down at her. But his next statement sure as hell wasn't charming quarterback. More like obey-me-*now* detention monitor.

"Follow me to the plane, sugar. No more questions, no more rebellion. Please, Sage. Not now."

Please, Sage.

He hadn't used the phrase once in the last ten days. Now that he had, it drew out mixed feelings. The tenderness in his voice was like a precious thread re-sewn between them. But that bond had been stitched with a needle of urgency and knotted off with dread.

"All right," she told him. "Let's go."

He ambled out to the Otter with her, though once more she got the impression he barely refrained from a sprint. Sure enough, as soon as they circled around to the plane's door, Garrett turned into the same daunting soldier she'd seen in Thailand. He swung up into the cabin in one smooth sweep. Once in, he strode directly to the back. Ethan was there already, and sliding out of his top. The olive and tan garment barely saw air before Garrett jammed his arms down the sleeves and started zipping up. If their plan wasn't clear to Sage before, it was now. Garrett was jumping as her tandem partner instead of Ethan, for reasons clearly above her pay grade. It seemed she was the first ghost in history bound to a security clearance.

Her mental trip into snark-ville didn't stop her from staring at the two of them and attempting to read their minds—though maybe that wasn't such a great move, either. Just getting into the plane had jumped her adrenalin a little higher, but now…

Oh, hell.

Ethan had already been pretty dashing in his combat top and bottoms, but the skin-tight brown T-shirt he wore beneath only amped the man's irresistible factor. His chest was a defined sculpture of muscle, and the long ropes of his arms continued that chiseled trend. All that hard-hewn glory, yet the man was always ready with a gentle smile and a mischievous

111

twinkle in his forest-green eyes.

Sage let out a conflicted sigh. Ethan was already dancing on the edges of flirtation with her, but just looking at him next to Garrett crystallized an epiphany for her. While Ethan was nice on the eyes and easy for companionship, turning her attention to Garrett did something…more.

So much more.

Even looking at him was a lesson in being consumed. From the moment they'd met, Garrett Hawkins was the blaze in her blood, the smolder in her sex, the molten magic in her heart. He was her fire. Period.

And damn it, she doubted if she'd ever be able to extinguish him. Or ever wanted to.

She found a seat, slid into it, clicked in and ducked her head so she could clench back the fresh slam of tears. Shit, she was a mess!

"Suck it up," she whispered fervently. "Do it, Weston. Get your shit together." *You want to make it as Airborne? There's no damn crying in Airborne!*

When Garrett took the seat next to her, she compelled her head back up. Well, at least enough to look at his knees instead of hers. She longed to wrap her hand around the inside of that knee, using it to pull herself over and curl against him. But rules were rules. And if crying wasn't allowed in Airborne, breaking the personal affection parameters *really* wasn't.

Still, in that sixth sense way of his, Garrett leaned a little closer to her. He angled his body, completely protective about the pose and not seeming to care who saw. "You okay?"

"Yeah." She glanced up in time to see Ethan make his way over. "But I'd be better if I knew what the hell this is all about with you two."

"Not gonna happen." Garrett and Ethan retorted it in unison. They followed that by locking palms in their gruff version of a handshake.

"Hey," Garrett stated. "I owe you, Runway."

Ethan chuffed. "You owe me shit, boss." He cocked a sideways smile at them both. "See you at the pit. Have fun, Sage."

She tossed back a grin of her own, but the expression faded as soon as the plane accelerated, gained air, and began to climb into the clear summer sky. She kept glancing at that sky, trying to think of how much it looked like Garrett's eyes, struggling to take strength from that as the earth began to resemble a watercolor below. Structures and landscape blurred together, a beautiful but daunting reminder of the fact that they were rapidly climbing to ten thousand feet—and that she'd be traveling back through that distance by hurling her body through it.

Shit, shit, shit.

What the *hell* was she thinking?

She tried another stab at thinking about anything except the fear pounding at her body. Had she turned on the dishwasher this morning? Damn it, she didn't think so. Maybe they needed to turn around and land so she could go handle that. Oh God, oh God, they weren't going to do that, were they? Okay, so maybe she'd cook dinner for Garrett tonight. They could grill something. She'd mash some sweet potatoes for him. He loved her mashed potatoes. No, wait. She was ticked at him. And Ethan. What was that all about again?

Her brain gave her nothing. It was official. It had checked itself out from her body down on the tarmac. The conclusion gave her a fabulous excuse to seize Garrett's hand and crunch his big long fingers for everything she was worth. The indentations at the corners of his mouth, normally so tight, loosened into twin brackets of mirth. She retaliated by whacking his shoulder.

"Dork," she yelled.

"Cherry blaster," he called back, making her heart do a backflip between its terrified convulsions. The slang term for a first-time jumper became four syllables of pure sex in his husky bellow.

Her moment of ease was short-lived.

The pilot pulled back on the engines, slowing the plane. A crewman got ready to open the door.

With a grin, Garrett unbuckled and got to his feet. It was a good thing he moved first, because none of Sage's muscles would budge. She didn't remember him unlatching her seatbelt, but suddenly she was on her feet and guided into position in front of him so their tandem rig could be connected. Next, she felt Garrett clip the heavy chute pack onto his back. He jerked a little as he double-checked the cords and parachute release. *Please double-check the release!*

The crewman pushed the door open. T-Bomm and Kell were first up in the rotation, a fact that apparently deserved ear-splitting war cries from both warriors. As the two of them careened out the door, their cries disappeared with them.

She and Garrett were next.

He nudged her closer to the door. Her vision filled with nothing but sky and the ground below.

Very far below.

She flung her hands backward, trying to grab him. Though Garrett was already pressed close and safe behind her, literally bound to her, she craved more. Couldn't they do this another way? Couldn't she flip around, burrow against his chest, squeeze her eyes closed, and pray she got to the ground safely? She had to pee. She longed to scream. She wanted to die.

"I—I've changed my mind! F-forget it, okay?"

Garrett's mouth was a warm, heavy pressure at her ear. His lips curled into a fervent kiss on her lobe before he said at a volume only she could hear, "I'm right here, sugar."

Somehow, the words sank in, though it was impossible to respond. She couldn't nod. Or speak. Or move.

This wasn't sane. This wasn't rational. Why did people do this? Couldn't they find an easier way to get troops places? Somebody seriously needed to talk to Armed Forces leadership about this. Somebody needed to talk to the *president* about this.

Garrett's voice was back in her ear. But it wasn't an intimate growl this time. Now, he yelled at her in full, commanding throttle.

"Go!"

She wanted to die. Instead, she stepped into thin air, and the breath-robbing force of freefall *whomped* every cell in her body. Her heart rate was a rocket. She was pure electricity.

114

She was raw energy. She felt everything yet nothing at once, all thoughts of past or future gone. There was only right here, right now, and in this insane moment, she was only certain of one thing.

Yeah. She was going to die.

Angel Payne

Chapter Eleven

Garrett had long ago lost track of how many jumps he'd completed, but like the best thrill ride, it never got old.

The exhilaration was even better this time, though. It wasn't every day that a guy got to take the woman of his soul on the world's most incredible adrenalin rush. Getting to experience the jump through Sage's eyes, even down to her terror, actually made him feel better than he had all week. He wished he could tell her that here, at ten thousand feet over the earth, she was the safest she'd been in seven days. In more than a year. He'd never been more aware or thankful for the hand of irony. Up in the plane, he'd actually relaxed. He'd gotten so sarcastic with Sage, she'd laughed and called him a dork. For a few incredible seconds, they were just a guy and a girl again, flirting with each other, falling in love.

But that thirteen hundred foot bonus dwindled fast.

He let the freefall go on for a few thousand more feet before yanking on the pud handle, which deployed the drogue parachute, preparing them for deployment of the main chute. The bigger canopy flowed out next, yanking them into the wild swoop of opening shock. As they swung forward again and he started to guide them toward the landing pit, Sage let out her first sound since they'd left the plane: a long, gleeful shriek. A bunch more followed as they rode the wind together, and Garrett couldn't help but laugh. He tried to remember that an hour ago, he'd been in the Taj Mahal of royally pissed at her. He struggled to dredge up what it felt like to see King's gutter dogs in that hangar, sniffing at her with their hungry eyes, looking at her as nothing more than a means to a fat payback. He fought to recall how the Otter couldn't take off fast enough, and how he'd breathed easier with every foot they ascended.

He struggled to remember all of it, yet the only thing that seemed to matter now *was* now. This moment. This pure, soaring, joy. For a few precious seconds, time was flung backwards and the only thing in the world was just him and

117

her, wrapped around each other again. Flying with each other.

Muscle memory took over while his hands pulled at the steering and brake lines, aligning their descent with the landing pit. The perfect jump conditions didn't preclude him from taking care with the task. The pit was a little sloped due to being lined on one side by a dense forest, a challenge the Army had created during the years units were being deployed every day to the Afghan mountains, and needed training on terrain like this. He slowed the chute down by increasing intervals, bringing them down for what was going to be a textbook landing.

"Legs up, Sergeant," he instructed Sage.

"Yes, Sir." A tiny giggle in her voice drained the respect from the words. His brain, already untethered from a number of its usual restraints, kicked in with a reaction that sent his senses on another freefall. He imagined disciplining that sass out of her—right on her tawny, smooth ass. Then he'd force an apology from her with his cock head, refusing to let her pussy have him until she said those two words with breathy, needing reverence…

Thank *God* he had the landing to worry about.

They hit the gravel at perfect velocity. Sage squealed with victory as they did. She squirmed with energy as Garrett unclipped them both from the rigging. T-Bomb and Kell were doing the same about twenty yards away. He exchanged upturned thumbs with them, indicating everyone had gotten in a good jump. Kell, as the unit's rigger, came jogging over to collect his chute and rig.

"The penguins will be here in about twenty with the van," he stated.

"Got it."

Garrett confirmed, reckoned it might be the longest twenty minutes of his life. He knew Archer would be riding with the ground crew and ready with an update about the assholes who'd snuck into the hangar. With any luck, the MP's would be able to detain the men long enough to discern how they'd tailed Sage onto the base.

Tension jabbed its way back into his muscles. He

grunted from the invasion, wistfully saying goodbye to those blissful moments up in the sky.

He looked over in time to see Kell crack one side of his mouth up at Sage while he sorted through the lines and deflated canopy on the ground. "So, Sage Mouse, what'd you think?"

If it were possible, Sage's glow got a little brighter. Kell was one of the guys who'd been around long enough to remember the unit's endearment for her, given instantly after Garrett had fallen for her. "For once, the prey caught the hawk," they'd joke. They got away with it because they knew it was true.

Thank fuck none of them had a door to his brain, allowing them to see how the woman proved it glaringly true right now. Damn, she riveted him. She was even more stunning now than before the flight, bouncing around like one of those dancers from the Irish fast-step troupes, even humming a silly tune as accompaniment. The brilliance in her eyes was a breath-stopper. Her dazzling grin hadn't faltered since they touched down.

"I—I *didn't* think," she exclaimed. "I couldn't! And that's what made it so—so—"

Kell chuckled. "Yeah. Pretty good, huh?"

"*Pretty* good?" She gaped like Kell had just grown horns, before spinning around and pumping her fists skyward. "Wow! Flipping, freaking *wow*!" When her pirouette placed Garrett back in her field of sight, she stopped. Her smile dropped a little, but the change was good. Very good. It was the way only Sage could look at him, shoving past those doors inside him that said No Admittance, diving over the barriers and the bullshit he gave everyone else, seeing him as nobody else did and loving him anyway. Holy fuck, he loved that look. And hated it. And right now, had no idea what to do about it.

Sage didn't abandon him to the dilemma. Before he could form another thought, she threw herself against him. "Thank you, baby!"

She clearly intended the embrace to be over as soon as it started, but Garrett's instincts, still on overdrive, forced another plan. He held her in return. He didn't want a damn hug.

He needed an embrace. As he wrapped his arms around her, he ducked his head against the side of her head. She felt so tiny. She felt so warm. She felt so right.

"You're welcome."

He knew how rough the sibilance came off his lips, and he saw the recognition of it in Sage's gaze when they pulled apart. He also saw what she wanted to do about it—if her lingering touch on his ribcage still meant what it had a year ago. On top of that, the celadon of her gaze deepened to a shade that matched her name, and her tongue snuck out in a tentative slide between her lips. Damn. Even if he wasn't smitten with the woman, he'd read her mind more cleary than a comic book.

She wanted his tongue to go in after hers.

The adrenalin from the jump fused with the new heat in his blood, spiking his heart rate. It became an anaerobic fun zone as his mind took things from there, working the image into a fantasy that ended with both of them naked, gasping and drained. *Damn* it, this was getting messy.

And impossible to deny any longer.

Somehow, he managed to let Sage step back. But even those two feet were intolerable. His body gunned like a dragster at the Start line, the key in the ignition and all cylinders ready to fire. If he didn't get to open the throttle soon, the engine was going to explode.

"Kell," he called without ungluing his stare from Sage. "We'll be right back."

"Okay. Where you going?"

"Yeah." Sage frowned in confusion as he dipped his head toward the woods, indicating for her to follow. "Where are we going?"

He willed his voice and his gait into feigned ease. "Maybe we can find that—er—house key. Yeah, your house key. You said it fell loose just before we dipped in over the trees."

"Oh." Suddenly she quickened her own pace. "Right! Yeah, that's right. Damn. I can't believe that happened. Hopefully we'll see it. Be right ba—"

He literally snatched the rest of the word out of her, pulling her through the underbrush at damn-near a run.

The second they were out of eyesight and earshot from Kell, he whirled Sage around. He picked the spot on purpose. A wide tree was right behind her. With one solid slam, he had her pinned between the trunk and him. Her mouth popped open in surprise, which he also didn't let her finish. Her open lips were the beacon for his, and he wasted no time smashing a deep, hungering kiss on her.

A high cry swept up her throat. The vibrations of it filled his mouth, pulling his tongue deeper inside her. And that was it. She set him totally afire with her open, incredible surrender. She fanned the blaze higher by stabbing her arms under his top, fisting his T-shirt, pulling hard on the sweat-soaked cotton.

"Garrett!" She pleaded it against his jaw when he dragged away to let her breathe. "Oh yes…"

He stopped her with another kiss, though he wasn't sure this still qualified as kissing. Conquering her mouth, controlling it completely, was a rushing, consuming exigency. He needed this. Fuck, he couldn't get enough of her.

He bracketed her face with one hand, holding her in place while he plunged, plowed, and explored with his tongue and teeth. His imagination went into hyperdrive again. It taunted him with the fantasy of her creamy and nude against the leaves and mud. *Ditch the dream, Hawk. Isn't going to happen here.* But the creative imagery exercise left its mark in his blood, torching him from head to toe so even the act of pulling down her jumpsuit zipper was a pure carnal pleasure. Her answering moan urged him on. In seconds, he found his way under her T-shirt and bra, landing his eager fingers on one of her erect nipples.

He finally pulled away from her lips, but didn't go very far. The soft column of her neck beckoned. He marked the skin there with his teeth while he continued to tease her breast. "Damn it, Sage," he growled against her jugular, "I should still be furious with you."

"I know." Her voice was a rasp, but her hands gave him

a different message. She tore at his back with her fingernails, her touch almost bestial with need. "I know, and I'm sorry…"

Garrett went at her mouth again, and she dug at his back even harder. He grunted from the new pressure but followed with a rough moan. If his endorphins weren't turbo-charging everything in his body, he imagined her ploughs would be painful, but the only sensation he cared about was the hotter, harder, heaviness between his thighs.

Hell. They needed to stop. The most dangerous prisoner in his psyche began stirring again. The dark beast paced the cage of his soul, demanding a little exercise. Okay, *a lot* of exercise. And his brain had run a goddamn mental obstacle course for the last two hours, depleting his strength to fight the monster.

He needed to push away. He needed to leave her the hell alone, or the cage was going to snap. This animal he didn't know, much less control, was going to break free. Seeing her like this, with her hair half-down and her eyes half-wild, didn't help. Not one fucking bit.

"Sorry," she offered again, lifting her lips to his chin, his neck. "Garrett, I really am—"

"No." The mix of the beast's voice and her plea was a double whammy on his dwindling restraint. He moved his hand into her hair and yanked her head to one side. As he sank his teeth again to her neck, he slid his hand to her other breast. No," he repeated in a seductive snarl, "I don't think you really are." Her peak came alive under his squeezing fingers. Her sharp gasp was exactly the reaction he sought. He could feel her hammering pulse through his questing tongue. "But if we were anywhere else, I'd make sure you *were* truly sorry."

A deep swallow undulated down her throat. "You—you would?"

"Damn straight."

Her head tipped deeper to the side, sending her hot, panting breaths into his shoulder. She nipped at the skin there, dipping her head as if trying to determine how to crawl inside him, before uttering one word of reply.

"How?"

Her sweet, quivering question sent a shot of lighter fluid into his cock. Damn, it had been four hundred forty five days since he'd last been inside her, not that he was counting. He let out a harsh breath as his BVD's chafed with a familiar wetness. Hello, pre-cum.

"I'd have this jumpsuit down past your knees." Acting on at least part of that fantasy, he unzipped the jumpsuit farther. Her body had warmed the inside of it, forming a perfect welcome for his wind-chilled hands. She let loose a gorgeous sigh as he swept his grip around, cupping her ass with voracious force. "Then this bra would be gone too. You'd be naked for me. Exposed. At my mercy."

He felt her thighs tremble. She scored his spine with her nails. "But I still wouldn't be sorry."

"No," he said, "you probably wouldn't be."

As he gripped her tighter, fitting the apex of her body against the center of his, he angled his gaze to lock into hers. Damn it, here came the animal again. It charged the disintegrating cage of his control, completely taking over his next words.

"That's why I'd have to get you over my knees."

Sage's lips parted. Her eyes glimmered like a tigress in heat. Feral. Magical. Thoroughly aroused. "Oh," she murmured. "Over your—"

"Knees." He nodded as she shivered again. Though he hated the animal, he adored the creature it set free in *her*. He was transfixed by the new softness in her face, living there right beside her wildcat. He was helpless against her sensuality, drowning in it. "Yeah, that's what I said. Over my knees. With your head against my calf, and your ass high and proud…waiting for me."

"W-waiting?"

"Yes." He curled his fingers deeper against her ass, scraping the flesh inside her cheeks with his nails. "What do you think it would be waiting for, Sage?"

She closed her eyes for a second. When she opened them again, the sun kissed her tawny lashes and highlighted her deep arousal. Holy hell, she was gorgeous, wildness and

123

tenderness together, a creature all but begging for his claim. Garrett had never remembered her so beautiful, and the realization that he'd caused it was better than ten shots of Patrón.

She was even more mesmerizing as she answered his query. "Your punishment," she whispered. "It—it would be waiting for your punishment."

"Damn right, sugar. It would be waiting for my punishment. For me to spank it hard, as many times as I wanted."

He ground her crotch along the bulging ridge of his, letting her feel what this forbidden fantasy was doing to him. Her head fell back against the tree as he pressed close, her heartbeat slamming at the base of her throat. "Garrett. Oh, hell!"

"Uh-uh," he commanded. "None of that, Sage. No words during your punishment. You'd take every blow in silence, to ensure me that you were thinking about how insane you'd made *me* today. When I got out of the shower, and you weren't there…" The memory of his terror twisted with the fever of his lust, making him thrust against her harder. "Fuck, Sage!"

"I *am* sorry." A couple of tears tangled on her cheek. "I never thought you'd be—"

"Hush." He slammed his mouth to hers again, reddening it like he craved to darken her ass. With his gaze planted on her face, he ordered, "Give me your hands."

She frowned, clearly confused. "What?"

"Your hands." He gave it harder emphasis. "Off my back, against the tree, over your head. *Now*." After Sage complied, he pulled one of his hands off her ass and raised it to her wrists, pinning them together under his grip. "I'd bind you like this too, Sage. Yeah, definitely. You'd be helpless, the same way I felt this morning, not knowing where you'd gone, not knowing who you'd gone with."

For the first time, the tigress in her struck out. "And if I'd told you, would you have let me go?"

"Damn it!" he snarled. "It's my responsibility to—"

"Protect me. I *know.* Though from *what,* I don't know. But protection is different than house arrest, Sergeant Hawk—"

She interrupted herself with her own high, aching cry. It exploded from her as he widened his stance in order to mash their bodies with more ferocious force. Oh, damn. Her yelp...he instantly craved to hear it again. He hated himself for the admission, but it resonated deeply as his fucking DNA. He'd never wanted to go balls-out fighting with a woman at the same time he had balls in other places too. This...fuck, this was new as boot camp for him.

That's not quite the truth, is it, Hawk?

He raged at the reminder note, courtesy of his past. At the same time, he couldn't ignore the truth that was in front of him, very much in his present. There was no denying the effect that this new "thing," whatever it was, had on both of them. Sage was an image of writhing, breathtaking beauty as she started to match his thrusts, her eyes closed, her lips panting, her body trembling. His anger from this morning, stirred with this week's nonstop apprehension, flipped his desire for her into pure need. It wasn't just his body that told him to conquer her now. It was his mind, his heart. He craved her surrender in every way he could get it.

The comprehension spurred his retort, flung with no apology. "'House arrest?' That's the line you're going with, huh? Seems you really do want me to paint your ass red."

Sage chuffed, matching him snark for snark. "It's your punishment fantasy, baby."

Again, he battled the simultaneous urges to spank her and screw her.

The former wasn't happening here. But they were doing a damn fine job of dress- rehearsing the latter.

"Well, maybe I'm not fantasy-punishing your ass good enough." He crushed her even tighter against the tree, shaking the thing so hard that a flurry of pine needles scattered on them. "You're still spitting that sass at me worse than a thirteen year-old on restriction. Maybe that means you've got to have the punishment fucked directly into you."

He didn't give Sage a second to try and interpret that.

125

He showed her exactly what he meant with his body. As he rammed more forcefully against her, he freed his other hand from her jumpsuit and grabbed her leg. Inside a second, he forced her thigh around his waist. His other arm remained raised, his hand still a shackle to her wrists, leaving her upper body open for his gaze and his lips. He took advantage of that opportunity, taking her collarbone, her sternum and her neck with his open, wet mouth. Every shiver she gave him in return was like a gift of molten gold. No matter what, he didn't stop rocking against her, pseudo-fucking her into the high gasp she finally erupted at him.

"Y-yes! Oh…yes, Garrett. Maybe that is what I need…"

He intensified the pace. The friction of their clothes was an agonizing, erotic surrogate for the bond their bodies couldn't have. "Tell me again," he commanded. "Call me 'Sir' this time."

"Yes Sir. Yes, you know exactly what I need."

He clenched his thighs, counteracting the pure flame in his dick. He kept his gaze twined with the verdant glory of hers, watching her arousal spiral higher, feeling her legs shake, her breathing quicken. "What, Sage? Tell me. Use the words to make my cock harder, so I can give you exactly what you need."

"I—I need you to punish me. To—to fuck the discipline into me."

"Yes," he growled. "That's beautiful. *You're* beautiful."

He took her mouth so violently, he lifted her head from the force. He added a rolling motion to his thrusts, drawing out an exquisite little whimper from deep in her chest. He spread his knees a little more in order to drive harder at her.

"Oh!" She gasped and bit his lip, too lost in her escalating arousal to even realize what she'd done. That was all right by him. Her fire fed his, blazing into the corners of him that had been freezing for so long, fusing the driftwood of his desire back into a searing rod of need. "Oh, Garrett! Please!"

He grunted in chastisement. "Re-phrase, Sergeant Weston?"

"Oh, Sir!" she amended. "Please, oh please. I need to—
"

"I know what you need. And I'm going to give it to you. The explosion's on its way, Sage. Your sweet pussy will have its satisfaction, I promise."

She whimpered and trembled beneath him. "Now," she pleaded. "God, please…I don't know how much more of this I can—ahhhh! Please! Now!"

"Don't think so, sugar."

"Garrett! Damn it!"

He speeded up their tempo, making her moan hard in protest. His own voice started coming in low, tight growls between his labored breaths.

"The punishment might have been a fantasy, Sage, but the lesson wasn't. Tell me what lesson I'm fucking into you, then you can come apart for me, *with* me."

"I—I can't even think straight! Are you freaking kidding me?"

As much as it killed him to do it, he screeched his body to a full stop. The only thing he moved was his top hand, twisting it harder to keep her wrists in place. "Does this feel like kidding?"

She let out an agonized moan, clipping his ass with her heel, which made him screw the hold tighter on her thigh. "All right!" she finally cried. "All right, fine! Uh—errm—the lesson was—"

"The lesson *is*?"

"The—the lesson is—" Her mouth gaped open as he started the cadence between their bodies again. She learned, at the same time he did, that the thirty second break made their new grind a hundred times more intense. "Oh, Garrett!"

He gritted out a harsh redirect. "Sage? The lesson?"

"I know, I know! The—the lesson—uh—" She licked her lips with delectable desperation. "Don't—don't leave the house again without telling you. There. We good now?"

She lurched her hips, blatantly fighting to get him closer. The vibrations squeezed his bottoms in exactly the right way to stroke the aching head of his sex. He shuddered from it, but found the will to demand, "Why? *Why* don't you leave the house without telling me?"

"Garrett! Please!"

"Tell me why, damn it!"

"Be-Because—it makes you feel—uh—"

"Like tearing the fucking neighborhood apart." The renewed viciousnes in his tone wasn't just because of the bonfire in his cock. His passion was intertwined with the other shit she needed to hear from him, to see in him. She needed to know how his heart seized and his blood became ice this morning when finding her note, how he'd wondered if she'd been forced to write it at gunpoint by one of King's wanksters, how he barely held the truck to the speed limit when driving to the base after finding the papers in the driveway. She needed to feel what had driven him to pin her here, and act like this. "It makes me feel like I've been cuffed in steel and can't get out, Sage. Like I've lost you all over again. Can you understand that? Can you understand what that does to me?"

Her face contorted. More tears slipped down her cheeks. Damn it, this hadn't been his intention when hauling her out here. He'd hoped for some fast necking and a grope or two, maybe to help take the edge off her sexual frustration, if not his. If a crystal ball had floated ahead of them through the brush and shown they'd be dry-humping each other through a mini psychotherapy session, he would've hurled the thing into the woods and told it to go back to the cheap toy store it came from.

"I'm not lost anymore."

She spoke it with the conviction of a courtroom oath. The solemn words resounded into the depths of his heart and chiseled at every aspect of his control.

"I'm right here, stronger for what I've been through, and you are, too. You came and found me, and now we've left the hell behind. We've left that bastard King behind...right?"

He heard the deliberate pause she inserted before that final question. When he didn't say or do anything to fill that gap, Sage fell into contemplative stillness. When she moved again, it was to test his grip on her wrists. Garrett let her slip free. She extended her hands straight to him, threading her fingers through his hair. "Garrett? Look at me. I'm here. I'm *here*. Do you get it?" Her grasp tightened. "Or is there something *I'm* not getting?"

He got in half a breath before the flames in his body turned to icicles. He went stiff from the impact, not in the great ways this time. The wind rustled through the pines, a sound so peaceful, it turned into a taunt at his heart and soul. He couldn't hide it from Sage anymore, either. He raised his eyes to meet hers. Her gaze, deep and lush as the boughs over their heads, didn't let him go. He witnessed every nuance of the conversion that took over her face, the lust dissolving, the dark bafflement taking over.

"Goddamnit," she whispered. "Tell me, Garrett. You don't get to walk back up the dock this time. What the *hell* is it?"

He stroked a steady thumb along her cheek. "What do I do for a living, Sage? You know I have to hide lots of things."

She ditched the confused frown for an outright glower. He'd backed her into an impasse and they both knew it. Nobody had more reverence for his SF secrets than Sage, and he loved her for that integrity. To push him would be taking a hammer to that foundation between them. But her eyes revealed her insight. She knew this had nothing to do with "work."

A bellow came from the landing zone. Kell had unknowingly perfect timing. "Are you two done sucking face? The van's here. We'd all like to get back to base and enjoy some of that yummy-ass brunch."

Garrett pulled Sage's zipper back up before readjusting the painful weight beneath his thighs. Despite having to walk out of the wood with a modified gait from unfulfilled need, he silently thanked fate for smiling upon him in this instance. All right, it sucked that he wasn't sure when he'd see a smile on his fiancé's lips again—but for now, he'd yanked her from King's tentacles again., and she was technically none the wiser.

He had no idea how much longer he could keep up this ruse.

The sooner they put the asshole away for life, the better.

Chapter Twelve

Sage sighed heavily as she stood in the kitchen, watching him from the wide window over the sink. Garrett paced the lawn, side patio and back of the condo with careful steps and a vigilant gaze. All he needed was a brain bucket and an M16, and she'd swear he was out on patrol. The strain didn't leave his body even as he sat at one of the chairs around the fire pit to strip off his T-shirt and get out of his boots. Every rope of muscle in his torso was still wound in tension.

None of it came as a surprise. Or a difference. He'd reinstated his mental smokescreen the second they'd climbed into the van with the other guys. Tait and Kell had led the bombardment of questions and general chatter, adding their embellishments about what their own first jumps were like, as well as their most harrowing jumps since then. Sage was glad some of their stories pushed believability, since she'd needed the distraction from the silence wrapped around the man who'd brought her such bright ecstasy just minutes before. Nothing improved during their drive home, when Garrett pretended to be interested in the entertainment news update oozing off the radio. Did he seriously expect her to believe the newest Hollywood hook-ups were a remote concern to him?

It was official. He was hiding something from her. And if it was an understanding about this new energy between them, she had a right to know about it. She'd burn through his whole damn forest to do it. *Let's do this, Smokey the Bear.*

She poured a couple of glasses of water as he came back inside. "Oh, hell yeah," he murmured when she offered him the drink. "That's good. Thanks, sugar."

He guzzled the whole glass in one swig, slammed it down, and refilled it. The moment provided the shot of courage she needed. There'd been a few others like this, where he'd poked through the smoke to give her glimpses of the brash, wild mustang of a man who'd first captured her heart two summers ago, when she'd been refueled to fight for him again.

131

To fight for *them.* It was worth it. She had to keep trying.

The mantra compelled her forward, next to him. As she expected, Garrett stiffened. She didn't back off. Instead, she lifted a hand and rested it against his chest, above the V formed by his dog tags.

He didn't retreat.

That was a good sign, right?

Sage slid her touch toward his neck.

He grabbed her wrist with the speed of a cobra.

"Don't." She said it from tight teeth. *"Don't,* Garrett."

"Sage—"

"You're not going to fire bomb me out this time." Though he swung away, she hooked a hand into the crook of his elbow and dug in, at least as much as she could against his coiled bicep. "I'm not going to let you." She got him to stop, though he only turned his profile for her to see. "Won't you even look at me?"

With slow resignation, he swiveled completely around. He hitched his grip backwards, palms against the counter. He raised his head, though his gaze only lifted far as her nose. His lips parted as if he were going to say something, but he just scissored his jaw at her.

"Damn it." Her rasp was more serrated than the knife stuck in the sourdough loaf she'd baked last night. "How long are we going to continue like this?"

Garrett's shrug was a maddening display of male evasion. "As long as it takes."

Sage dropped her hand from him. Fury eclipsed even her urge to leave a good scratch behind. "To quote someone near and dear to me, Sergeant Hawkins, *that's* the line you're going with?"

That got him to pin his stare directly into hers. Nothing had changed about the dark cobalt edges in his eyes. "Were you listening to me today at all? You know there's information I'm entrusted with, Sage. Information that can't be—"

"And *you* know that's not what I'm talking about!" She shoved past him, storming into the living room, where there was more room to fling out her arms in frustration. "Keep all your classified secrets, Garrett. I get your job. I always have. But you're not getting off that easy. You're not going to hide behind your security clearance to avoid talking to me at all. Uncool, Hawkins. And completely unacceptable."

She watched a deep breath fill his chest. "You're talking about what happened this afternoon." He didn't look at her as he said it, his tone even as his gaze. "*After* the jump."

She swallowed hard. "I'm not letting you pretend it didn't happen, Garrett." Her chest tightened as the memories, hot and sweet, flooded her mind's eye. "I don't want to pretend it didn't happen."

She dropped her arms. Held her breath. For a moment, she let hope bloom in her heart and gut again. She openly offered that longing to him, letting it paint every inch of her face.

Garrett's shoulders heaved as if she'd dragged home one of the trees from their forest and dropped it on him. His lips twisted. Conflict roared across his features. Still she waited. She prayed for that dark haze in his eyes to give way to the brilliant cyan stare of the lover who'd revealed himself to her beneath the pines today. Maybe if she envisioned him that way again, trapping her, consuming her, taking her in whatever way he could get her...

"I liked it, Garrett."

Her voice quavered. The words were dangerous. The last time she'd spoken them, he'd been marked with scratches from another woman, and they'd fought like hellcats. That night, they'd slept back-to-back for the first time in their relationship—"slept" being a really loose term for those fitful hours.

This time, his reaction was different. Really different. Garrett didn't bellow or growl back at her. By this point, he barely moved. He'd either shoved the invisible tree free, or decided to die under it. By the way his eyes slowly squeezed shut, Sage guessed the latter.

Damn it.

Fine. She knew how to light fires. Spark by excruciating spark.

133

"I liked it…Sir."

She had nothing to lose anymore. If he was going to slip away from her, if he was going to let her rot in sexual and emotional frustration on the pedestal of his "protection," she wasn't going to let him go without knowing she'd risked it all, including his ridiculous misconceptions of her. If he stomped out of here now, she'd at least know she'd thrown every stick of emotional dynamite that she could at his stubborn, beautiful soul.

He finally moved again. He went nowhere near the door, thank God. He pivoted back into the kitchen, grabbing his water glass on the way. He set the tumbler into the sink then braced his hands on both sides of the basin. The pose made her ache. It was only a slight modification of how he'd spread himself across the window of their room in Bangkok. As he gazed out the window, she only saw the spread muscles of his back, but imagined his face was stamped in a similar grimace to that day. His glare likely probed the horizon, reflecting a mind lost in a conflict she couldn't comprehend.

"I know you liked it, Sage."

She tamped her lips together to keep them from shaking . His tone was still shadowed, but the words were a caress instead of an accusation. Maybe this was a bit of progress.

"If I remember things correctly, you did, too."

Tension invaded his stance again. "What happened this afternoon …" His head sank. "Look, between the adrenalin from the jump, and watching your own excitement about the experience, and having you against me again—" He finally turned around, but made no move to leave the kitchen. "I should've controlled all that better, okay?"

Had the word "progress" actually crossed her mind a minute ago? Sage folded her arms, trying to muster a composed nod but feeling more like a bobble head doll on the dashboard of a lurching VW. "You should've—" Her lips stopped wobbling. She locked them together instead, hoping the action helped her clamp back a horridly familiar sting behind her eyes. "Right. Sure. I understand. Because God help your sorry ass if you lose control with your fiancé, of all people. Oh yeah, her. The one who's *supposed* to make you feel like taking her hard and fast and dirty against a tree."

His eyes slid shut again. "Hell, Sage."

"Nice choice of comeback, Hawkins. Is that where you think you're headed now, because we did what we did?" She watched two waves of awareness crash across his face. The first was raw arousal. The second was unfiltered shame. Nothing like that juicy combo to tempt her into playing with fire again. "Or is it because of what you were thinking about while we did it?"

"I *wasn't* thinking," he bit back. "Don't you get it? We were in that forest. Everything felt so surreal. Finally, everything just...went away. I lost rationality."

"Why? Because nobody who's 'rational' would have half a kinky thought about their woman?"

He surged forward, stabbing a finger at her. "*Not* about the woman they love. Damn it, Sage. We've been over this!"

"No. *You've* been over this." She uncurled her arms and planted her stance. Every step of his approach brought dual bites of anger and fear. Good Lord, he really had gotten huge over the last twelve months. But he wouldn't hurt her. Shit, they were here like this because he was spooked about touching her at all. Her fear stemmed from the very real possibility that they'd leave this room standing on the exact same game board squares, separate pawns at the mercy of *his* dice. Do not pass *Go.* Do not collect two hundred dollars. Stay in Jail. Stay in Jail. Stay in Jail.

No way. Not this time.

"What the hell?" He fired it back at her with what looked like confusion—on the surface. But they'd always been able to stab through each other's one-liners, whether they were joking or fighting. The fact that this was the biggest skirmish of their relationship didn't change a thing. Garrett knew it, too. One look up at the blue flames in his eyes told Sage that.

"You heard me," she retorted. "I said *you've* been through this. That wasn't a two-way conversation we had in Bangkok. It was the Garrett Hawkins sermon hour, concluded when you decided the gospel had gotten pounded into me enough, and it was time to ram your close-minded brain back into the quicksand of denial."

He stopped in front of her, eclipsing with the force of his presence. "I'm not in denial about a damn thing here."

Sage sneered. "Is that so, Preacher Boy?"

With no warning, he clutched her by the shoulders. The move was so sudden, her head snapped back. That was a good thing, since the searing intent on his face said far more than the gravel in his reply.

"You don't think I know what I'm talking about, Sage? My best friend is a hardcore Dominant. Half the unit practices the dynamic too. I've trusted these men with my life, and I'll do it again. You think I'd toss a single one of them into hell?" He pulled her an inch closer. Both their chests clutched. His jaw tensed as if her body was a stem of Belladonna, breathtaking but deadly. "I don't damn anyone for enjoying Power Exchange, okay?"

"Just yourself," Sage whispered. When his hold tightened, she persisted, "I'm right about that, and don't you dare deny it." She pressed her fingers to his sternum. His heart thundered against the taut skin. "Why am I right, Garrett? Why are you denying yourself? Why are you denying both of us something we clearly want to explore?"

He curled his fingers harder against her skin. His touch turned into scrapes of rough possession, marking her along the backs of her arms. A shiver coursed through her. She wondered—oh God, she hoped—that her words would unlock the chains so clearly weighing his gaze too. But as she searched for that freedom in his eyes, she saw devastating truth to the contrary. His mind was barely here anymore. He looked at her, but didn't see her.

Sage endured another tremor. This vibration wasn't singing a sunny Beach Boys tune. *Where are you, Garrett?* Where had he sent his thoughts? Had he taken a mental vacation back to Bangkok, maybe? If so, to where...or damn it, to whom? When he'd come back to the embassy drenched in perfume and marked with fingernail scratches, Sage had assumed he'd gone to see a call girl. What if that "stranger" hadn't been such a stranger?

His heavy swallow tossed icebergs into the freezing lake of her fear. The way he let her go, as if she were a treasure he didn't deserve, added more.

He skirted around her and walked to the window. *Shit.*

Sage stumbled in a semi-circle, forcing herself to turn toward him. He stood with his legs parted, his arms at rigid angles to his sides. The sun was setting over the lake, casting a deep bronze glow that turned his honed torso and long legs into a silhouette that resembled a demi-god rising from a pool of fire. Damn it, if this was the moment he was going to break her heart, could he look a little less magnificent doing it?

After a minute of torturous silence, she forced three words out.

"What is it?"

Her ragged rasp seemed to impact him harder than any shriek she could have mustered. That was a good thing, because Sage barely had the strength to stand, let alone speak.

"What is it." He repeated it as a statement instead of a question. "I think the proper phrasing query here, sugar, is *who,* not what."

Sage gripped the back of the couch. Okay, this *really* wasn't boding well. "All right," she said tightly, "if you say so."

Garrett dragged a hand through his hair.

"Fuck."

The word was horridly ironic, a jut of breath into the air, but carrying the weight of so much more beneath the surface. Sage did fight back the urge to scream now. "Garrett, damn it! Just spit it out, okay? I've pulled on the big girl panties. Who the hell is she?"

He laughed. The sound didn't possess a single note of mirth, but yeah, the bastard actually laughed at her. As Sage battled the urge to tackle him out the window, he closed the distance back to her and yanked the option from possibility. Suddenly, he had her wrapped against his chest with her cheek between his pecs and the top of her head locked by his lips. "Is that what you think?" he whispered.

She couldn't stop shaking. "I don't know what the hell to think anymore."

"I know." His breath heated her scalp. "And I'm sorry."

She squirmed. This contact would've been a glimpse of Heaven, if he wasn't using it to evade the obvious. "Stop stalling, Garrett, and just give me the damn name. If you're going to let me go, let's get—"

"Wyatt."

Sage froze in the middle of trying to shove against his shoulder. With her fingers locked on his collarbone, she tipped her head up, openly bewildered. "What?"

Garrett's face was still a study in concrete control. Only one part of his regard went soft by any degree. His gaze.

"You wanted a name." He tucked a strand of hair behind her ear. "Command granted, Sergeant. There's your name."

"Wyatt?"

"Yep."

"As in…your uncle? The one back in Iowa?"

"Yep."

"Funny," she snapped. "Ha ha. Way to pluck that one out at random." She started pushing from him again, but for the second time in the last minute, her instinctual bullshit meter for him registered at zero. Sage straightened her head now, directing a deeper scrutiny into him. "Wait. That wasn't so random at all, was it?"

Garrett dropped his head as he descended his hold. He grabbed both her hands into his then looked at the union of their fingers as if it were the first time he'd done this with her. His resigned energy turned Sage's heartbeat into turmoil against her ribs. Hell. Why did she feel like Oprah Winfrey, about to have a celebrity spill their darkest secret?

Garrett didn't ease her trepidation by pulling her to sit on the couch with him. Her toes sank into the thick shag of the chocolate brown area rug that stretched to the hearth. She loved this rug. The memories Garrett and she had created on it had carried her through a shitload of dismal nights, especially after she and Ray had gotten free from the pirates and had no idea what country they were in or who they could trust. She spent thousands of long nights replaying the way Garrett had teased her, touched her, thrilled her in this room.

She had no idea how he was going to change those memories now, but his continued demeanor, too damn composed for "normal" Garrett mode, confirmed this wasn't going to be some cozy fireside chat. Sage struggled to borrow his calmness as he wove their fingers tighter together. More silence stretched while he stared into the grate where so many logs had burned into ash while they loved the night away.

"How much do you know about my relationship with him?" Garrett finally asked.

"With Wyatt?" At his short nod, she tilted her head and continued. "Well, I've only met him once. He seems like a generous man, though there are parts of him that are closed off, that's for sure. He seems proud of you, but he's afraid to show it somehow."

Garrett emitted a rough snort. "Afraid to? How about just won't?"

Sage peered harder at him. "I'm officially lost here."

He stabbed his free hand into his hair. As he lowered it, he balled it into a fist. "Guess I never told you how I used to idolize him more than Dad."

Sage felt her eyebrows jump. "You certainly didn't."

He nodded. "Yyyeahhh, I tend to leave that part out of the life story most of the time."

Sage searched her memory for a recollection of Wyatt Hawkins. When she'd met him during their trip to Iowa just before Garrett proposed, it had been during a big family barbecue at the home in which Garrett grew up. Wyatt and his wife, Josie, hadn't traveled far. They lived next door. Like Garrett, his dad, and his two brothers, the man was tall, tawny-haired and all muscle, even for a guy closing in on his late thirties. Josie seemed completely smitten with him. Wyatt clearly returned the sentiment, always kissing his wife, or pulling her onto his lap. But around the rest of the family, the man was guarded, even a little aloof.

Like a man who had to keep a lot of secrets.

Comprehension hit her like a tidal wave. "Damn," she murmured. "He's ex Special Forces, isn't he?"

Garrett preceded his confirmation of that with a resolute jut of his jaw. "When I was a kid, Wyatt was larger than life. I didn't watch the Transformers or the Ninja Turtles or fucking G.I. Joe; I had a real-life version of them rolled together in my uncle. He upped when he was nineteen and was damn-near plucked out of Basic for the Special Forces track. A lot of folks said they'd never seen anyone like him. The guy loved being a soldier. He was stationed with the fifth SF group, down in Kentucky, before getting sent up to Ranger School and graduating top of his battalion."

A grin peeked through his lips, turning back the clock on his face by at least five years in two seconds. Sage smiled back as he shook his head wistfully. "They threw this wild-ass party for him when he made Triple Canopy in record time." He broke out in a full chuckle. "Not every day a town had a guy who kicked ass in Jump School, the Special Forces funnel, *and* the Ranger course, right? The bash went on for days, and they used a cleared field on the west side of the farm for what was quite possibly the biggest mud football game ever played. I was only eleven, but I could've died that day thinking I'd hit Heaven."

Sage laughed softly. "I can imagine you had."

The faraway haze in his eyes got a little thicker. "For a bunch of years, we didn't see him a lot. His deployments were long. But man, when he got a chance to make it home…it was better than Christmas. I'd beg Mom to let me skip school. I'd spend the days at Wyatt's heels, worse than a damn puppy, drinking up his charisma, letting him kick my ass in mock 'training battles.'"

"Oh boy," Sage murmured. "The dynamic duo, Hawkins style."

"Yeah." Garret laughed. "Yeah, it was…well, it was awesome."

Before she spoke again, she repositioned one of her hands so she could run her fingers over the hills of his coiled knuckles. With the same care, she studied his face. His rugged features had never snagged her breath more. Finally, he was letting her see everything, a fast-shifting landscape of emotion as years of memories bombarded him at once.

"So what happened?" she asked at last. When he gave her only a tighter scowl, she pressed, "Garrett, *what happened*?"

He captured her hand beneath his again. The hot, dark haze in his gaze went thick as grenade smoke. "Iraq happened."

Sage nodded. "And he was likely in the thick of it."

"No 'likely' about it."

She winced. "How bad?"

Garrett took in a heavy, shaking breath. "I'm not sure. He never talked about it in full. From what I can logically snap together, he survived at least three roadside attacks. The one that sent him home for good took out everybody in his unit but him."

She leaned heavily against the cushions. "Wow."

His face, now in profile to her, settled on a strangely serene expression. It was almost like he prepared to bow his head and pray—and it scared her. She knew that look. It happened when someone went on agony overload and had to detach from what they talked about in order to remain halfway sane. She'd never seen it on Garrett's face before, not even after he returned from missions that had been brutal to his body, his uniform, his energy. But right now, recalling how the war had taken his beloved hero from him, the grief gouged too deeply.

She squeezed his fingers harder. She let him know she was still there with everything she was worth.

"By then, it was no secret to any of us that the war was carving bigger and bigger pieces out of him. But I was thirteen and filled with all the never-surrender bullshit the man himself had filled me with. I thought that as soon as Wyatt was home for good, I'd single-handedly rehabilitate him back into Soldier-God Hawkins. Only this time, it would be better. There'd be no deployment to take Wyatt away from me. We could just—" He halted as the church-worthy expression

141

dissolved off his face. His lips curled, his nose flared, and he huffed heavily, closing his eyes to reveal the sheen of tears on his lashes. "Well, we didn't. Wyatt decided that the National Geographic channel and Jeopardy marathons were more exciting than hanging out with the kid who still remembered the night he'd scored five touchdowns in the mud.

"Slowly, he realized he was pretty much being a brokedick. He started helping Dad run the farm, but he picked all the one-man jobs that didn't require him to speak to anyone. He also told Mom not to let me play hooky anymore, because by that time, I'd made it damn clear to anyone who'd listen that I wanted to make SF when I grew up."

Sage unhooked a hand long enough to give a reassuring stroke down his arm. "I'll bet he was really proud when you did."

Garrett shrugged on shoulders taut with bitterness. "I have no idea if he was or not. Frankly, I stopped caring—especially after one pretty memorable summer night."

Until now, the conversation had clearly been uncomfortable for him. But his uneasiness took on a new strand of tension with that statement. Sage had the distinct impression that the Oprah confession was about to get an R rating. Or worse.

"Memorable…how?"

For the first time since they'd sat down, Garrett looked like the words in his mouth were chunks of something vile.

Oh, yeah. This was going to get awkward.

"We all pitched in and got Wyatt a new Nintendo console for his birthday. He'd play on it at night when the flashbacks from Iraq kept him up, which was pretty much every night. When I couldn't sleep myself, I'd sneak down the rain gutter and go join him for an hour or so. It was barely a connection, but I clung to it. I hoped we'd work our way back to at least a friendship."

"Of course you did," Sage assured.

"Well, that night…I only got as far as the barn."

She accessed more memories. "The big brown storage one, between the two houses, right?"

"Roger," he confirmed.

Sage's instinct started kicking in. There was no way it couldn't. The nervous flicks of his gaze, the color climbing his neck, the finger he drummed on a knee… Oh, yeah. This wasn't just uncomfortable for him. It was torture.

She tried to ease things for him with an thoughtful tone. "You only got to the barn…because Wyatt was inside?"

He took a prolonged second before answering. "Yeah."

"Was he alone?"

He rolled his head, looking like she'd punched him. "No. Josie was in there with him."

She could've filled in that blank too. Moreover, with that new slice of the image, she started filling in details for herself. But she didn't voice them aloud. Garrett needed to tell her himself. The words needed to come out of him, if his perception of them were ever going to change. If he was ever going to heal.

"What were they doing?" She rubbed his knuckles again in a gentle coax.

"They—he—*fuck*."

"It's me, Garrett. I'm not going anywhere. Tell me."

He pulled in another hard breath. "Josie was kneeling over a hay bale. Her wrists were hooked together, locked in leather cuffs. She was dressed in this corset outfit, also black leather…with panties that might as well have not been there, and a—a collar that was attached to a chain." He twisted his hand against her, and shoved a foot so hard that the rug bunched up. "Wyatt had his *wife* on a goddamn leash! And he was—"

"He was what?"

He looked away. "Shit. No. Forget it."

Sage hung on to his arm like it was a damn parachute rip cord. "No way, Hawkins. Spill it or I'll just pick up the phone and call Josie myself for a little girls' chat."

He swung a hot glare at her. She jabbed her chin out and met that cobalt blaze without blinking.

"You're not kidding, are you?"

"I've had to eat bugs to survive, Sergeant. Do you think

I'm kidding?"

His head fell against the cushions. A hard gulp rolled down his throat. He dragged his hand down his face. "He had a riding crop, okay? And he was striking her ass with it. Repeatedly. And hard."

"Okay," Sage answered evenly. "And was she liking it?"

"Hell, Sage. I wasn't in a position to take a fucking survey!"

"You remember a hell of a lot of details already. You want to tell me that you didn't notice whether Josie was begging, 'Get me out of here now' or 'Get inside me now?'"

"Did you really just ask me that?"

"Are you really still avoiding the answer?"

He threw her another glower. "Fine. Okay, she was—enjoying things—I suppose." He lurched off the couch, slamming his hands to his hips as he stormed to the hearth. "I didn't stick around to write a full report."

Sage rose, too. He didn't turn when she did. She lifted a hand, yearning to touch him, to make sure he knew she hadn't suddenly turned to dust at his illicit revelation. Truthfully, she felt the opposite. For the first time since they'd gotten back from Thailand, she felt clear about her connection to him. This was them, tearing down walls together. This was them, forging into new territory together. *Together.* God, it felt wonderful to hear that word ringing in her conscious.

"I've never told that to anyone." Garrett dropped his hands as he muttered the confession. "I was afraid of it. Afraid…of what it had done to me."

"What *did* it do to you?"

"You've been the firsthand witness of that, sugar. A couple of times now."

She took a tentative step toward him but stopped. Conflict sat on her shoulders as she carefully considered her next words.

Who was she kidding? There was no "careful" to be had here. He was either going to understand, once and for all, that his burgeoning Dominant was one of the best things that had happened to their relationship, or he'd choose to dive back in to his sludge of self-condemnation. She refused to stick around for that sight anymore.

"I don't think you turned out so bad, Garrett."

"Really?" As she half expected, he wheeled back around. His shoulders were stiff and his face was gaunt. "You don't think so, huh? Well, isn't that special."

Had she been tempted to hold him a second ago? "It should be special," she snapped. "I'm your *fiancé*. Does that count for anything anymore?"

He snorted at her like a pissed-off bull. "Don't you get it? After so many years of swearing I wouldn't be like Wyatt, that I wouldn't become him, that I'd be *better* than him at handling my shit…and yet I've tromped down the same damn path as him." His lips twisted. "The only thing I didn't fuck up was letting some starry-eyed kid get obsessed with me, only to have their hero fall and crumble as they watched."

Sage dug her nails into her palms. Gazing at him was torment. It was worse than watching him get beat up, because he was the one doing the damage. And nothing she said could make him stop.

"You're right," she rasped. "On *one* thing. There's no kid this time. But there *is* someone here who calls you hero."

He blinked, clearly understanding her. And clearly not happy with that. *Tough beans, Sergeant Hawkins. You're going to listen to this.*

"You think it's just a cute catch phrase for me, Garrett? You think it's something I don't believe with all my heart? *Still?*" She couldn't stand the distance anymore. In two steps, she was pressed against him. She looked up and spread a hand to the side of his head. "And no, you haven't crumbled. Dear God, in this moment, you're more strong and amazing to me than ever. You're my hero in a million more senses. Confronting your truth takes as much guts as facing insurgent fire or an enemy grenade." She smiled. "Or a slime bag in a jungle, selling women into slavery."

His eyes went stunningly wide. In their blue fire, Sage caught the intensity of real horror. "Shit, Sage!"

He tried to turn away. She grabbed him harder. "No!" she pleaded. "Don't close me out, damn it! Don't run from this, Garrett. Don't run from *us*."

He curled his hands around the backs of her elbows. His fingers quivered, keeping time to the hard breaths pumping beneath his chest. "Sage." He dipped his face, every cliff and valley of his features etched in the agony of a new creature bursting from its chrysalis. "Sage, I love you so much."

"And I love you." She flattened her hands to the ridges that defined his lower torso. "But right now, I also need you." Using his body for balance, she slid downward. Then down even more. She didn't speak again until she kneeled fully, her head dropped between her upstretched arms. Just achieving that position made her mind shift into another place, where peace and power mixed together in a beautiful ambrosia. The elixir started spreading through her body, igniting her nerve endings, feeding the pulsing need in the deepest tissues of her sex. "I need to give it all to you, my hero. My body. My heart. My power. Take them. Use them to transport me. To transport you. You have all of me, Garrett. Everything."

She felt and listened to every part of his reaction. The tremors in his thighs, shaking like the tree he'd pinned her to this afternoon. The breath entering and exiting his body like whooshes of a wind storm. The sound that vibrated up his throat, rough and tortured, as he stroked the top of her head.

"You really want this?" His growl was part savoring predator, part intent lover. Oh *God,* that voice. If that's what the devil sounded like when he'd approached Faust, she didn't blame the guy for inking the deal on his soul.

"Yes." She finally got the word out on a dry whisper.

His grip on her head changed. By slow degrees, he tightened and twisted until he had her more by the hair instead of her scalp. "Tell me again, sweet sugar."

Oh, God. The growl that took over his voice…it belonged to the same beautiful, dark creature he'd untethered that first night back in Bangkok. Between that tone and the increasing torque of his hold, her skin began to tingle, her heart began to soar.

146

"Yes, Sir. I want this."

Another rough sound reverberated from his chest. The creature in him was prowling, assessing, approving. Sage sighed in bliss. To know she was doing this for him, giving him this dynamic that his soul and his body had craved for so long...she was joyous, floating.

His hand jerked harder on her hair. Her sigh turned into a sharp cry. She held nothing back from him, and it felt amazing. After a year of checking every move she made and controlling every sound she emitted, this freedom was a miracle. A gift.

He brought his other hand up to her head. When he had her braced in his dual grip, he pressed her face into the apex of his thighs. Sage bit hungrily at the fabric, reveling in how the ridge beneath his khakis jumped and surged for her. As his hold coiled tighter, she whimpered higher.

Until the next second, when he pulled back with a harsh grunt. He wheeled away from her, spitting the *f* word like it was about to get pulled from the world's lexicon forever.

Her heart dove back into her stomach. Searing heat invaded the back of her eyes. She fell back to her heels in a shaky heap.

Dead end. Again.

Garrett locked white knuckles to the mantle. Sage curled similar fists into her lap. They remained that way through interminable minutes, frozen at opposite ends of the rug that might as well have turned into a chasm, in a silence just as deep and divisive.

The doorbell rang.

Garrett looked to her. Sage shook her head. Neither of them was expecting anyone. She rose, wiping her cheeks as she did, and joined Garrett as he went to the door.

"Surprise!"

The couple on the front stoop exclaimed it unison when Garrett opened to them. The woman's pixie-like features were enhanced by a cute contemporary style of her black hair. The man was at least a foot and a half taller than her, and looked so much like a bearded version of Garrett that an outsider would've taken him as Garrett's dad. But he wasn't.

The tension in Garrett's body tripled inside ten seconds. Sage was proud of him for forcing a smile, and extending his hand in greeting.

"Uncle Wyatt."

Chapter Thirteen

The last time Garrett had been this uncomfortable, the squad was on recon in an alley in Aleppo, and they'd spent the night getting silently sized up by a group of local kids. They'd had to consider every damn move they made, turned into star specimens on one of life's stranger Petri dishes, whether they liked it or not.

Wyatt was giving him the same spare-no-details scrutiny.

The man hid it better than the Syrian kids, but Garrett felt every turn of the man's mental focus knob just as acutely. To anyone else, he simply appeared a proud uncle shooting the shit with his nephew in front of the backyard fire ring, sipping on a beer, enjoying the sunset. It was a façade and they both knew it. Garrett was pretty damn sure that if he asked, the man could tell him exactly how many egrets were out on the water, as well as which ones were there for food and which ones were trolling for a hump.

God only knew what specifics Wyatt had gathered about him in the moments he'd been too stunned to watch his composure. After the initial shock of their greeting, Sage had welcomed the couple inside. The second the door was shut, Wyatt pulled him into a gruff guy hug—the first heartfelt contact he'd had from the man in ten years. The move shaved off that much time from his spirit too. For a few awesome minutes, he was a Wyatt-worshipping puppy again, showing the man around their place, bragging about the new grill he'd put in himself, which was now filled with cobwebs because he hadn't used the thing in the last year. What would've been the point?

Sage instantly decided that the webs wouldn't do. She'd declared a family barbecue was in order, and it was happening tonight. Garrett, still giddy, had grinned and agreed—until his fiancé hooked arms with Aunt Josie and started making lists for their food shopping trip. That was when the ten years slammed

149

back in again, along with the shit that made those one hundred twenty months feel like twice that much. The memory of King's shrewd leer at Sea-Tac. The regular updates from Zeke, confirming that the girls remained a hot ticket on every bounty hunter's list, despite King's solitary confinement status at FDC. And damn it, that too-close-for-comfort house call made at the base this morning by the pair of King's minions.

Garrett snatched the list from Sage inside of five seconds. When she gave him a glare poured of solid sass, he'd been ready with both arched brows, along with the command that he and Wyatt would do the shopping. The long giggle she'd joined to Josie's didn't affect her own reflexes. She nicked the list back before he recovered from seeing her in a full laugh again, declaring that her house arrest didn't have jurisdiction over a food run chaperoned by his own aunt. She'd gone on about how their dinner needed to be something more than cold cereal, frozen pizza, and peanut butter from the jar, but he'd been busy trying not to look like an overprotective asshole to formulate a decent zinger back to that.

So here he was, faking his way through the guy bonding commercial, trying to numb some of his anxiety with the dark ale in his hand while keeping part of his brain heightened to what Wyatt's purpose was here. He and Josie had spouted the ideal excuse for their surprise drop-in: they'd seen the news coverage about Sage's miracle rescue, and couldn't sit still about it. Garrett had riveted his gaze to the floor after that, not having the luxury of sunglasses to hide his bullshit meter. But the current conversation wasn't lending itself to the Wyatt and Garrett Open 'n' Honest hour. So far, they'd talked sports, smart phones, and the newest Michael Bay movie, executing a perfect verbal waltz around the emotional bear trap neither of them wanted to set off first. Now the safe subjects were thinning out, the silences stretching longer. And the man sitting four feet from him seemed a more distant stranger than ever before.

Maybe, he mused, it was time to kick their "conversation" inside. He could click on the TV. The numbing savior of ESPN was just a dozen steps away.

His cell danced across the redwood table with an incoming call. The peppy dance song that blared from the device told him it was Sage. It wasn't as lasting a fix as ESPN, but he'd take it. As he reached for the phone, Wyatt flashed him a sympathetic smirk. Seemed Josie programmed her own ring tone into his cell too.

"Hey, sugar."

She stopped herself in the middle of a laugh. A smile tugged at his lips despite the status of his nerves. Letting her out of his sight might be playing havoc with his stress levels, but it was damn good to hear real joy in her voice again.

"Hi there, Sir Hero!"

He chuckled. "Right."

"It's true. You *are* my hero." She let out a long sigh. "You always will be."

His laughter slipped. The second sense he'd been honing on Wyatt launched a redirect at her—more specifically, her mushy words and slurred inflection. "Sage, are you a little juiced?"

A spluttering giggle came through the line. "Maybe. Just a little."

"At the base commissary?"

"Ummm…maybe we're not at the commissary anymore."

"What?" It shot out of him like a twenty-five millimeter bullet. "Sage, I told you this trip was fine as long as you and Josie went to the commissary." After the incident with King's goons this morning, both Ethan and Zeke had confirmed the base was beefing up security patrols, credential checks, and license plate scans. Adding all that up, he'd finally relented to Sage's enthusiasm, figuring an hour's trip to the commissary would be the safest solo trip she could make. Now, she'd just tossed *safe* to the roadside. Damn it!

"Don't yell at me," she blurted back.

"I'm not—" He lurched to his feet, and tried to get in a deep breath. "I'm not yelling. So where are you?"

"The seafood at the commissary sucked," she babbled on. "I should've known. They never have good prawns. God, I can't *wait* to have these prawns tonight, baby. They're huge! Really amazing! Wait'll you see—"

"*Sage.* Where. Are. You?"

"The Market, silly. Where else would we get great prawns?"

"The Market." He muttered it as his chilly unease turned into the ice of dread. "The Pike Place Market?"

"Now you're yelling."

"Damn straight! I told you to go to the base, *only* the base, and now you're downtown, shopping with half the goddamn world?"

Her answering laugh dug into him like razor blades. "Yeah. I've been naughty. You'll probably have to spank me."

Every syllable of his retort came gritted from between his teeth. "Not funny, sugar."

"Well, Josie thought it was. So did Rayna." There was scraping on the line, as if she turned her head. "Didn't you, Ray?"

He sank back into his chair, frowning in confusion. "Rayna? She's there too?"

"Yeah! Isn't that great? We just bumped into them! They're gonna come for dinner too, okay?"

"Them?" The air slowly returned to his lungs. That didn't mean it still wasn't painful to breathe, but the extra oxygen to his head helped with clarity. "Who's with her?"

He prayed for one specific word in answer. At last, God heard him.

"Zeke."

"Thank fuck." He pinched his nose. "Baby, let me talk to him."

More rasps grated in his ear. The throb of heavy wind. At last, a heavy grunt he'd never been more happy to hear. "Yo, Hawk."

"Christ," he muttered. "I ordered her to hit the commissary then get her ass straight home."
"I see how that worked out."

The implication in Z's voice was plain as a fly on a trap strip. "Look, after this morning, she started calling me the prison warden. There isn't a Broadway cast of brothers around to help me with this shit, either."

"I feel you, dude," Z replied. "But it's all good, okay? Fortune owed us one and decided to pay up. There's a Seattle PD officer nearby, and I've filled him in on King's witch hunt for the girls. He's adding his eyeballs to the cause. It's handled."

Garrett snorted, his shorthand version of a thank-you. "So why are *you* two there?"

His friend let out a low grouse. "Rayna started calling me the warden too."

He couldn't help a sharp laugh. No wonder Z was being Mr. Understanding about his frustration. "And the story on the tipsy status?" Another jolt of alarm hit him. "Hell. If Sage drove there from the base in that condition—"

"*Relax,* man. There's a bunch of Yakima Valley wineries here having a tasting thing in the restaurants. Your Aunt Josie has grabbed Sage's keys already. She can follow me back to your place. It seems we've been invited to dinner."

"Seems so."

"We'll be buggin' soon, Hawk, I promise."

"Thanks, Z."

"Peace out."

He settled the phone back on the table and released a weighted whoosh. Though he'd been aware of Wyatt's watchful silence through the whole conversation, Garrett's brain officially jumped back into the symbolic Petri dish. He had a couple of choices now. Try to hide the relief on his face, or simply wait for the question he was certain Master Sergeant Wyatt Hawkins was about to lob his way.

"The troops aren't cooperating today, eh?"

There was enough of Wyatt's old bravado in that to make Garrett smile. "You could say that."

His uncle stared over the water again, rubbing a slow finger across his lip. Added to his beard and the sunglasses he wore, the motion made it impossible for Garrett to read what he was thinking. It was likely by design.

"And how's Zeke? Still getting you into some crazy-ass

Charlie-Foxtrot missions?"

"Well, he's still crazy." Garrett tossed back some more beer. "And he's still an ass sometimes. But as you know, I get hard for the cluster fucks."

"Yeah." Wyatt's murmur was low and tight. "So did I."

Garrett didn't say anything. Words would have diluted what his silence said louder and better. That he understood. That his addiction for the tough missions, the batshit bullet fights, and the tore-up-from-the-floor-up adventures had been pre-written into his blood from the first battle story Wyatt had ever told him—and that he wouldn't have changed a damn thing about it, either. Like he even could have.

As if Wyatt read that exact thought, he cocked his head toward Garrett. "Guess everyone in Adel was right when they called us two of a kind."

The reaction for that didn't come so easy. There was a time when the words would've had Garrett beaming. That time was pretty damn long ago—and seemed even more distant after this last year. After this last *month.*

"I guess so." He hated himself for sounding as thrilled as a grounded teenager. But faking the happy-happy-joy-joy with Wyatt was like trying the effort with Zeke. That's what sucked about hanging out with guys who'd been trained to spot a lie on your face better than a wart.

"Yeah," Wyatt muttered. "Just as I thought."

Garrett glowered. "Just as you thought *what?*"

"You really are my goddamn Mini Me."

"All right," Garrett snapped, "now that we've established the obvious, what the fuck is your point?" He grabbed his empty beer bottle by its neck and flung it into the trash can next to the barbecue. Glass shattered in the can with satisfying violence as he uncapped his second brew. "For that matter, why have you even come here, Wyatt? I'm not buying the excuse that you and Josie volunteered to be Sage's welcome wagon back to life on behalf of the family."

His uncle leaned back again. Every inch of the move was a slide of smooth, careful assessment, acting like a Bowie knife to Garrett's gut. *I'm not some interrogation subject. I'm the guy who grew up worshipping you, damn it, and now you won't even take off your sunglasses to meet me in the eye.*

Still, like an imbecile himself, he waited and hoped that this time would be different. That maybe—

Wyatt would yank off his glasses, like he did now. His uncle would stare at him with pure pride and affection, like he did now.

Garrett dipped his own gaze. He'd dreamt the moment, right? But when he lifted his head again, Wyatt's pure blue eyes looked back, now attached to a sincere smile.

"We came because I wanted to, Sergeant." He used the rank with purposeful respect. "Because I needed to see you. To talk to you."

The confession pushed a weird overload button in his brain. Was this *seriously* happening? He couldn't remember the last time he'd entertained this fantasy, before finally shoving it down into that dark pocket of his psyche called *better to just forget.*

"Why?" he finally challenged.

"Besides the fact that I'm about twelve months too late on doing it?" Wyatt answered. "Oh, hell. Who am I kidding? Later than that, right? But I started thinking about it in earnest right after they declared Sage K.I.A." His fingers went white where they still hung on to his glasses. His other hand balled into a fist on top of his thigh. "My God, Garrett. My soul cracked for yours."

Though a moist twilight breeze blew up off the water, Garrett felt like he'd been thrown into the desert. Heat blasted him, especially north of his neck. He opened his suddenly-parched lips, trying to suck in some air. *Yeah, right. So not happening, man.*

"It's probably best you didn't come around," he muttered.

Wyatt's reaction wasn't what he expected. Did the man really laugh? No. The sound was more a mocking snarl. "Well, fuck," he spat. "Didn't you rattle that off like a damn fine soldier?"

Garrett sat up straighter, yanked that way by a rod of

155

tension up his spine. "I have no idea what you're—"

"Of course you don't, Sergeant." He didn't invoke the rank with such reverence this time. "Neither did I, when everything in my world unspooled beyond my control." He stared at the water again. The line of his jaw hardened into an anvil of antagonism. "So many people reached out to me… Your dad. Your mom. Pastor Dooley. All my goddamn doctors. And at least three head fucking shrinks."

Garrett interrupted him with a snort. "I *hate* the head fuckers."

"Yeah, so did I." Wyatt shook his head. "Even going to see Dooley was preferred torture over them."

"You mean Drooley?"

Wyatt spat the mouthful of beer he'd just gulped. "Holy shit. That's good."

"And accurate."

"Yeah, that too." The man took in another swig of beer and kept it down this time. When he lowered the bottle, his mouth was re-set into a somber line. "But I shoved them all away, Garrett. I locked myself in a box of mental steel, forging the thing out of my anger, my fear, my goddamn guilt. I was the sole survivor of that attack, yeah? So how could anyone get that? How could anyone understand? How could anyone know what the fuck I was going through? How could any kind of therapy or prayer touch the depth of my shame? Psychology certainly wasn't set up for my shit.

"And God? Well, in my mind, God had thrown me away, too. He'd intended to take everyone in that explosion, but got his hands full with the load, so he asked himself, which one could he do without for a few more years? Certainly not Mason, who had a wife and two kids at home. And not Searle, who spent her free time on base taking care of the stray dogs in the neighborhood. Looked like it was my pathetic ass."

Garrett clenched his jaw. The heat engulfed him once more. He didn't want this. He didn't want to be listening to every word from Wyatt's mouth, and admitting the same damn thoughts had relentlessly drilled his own mind over the last year. He sure as hell didn't want to accept the disgusting

156

conclusion to which Wyatt had led them both, and he fought the mental shit bath of putting it into words. But somebody had to be the voice of this truth. *He* had to be that person.

"But you didn't tell anyone, because that's not what Special Forces does, right?"

Wyatt said nothing. He didn't have to. The gripping fist in Garrett's gut confirmed his call had hit the bull's-eye. He closed his eyes, trying to process the blow like he had a thousand times before—and failing, just like he had a thousand times before.

"We take the pain, don't we, Uncle? That's what we're trained best for. We take it through boot camp, through Assessment and Selection, through Final Qualification, through every op in every shithole they can throw us into. Then when the agony attacks and the spool starts unraveling, we search the database in our heads, certain we had to have missed the training about this shit—because surely they didn't just leave it out of the curriculum."

"And God forbid that we ask anyone what page it's on." Wyatt flung his own empty bottle into the trashcan. "Even when the book is open and in front of us."

Garrett stared down the neck of his beer bottle. He wasn't certain what to say to that, or how to say it if he did know. Just two hours ago, he'd vowed to Sage that he'd never turn into the man who'd crushed so many fantasies of his youth. But this twist on things was…fucking bizarre. Wyatt himself was telling him exactly how to keep that promise.

It was an act of bravery that hauled the fist from Garrett's stomach and up into his throat. The man could've laid down his life for Garrett with more ease than what he did right now. Opening every inch of one's heart to another human being was one of the first behaviors they pounded from a guy in Basic, let alone what he went through on the way to Special Forces.

"I saw the book, Garrett," Wyatt continued. "And I saw *you,* okay? You need to know that. I saw everything, all the havoc my asshole act wreaked on you. I just didn't—" He leaned forward to brace his elbows on his knees. His shoulders slumped. "I didn't know how to climb off that damn pedestal you had me on. I'm—I'm not sure I wanted to. After all, I helped you build the thing. And I'm sorry for all of it, Garrett. I'm so goddamn sorry."

The knuckles at Garrett's throat grew brass battering rings. Apparently, his soul knew what to do with them too. The pain barely made breathing possible, let alone speaking. Why was this moment such a torment? He'd wanted nothing more than this from Wyatt for so long, words that hammered down the beginnings of a bridge between them once again. But it had been so long since he'd believed this would ever happen...
He'd filled in the cracks in his spirit with the no-fuss mortar that let in no more light, and let out no more feeling. He liked it so much that he piled on years' worth of the gunk, letting it harden into layers of a warrior they called the Hawk. The guy with the surprise claws. The indispensable killer.

If he believed Wyatt's words, he'd have to tear off all that mortar. He'd have to look at the cracks again. He'd have to feel them again.

"Fuck." He muttered it before finishing his beer in one chug. "Why?" he finally growled at his uncle. "Why are you doing this now?"

Wyatt tilted his head again. A broad smile spread across his lips.

"Josie's pregnant."

Garrett gaped. Wyatt chuckled at him. "Yeah, that was my reaction at first too. We're not exactly youngsters, and this was definitely a surprise. A pretty awesome one." The smile faded but the gentle lines remained on the man's face. "After the shock wore off, I realized that I couldn't think of being a proper father to this kid until I set things right by you. When we heard about the miracle of you finding Sage, I knew I'd been given a perfect chance to do that."

Garrett felt his eyes narrowing. Wyatt had never been this open with him, even on those blissful deployment breaks, and yet an undertone still clung to the man's voice, a layer of mortar *he* wasn't peeling off. He issued his reply with an air of careful casual. "A *perfect* chance, eh? Now how did you figure that?"

Another low laugh rumbled from the man. "Son, if burying your woman didn't deplete the control spool, getting her back surely fucked the thing to hell." Wyatt's gaze darkened by a couple of shades. "Like I've been saying in my not-so-elegant way, I've been there. Maybe not the exact miles your boots have gone, but close enough, Garrett. Close enough."

Garrett pulled in a deep breath and gazed across the water. The sky was turning lavender now. He thought about getting up and flipping on some lights, but the darkness felt better. Way better. It helped hide things like falling chunks of emotional cement.

"I'm fine." He forced confidence to the words. "Sage and I...*we're* fine."

"Okay. Sure."

The man's snicker was unsettling. Screw that. Enraging filled the bill better. "What now?" Garrett barked.

"Nothing, son. Not a damn thing."

"Why don't I believe you?"

"Probably the same reason I don't believe *you.*" He shook his head. "But you go ahead, Garrett. Keep up with the 'we're fine' line. But repeating it a thousand more times won't make it true."

Garrett chucked his new empty at the trash can. Incomplete pass. The bottle shattered on the patio stones. *Perfect.* "Fuck. Off."

"Check," the man replied. "I'll do that. And you keep up with your 'fine' thing. Ordering your woman around like she's on some weird probation but giving her little reason to feel connected or safe in the prison you've confined her in— her own home, at that. Jo and I didn't notice all the tear streaks on her face when we got here, either. Of course, I won't bring up how you barely touch her—"

"Shut up." Garrett surged to his feet. A bitter laugh exploded from him. "You have a couple of big ones in that nut sack, Uncle, coming here and trying to call my shit about 'connection.' I'd laugh, but I'm too busy getting over the shock."

Wyatt tipped back and touched a finger to his lips again. "Don't forget the energy suck of keeping all those kinky fantasies under control."

Garrett froze. The action reflected exactly what the man had done to every blood cell in his body. He glared at Wyatt, but damn it, thanks to the lights he *hadn't* turned on, his uncle's face was draped in shadows. "What the hell is that supposed to mean?"

The fucker made him wait through a tortuous silence. The only thing about Wyatt that moved were the flames in his eyes, billowed into a full bonfire now. Ironic, that. The fire didn't do a damn thing for Garrett's frozen bloodstream. This really, royally sucked.

"Garrett...I know you were there." The man finally shifted. As he leaned forward to his knees again, he let out a rough cough. "That night, in the barn...when you saw Josie and me—"

"Fuck." Garrett clawed at his hair and spun away.

"It wasn't like I had an ear peeled for you, son. You scrambled outta there with the grace of an ox on an ice rink. Man, I sure hope they gave you dance lessons in training."

"I can't believe you're trying to joke about this." He veered around and rushed at his uncle. "No, what I really can't believe is how you never, in twelve years, chose to *really* grow a pair and talk to me about it!"

"Right. That's such a great conversation starter for post-Drooley Sunday brunch. 'Hey Garrett, did I ever tell you how your Aunt Josie saved our marriage by suggesting I tie her down, flog her then fuck her until she screamed through four climaxes? Oh, and pass the coleslaw, buddy; thanks.'"

"You lived *next door,* Wyatt." He spread his arms. "I was fifty steps away!"

"You were also a goddamn pup."

"No." He swept an arm back and stabbed a finger at the man. "That's what you wanted me to be. That's what you saw because of the fucking pedestal you couldn't climb down from. I was a young man. And," –he watched his finger shake—"I was confused." More mortar tumbled off his heart, this time in chunks. It hurt. Holy hell, it hurt. "I was so fucking confused."

He dropped his arm. He let his gaze follow that direction too. Wyatt's continuous regard still weighed on him like a wool blanket. The guy picked *now* to fork over his undivided attention?

At last, his uncle gave a low sigh. "Yeah," he murmured, "I was confused too."

Garrett nodded tightly. This transparency had taken twelve years to come, but the man was giving it his all and a little more. On any mission, that was all you could ask of someone.

Garrett turned up the gas-fed flames beneath the rocks in the fire pit. Zeke would be bringing the women home soon, and he knew Sage would be chilled. Her endurance against the Puget Sound moisture had been whittled away by a year in the wild. He paced across the patio and glanced through the living room toward the front door, half from the hope she'd be coming through it and half to buy some time to form a clear thought.

No-go on the Sage appearance. But he did connect with the curiosity that burned at him from Wyatt's confession. He sat again, voicing his question with more than a little amazement.

"So that's really what happened? *Josie* was the one who—who saved your marriage?"

Wyatt gave back a slow, sure smile. "Damn straight she did."

"By offering herself to you." Garrett felt his brows crunching in incredulity. "By asking you to…"

"Be her Dominant. Yes."

Garrett emulated his uncle's pose, settling elbows on his knees. "With all respect, Sir, that's not the first thing wives usually bring up as a quick fix-it for matrimonial woes."

"Oh, we were way past the easy repairs, Garrett." The man's grin twisted into an uneasy grimace. "Your dad and I started scouting bachelor apartments for me. I even thought of going back into the big green government machine as a trainer, maybe a desk jockey somewhere."

"That would've killed you."

"I was half dead anyway." As the man peered into the flames, Garrett noticed things on Wyatt's face that had never been there before. Deeper grooves around his mouth. Gray tinges in his beard and hair. A well-earned wisdom in his eyes. "My spool was at its end," the man went on. "I wasn't super soldier anymore. I wasn't super *anything* anymore. And when Josie first talked to me about the lifestyle, I have to admit that I wondered who she was, and what she'd done with my wife. Turned out she'd been in some online support groups, and made a friend who swore to her that BDSM was better than Xanax, and a hell of a lot more satisfying." With that assertion, his lips curved up again. This time, the expression came with a wicked twist. "Turned out she was right."

Garrett snorted. This still felt like some strange fourth dimension, where nothing was real. "So…what happened then? You just took her to the barn one night and—"

"Shit, no. There were conversations. Lots of them. I had to be convinced I had my real wife, remember?" A soft chuckle vibrated the man. "But I'll never forget the first night that beautiful woman kneeled at my feet and surrendered herself fully to me. It was a gift, Garrett. A treasure for which I'm grateful every day."

They were words for a song lyric. That was all great and dandy. But nobody was paging Springsteen here. Wasn't Wyatt leaving out a huge chunk of the debrief? Garrett shifted restlessly. "Okay, that's fine and fantastic—for *you*. But what about her? What does Josie get out of all this? Is she really doing this and—"

"Enjoying it?" Wyatt laughed with heartier emphasis. "Ohhh, yeah." He sobered fast before tilting a long look at Garrett. "Think about it for a second, would you? Wrap your head around what a soldier's woman has to go through. When the plumbing busts, we're not there. When there's a scary noise at night, we're not there. And during the shittiest times, when the hormones rage, we're still not there. Now multiply that by months, by years. When you ask her to hand over everything to you, you're offering to set her free from all that crap, if only for a little while. The decisions are suddenly not hers to make. The control is gone. The pressure is gone. And she feels completely safe about letting it go, because the man she loves is the one who's taking care of it."

Garrett pushed back his hair again. He stared at the fire, wondering if the flames had sprouted an invisible fire bolt and thrown it into his brain.

"Shit," he blurted. "Holy shit."

The pictures Wyatt had just painted were the frustrations of a regular battalion wife. But Sage was no normal anything. It was why he'd fallen in love with her inside a month. It was why he'd gotten his ring on her finger as fast as he could. It was why his soul had never truly believed she'd died—and true to her no-normal self, she'd proved him totally right. But in doing that, had he ceased to see her as a real woman, with real passions, fears, insecurities? When she'd begged him to control her, had his soul insisted on worshipping her instead of loving her, of meeting her deepest needs? He'd practiced plenty in the art of pedestal-building, hadn't he?

She'd needed him. Really needed him.

And he'd just kept pushing her away.

Why hadn't he seen it that way before?

A breath fell out him that felt like a boulder. Like it did any good. Another stone rolled into place behind it, lodging itself at the base of his throat. "I've been such an ass."

Wyatt huffed. "Oh, hell. Cut yourself some slack, you cocky whelp. You don't have all the answers." He flashed a grin Garrett hadn't seen on his face in over ten years. "That's my job."

Garrett smiled back. It felt good; damn good. He was suddenly soaring at ten thousand feet over the earth again, with his pulse pounding like he were about to toss his ass out of a plane. But this time, he didn't have a parachute, nor did he need one. He had wings of revelation. Wings that would carry Sage and him into a future full of illicit, incredible possibilities.

Fuck. How was he going to keep his hands off her during this impromptu dinner party?

He indulged an inner smirk as he answered himself.

He wasn't taming himself at all. He was going to drag her naughty little ass upstairs, lock them both into the master bathroom, strip her naked from the bottom down and order her to bite back her screams as he drove into her with every full, throbbing inch of his cock. And she'd control those shrieks while he described every detail of every punishment he planned on meting out for her trip to downtown without his consent.

He shifted in his seat with a grunt and tried to relax by looking at the lake. The only thing he could think was how dark the waters had gotten now—and how his balls were an even deeper shade of blue.

He snatched up his phone, getting ready to punch in Zeke's number. How long could a stupid wine sampling take?

Perfect timing. The device rang with an incoming call from Z himself. Garrett jabbed a thumb at the green key.

"Did you forget the access code to our gate again, man?"

Zeke's response sounded distracted. "Wh-what?"

"The gate. It has a code, remember? The code you never remember, assface?"

The zinger he expected in return from Z never came. In its place were words in a tone he'd heard so rarely from his friend, he could count the occasions on one hand. It was chilled. Choked. Afraid.

"Hawk." A rough sigh grated across the line. "Garrett. Fuck. You'd better—"

The guy just stopped, like he couldn't go on.

"What?" Garrett barked. "I'd better what, damn it? Zeke, what the hell—"

"Just get your ass in the car, and get down here." A tormented growl ripped out of him. "Aaaggh! God, I can't fucking believe this!"

"Z. You're not making sense." But the second the words spilled from him, instinct clicked into place. A damn few things could do this to Zeke. Losing at hockey. Losing a guy on the team. Losing *anyone* he cared for. Like a certain dark redhead with whom he'd spent nearly every hour of the last ten days.

"Shit," he muttered. "*Shit.*"

"I only turned for a second. One of those fuckhead fake cops asked me a question, and when I turned, the other one had three goons with him. They were already throwing Rayna into a van." His growl escalated into a snarl. "Goddamnit!"

"What about Josie? Did she observe anything?" He fired off the questions as mandates while shutting off the fire pit then whirling back toward the condo. Wyatt followed, his attention officially engaged the second *his* woman's name was mentioned. "And what do you mean, 'fake cop?'"

"I mean just that. The bastards were planted there. Goddamnit, there's no end to the toilets King can send his shit up around here!"

"That doesn't add up. He didn't know Sage was going to end up at Pike Place today."

His friend let out a leaden sigh. "Rayna and I made plans for *our* trip yesterday."

That added up. "Fuck."

"Yeah. That about says it all."

A cobra of terror slithered its way through his chest and sank fangs into the base of his wind pipe. Garrett paced into the kitchen and slammed his fist into a cupboard, answered with the din of shattering glasses from inside. He forced himself to breathe. He forced himself to *think.* He wasn't standing here with Sage's death certificate in his hand again. They had hope. It was only a thread, but he'd take it.

"Josie," he gritted again. His aunt had a damn good head on her shoulders. Maybe she remembered something vital. "You've questioned her, right? What'd she say?" Wyatt braced himself to the other side of the counter. "Questioned her about what? What the hell is going on?"

"Hawk...she's gone too."

He turned from his uncle. "Shit."

"Garrett, don't you dare turn your back on me! What's—"

He silenced his uncle with an upstretched fist. "What's

your twenty?" he demanded of Zeke. After committing the cross streets to memory, he barked, "On our way."

After punching the line shut, he swung his attention to Wyatt. The man's face had hard angles that could've formed the fifth profile on Mount Rushmore. He hadn't seen the look since Wyatt got back from his last tour in Iraq, and he hated being the one to evoke it again.

Remorse wasn't going to serve either of them right now.

"Are you carrying?" he asked his uncle.

"Does a pig blow mud for snot?"

Garrett nodded. "Grab your heat. I'll fire up the truck. We're on full ready mode as of *now.*"

"Are you going to tell me what the fuck is going on?"

"Yeah. On the way." *When you won't be so tempted to choke me to death as you think of your wife on a barge headed for Thailand.*

Chapter Fourteen

"Well, we could do worse for accommodations."

Josie was giving the situation her best, including little quips like that. Sage tried to give the woman at least half a smile, especially because Josie had spoken the truth. She peered around again. The space was nearly as big as the backstage of King's Thailand hut, only the floor swayed beneath them and she could hear the faint horns of the Bainbridge Island ferry boats. The single light they'd been given was attached to a polished teak hull, and they'd been thrown onto a plush bed with satin pillows. She guessed they were on one of the luxury yachts that were moored at the private marina north of the city.

But being surrounded by a music video fantasy didn't make her feel like dancing. That could have something to do with the dread. It returned like a creepy ex-boyfriend— wielding a knife and a shotgun. Though she fought to hit the off button on her memory, the damn thing returned to that wrenching moment in the Market, when she realized their fun girls' field trip had suddenly taken a wrong turn. She'd seen their fate written on the face of the cop who stepped in between Josie and Zeke. Within a second, he'd gone from friendly to feral, a hunter with his prize meat in range. She'd barely been surprised by the hand slapping the duct tape on her mouth, the grip that nearly yanked her shoulders from their sockets, or the body slam that took her from the afternoon sunshine into the dank gloom of a van.

That was when the hard part had begun. Again. The wild wondering of what had just happened. The pounding terror of predicting what would happen next. The enraging silence of the two men who watched over them with aimed pistols, and the third who sped the van through traffic with fluid expertise, no doubt experienced at the art of the getaway.

She bent her head back into the pillows, wishing the thoughts would tumble out the back of her head. The only thing that toppled was her equilibrium, thanks to the pitch of the boat and the aftereffects of the wine she'd "sampled." But the moment also brought clarity. She winced from the blinding force of it. All of Garrett's guard dog behavior—the paranoia, the monitoring, the needing to know her every sneeze and step—made sense now. He'd felt, probably even known, that throwing King into a jail cell anywhere in Thailand was going to be a temporary fix. She'd been held by the monster long enough to see how far his money flowed, what kind of people it turned into dancing monkeys for him.

A hard snort escaped her. Shit. It all made sense now. She should have put the pieces together long ago. She should have realized all Garrett's freak-outs weren't normal. But their absence from each other had stripped her baseline for clear judgment. He hadn't been such an ogre before Botswana. A growling grouch from time to time, but not a creature who snarled when she so much as hinted of taking a morning jog on her own. But she never questioned the ogre. She'd figured it was just part of how the last year had morphed him, the same way it had changed her. All the fear in his eyes…she'd yearned to douse it, not deal with it. For nearly fourteen months, she'd lived with more fear in her belly than food. Now that she was home, she'd only yearned to leave all the terror, desperation, uncertainty and ugliness behind. She'd longed to return to reality, and finally be free of the nightmare.

A serrated breath tore apart her throat. Return to reality? That was where she'd slipped on life's big fat banana peel, wasn't it? And life was sitting nearby, sipping a mai tai, laughing its ass off at her.

The nightmare *was* the reality.

She squeezed her eyes shut, unable to hold off the attack of the words, worsened by their leaden truth. In the darkness that encased her vision, she embraced a place where she could be free again. She knew that place before it even formed fully in her imagination. She could feel the deep shag of the rug under her knees when she dipped there, offering herself to Garrett. She could feel the response of his body, all its hard striations above her and against her, a refuge that would let her be simply woman again. Simply his again.

A dream that was never to be.

She ripped her teeth into her lip until the pain prevented her from shedding a single tear. These shitheads weren't getting a drop of her weakness or an ounce of her fear. She dug deep, lowering a mental bucket down her well of resolve, and praying there was enough to get her through the trip to Thailand. She'd worry about getting more after that.

Especially because it seemed Rayna was going to need a loan.

Her friend's ragged sob tore the air. Rayna was scrunched against the wall with her head between her knees. Her shoulders formed a horseshoe of taut agony. Sage's heart wrenched as Ray choked. The two of them had shared enough tears over the last year to fill this bay thrice over, but this was the first time her friend's grief sounded like this, coming in bursts of unfiltered pain. Even Josie winced from it. Every woman on the planet knew the discord of a breaking heart when she heard it.

"Sweetie." Josie stretched her bound hands over, trying to stroke her hair. "It's all right."

Rayna jerked away. "The *hell* it is."

Though her friend wasn't looking, Sage jutted her chin. "Ray, you can't give up now."

She had no idea where the bravado came from. Maybe she was just fronting it for Josie's sake. She remembered having that same Little Orphan Annie hope after the tribes had first taken them in Botswana. She'd managed to keep it as the bastards bargained them back and forth in exchange for fighters taken prisoner during the skirmishes. It had lasted until the day they overheard two of the rebels chuckling about how they could keep she and Rayna as bargaining chips for years, because no rescue team was coming for them. That was when Orphan Annie got replaced with Xena. Ray herself had given her the nickname, as she'd quietly started to plan their escape.

As if her friend had just traveled the same path of memory, Rayna lifted her tear-streaked face. "Save the pep rally, Sage. These guys aren't a bunch of jungle boonies rebels with no clue what they're doing."

"This also isn't the boonies," she countered.

Her friend rolled her eyes and let out a dark laugh.

"Damn it, I'm right and you know it. *Look at me,* Ray. You've seen it too, haven't you, in Zeke? The protectiveness that seemed just a little gonzo? The watchfulness that bordered on weird? The looks that were on you but not *on* you, like his mind was somewhere else, and that place wasn't too pretty?"

The dark green of Rayna's gaze rustled in recognition. "I just thought he was being a super soldier boy, suddenly without anything to do."

Josie nodded. "Been there, done that. They get one of those episodes, you either go shopping or find something for them to blow up that's *not* the house."

Sage shook her head. "This was more than episodes, Josie. This was pervading. Twenty-four and seven." She fixed her stare on Rayna again. "It makes sense now, right?" she asked her friend. "Garrett and Zeke…maybe it was just premonition for them, or maybe they got more substantial intel about it. Maybe King bought off people in Thailand and got sprung, or maybe he set the nets back out for us straight from his cell."

Rayna grimaced. "Anything's possible with that monster."

"Unfortunately, he's a monster with money, who doesn't like to lose."

Rayna's expression crumpled into a wince of understanding. On many nights during their confinement in his warehouse, King and his men would play card games. One night when he'd lost the big winning pile, the asshole shot the winner's kneecap off. Another losing night had ended with Rayna's brutal piercing.

Josie emitted a fierce huff. "All right, for argument's sake, let's say they knew something. Why the hell didn't they say anything to either of you?"

Rayna echoed the snort. "Because they're stupid, he-man chest beaters."

The older woman nodded. "That's a good one. Can I borrow it?"

"I may have to do the same," Sage added. She curled her knees beneath her, so she could concentrate harder on Rayna. "But now you know why I'm not giving up the pom poms, Ray. We're still in Elliott Bay. We're not on a barge bound for Bangkok. And even though the guys have pulled a stupid Fred and Barney on us, I have to believe they've got a direction to go in. We've just got to keep it together until they hone the coordinates a little better."

Angel Payne

Chapter Fifteen

"We don't know where to start, do we?"

Garrett hated how the words sounded more like an accusation than a question. Even more, he hated the pit of despair in his gut from which they'd formed. Worse than that, he hated what they did to the face of his best friend. Clearly, Z had mentally executed himself a thousand times already for this.

"They fucking disappeared." His friend beat a figure eight into the sidewalk at the south end of the Market, as if performing a ritual that would open up the concrete and give him a vision about what had happened. Or maybe he was just judging how to best slam his head against the walkway and crack open his skull. Garrett bet on the later, judging by the white-knuckled grip Z had on the back of his neck. "I turned for one second, and then—" He whirled, making even his leather bomber jacket billow. "Goddamnit! Those filthy fuckers!"

Wyatt had dipped into silence during the drive here, when Garrett gave him a fly-over of the situation that was as fast and furious as his driving. He'd started by recounting their bizarre sighting of King at Sea-Tac, filled in with the Cliff's Notes version of King's criminal past, and ended with the harrowing update about the asshole's vengeful vendetta against the girls. The monster's crusade had finally succeeded this afternoon, with one bonus prize included in the form of Aunt Josie.

After that, Garrett had sucked in a breath for the hardest apology of his life. Before he could get out a word of it, Wyatt had barked one word across the truck's cab. *Don't.* If the command weren't enough, the anguish in his uncle's eyes finished off the job. After that, the man's face had barely changed. Until now. Wyatt's gaze was now afire with alertness, scanning the entire area, including the burned tire marks the bastards had left them as a souvenir. He paced the sidewalk slowly, hands locked on his hips, head sweeping from side to side.

"Bottle it up, Sergeant Hayes," he finally said to Z. "That anger isn't going to do you any good until we find these pussies and teach them a lesson. When that happens, I'll gladly hold them while you get in a little punching bag practice."

Zeke straightened, and a little of his old fire sparked in his eyes. Despite this gut-muncher of a situation, Garrett nodded a thank-you at his uncle. Z didn't wallow well. Hell, he barely sat still with any degree of grace. By spinning up a fantasy the guy could focus on, Wyatt restarted Z's productivity. And damn it, they needed Zeke right now. To catch street thugs, it helped to have a guy on your side who used to be one.

"I would much appreciate that, sir." Zeke cocked a dark grin at Wyatt. "And I'll gladly return the favor, so you can fuck up an ass-licker of your own."

Wyatt straddled the van's skid marks. "Done deal." He lifted his head as Z walked over. "Now what can you tell us about the van?"

The question was quiet, but its implication was huge. In any branch of Special Forces, a squad member's life could depend on his brother's ability to recall details under pressure. Colors, textures, smells, sounds, temperatures, words, distances, equipment…any or all of it could become a vital game-changer. All three of them knew this, but Garrett exchanged a heavy glance with his uncle as they waited for Z's response, hoping for the best. Emotions were the memory's chokehold. And whether he openly admitted it or not, emotions drove the chariot of Z's brain right now.

"It was a custom job," his friend began. "Nothing wacky or foreign. It was likely a Chevy or Dodge, though hard to tell because the body was modified and skimmed low to the ground. The rims *were* imports though, blingy Italian shit. But the paint job's what I noticed the most. It was gorgeous. But it didn't match. It was…"

"It was what?" Garrett urged it in response to his friend's puzzled frown. "And what do you mean, it didn't match?"

An anomaly of any kind could be their key to busting this open. They were moving on the search without police support, in obedience to Franzen's orders. Their CO had been part of the information loop since the second Z called him, right after hanging up with Garrett. Since King was clearly still running at least part of the show from prison, enough to get an audio tap into Rayna's place and insert two fake cops at Pike Place today, the Seattle PD was blacked out on the trust grid right now. Even the Feds would be brought on board once Franz deemed it appropriate. Their sole purpose right now? Gather the facts. Follow up on everything credible. Find out everything they could from whoever they could.

Right now, that meant getting a hell of a lot more information about the damn van.

Garrett clenched back his impatience in order to prompt Zeke as calmly as he could, "What did the paint look like, Z?"

Zeke turned and looked at him. Damn. His friend's eyes were hollow, his lips tight. Maybe things with Z and Rayna had proceeded faster than he assumed. Garrett felt shitty for his friend, though on a selfish level, misery did love company. And goddamnit, he was sick with misery. He couldn't lose Sage again. He *wouldn't*. If he had to, he'd rip this fucking city apart to find her.

"The paint looked…feminine." The last word left Z like it was the zinger in a whodunit plot. Garrett didn't get the significance. But Zeke sure as hell seemed to. His gaze ignited like he'd become Fort Lewis' answer to Sherlock Holmes.

"Feminine?" Wyatt echoed. He was clearly as nonplussed as Garrett.

"Yeah," Z returned.

"What the fuck?" Garrett muttered.

"I'm serious. It looked like a tampon box."

"What the *fuck*?"

"It looked airbrushed. Lavender and pink. There was a pair of hands touching along the side, and…" He stared across the street, again pulling the Sherlock Holmes act. "There was a white cat laying across the back wheel well."

"A white *what?*"

"A white cat. That's really weird."

"Thanks for clearing that up, man."

Wyatt stomped back onto the sidewalk. "This isn't the time for jokes, son."

"No, sir." Zeke began to pace again. This time, his strides were wide and strong—and excited. "No joke at all. Just a lot of pieces sliding together."

"Awesome," Garrett inserted. "You want to enlighten *us* now?"

Z spun back toward them, arms folded, determination stamped across his face. "The paint job wasn't real."

"Huh?" Wyatt grunted.

Garrett narrowed his gaze as comprehension kicked in. "You mean it was a wrap?"

Zeke nodded. Wyatt threw a frown at both of them. "A what?" the man asked.

"An automotive body wrap, Uncle. They use them a lot around the city, mostly on buses, as advertising gimmicks. They have special machinery that can laser print an image onto plastic 'wrap' that's adhered to the bus, turning it into a rolling billboard."

"After the campaign or event is over, the plastic is peeled off," Z finished.

"We've been toying a little with the technology on our ops vehicles, but the wrap is still a little prissy. It doesn't like dirt."

"Small problem there," Z confirmed.

Wyatt snorted. "So the pussies were only pretending to have pussies. And that van is sitting somewhere now, decked in a completely different design."

Zeke snorted. "I'd bet my left nut on it."

"Fuck," Wyatt gritted.

"Seconding that," Garrett added. He looked back to Zeke. "How does this get us anywhere, man?"

Zeke's face resembled a kid about to go on his first roller coaster. Sheer excitement and blatant nausea warred for control of his features. "Because I wasn't looking at the hundredth ad for the Balloon Festival on that van. The art was *custom,* hand-painted."

"Still in the dark, dude. There are a lot of artists in this city."

"And they're all sitting in their studios with the extra flow to buy one of those big-ass machines that makes the wrap panels, right?"

A jolt of new energy made Garrett surge forward. "Hell. That sure thinned out the haystack."

"I'll give you one better." Again, that weird mix of feelings rolled across his friend's face. Zeke looked ready to do a touchdown dance and then puke about it. "I think I can find our needle."

* * * * *

This was their needle?

Garrett swung fast glances up and down the narrow passageway alley in which they stood. At least that's what he was calling it for the time being. Truthfully, "alley" would've been an upgrade. String a few lanterns and clothes lines between the roofs, add the scent of roast pig instead of impending summer rain, and one could give it another title: East Asian ambush zone. Some instincts were pounded into a guy's brain cells forever, and his were currently on high alert.

He felt more normal when he caught Wyatt doing his own surreptitious recon. Z didn't join them. These alleys had been the man's childhood playground. Beyond that factor, his friend was clearly familiar with this specific address—though like its neighborhood, the word "address" was given a wide berth for definition here. Z reached for a spot behind the grimy door frame and pressed in. The hidden doorbell let off a series of bell chimes inside the building, making the place sound like a cathedral being readied for worshippers.

"Should I have worn a tie?" Garrett cracked.

Zeke let out a dark laugh. "Only if you want her to whip it off your neck, braid it into a whip then beg you to open her up with it."

Wyatt coughed. "This should be interesting."

Two seconds later, a toned woman's arm shoved open

177

the door. Tattooed angels and demons danced their way up it, reaching for another piece of ink that took up the top of her shoulder, a diamond wrapped in thorny roses. Garrett's gaze was distracted from the artwork by a face that was surrounded by a sleek mane of ebony hair, broken up by silver and lavender streaks. In spite of all the distractions, the woman's face was striking. She used minimal makeup, which was a good thing. Her huge purple eyes, prominent bone structure and full mouth didn't need much enhancement.

At the moment, that mouth curved up at Zeke in a grin that truly defined the cat about to eat the canary. The metaphor wasn't tough to come by, considering the woman wore a skintight black outfit—and had Zeke responding with a very visual, gulp.

"Well," she finally murmured. "Ezekiel Gabriel Hayes. What's an angel like you doing in my naughty corner of Hell?"

Before Garrett could let out half a snort of derision, Zeke horse-kicked backward. His heel caught Garrett's shin with perfect precision.

Without skipping a beat, he lifted the woman's knuckles to his lips and replied, "Luna honey, my halo got shot off before I busted my sixteenth birthday."

He dropped her hand but determination didn't just live in the woman's gaze. Luna latched a finger into the V of Zeke's shirt before he could step back. "What about my horns?"

Garrett joined Wyatt in stunned silence as the woman lifted an angular leg and wrapped it around Z's waist. For a fleeting moment, Garrett wondered why this woman's name never left his best friend's lips, even after three years of their tight camaraderie. That was before he caught the terse lines of his friend's face, along with the invisible screws that tightened along Z's jaw. Slivers of understanding formed. Garrett *had* heard about Luna, though not by name. She was—how the hell did Z put it?—a "unique" sort of girl. A submissive with appetites that were beyond the edge coupled with a personality that didn't have a proper off switch. Z had actually shuddered when talking about girls like her. Their refusal to call a safe word could land an unsuspecting Dom behind bars for abuse, assault and battery, maybe even murder.

Zeke grabbed Luna by the waist and pried her off. "I think it best we keep your horns safely tucked away, girl."

She narrowed her eyes, flashing an energy out that really did seem a little demonic, before pivoting toward him and Wyatt. "Maybe your friends want to see them."

"No." Z tightened his hold on her waist to keep her in place. "They *don't.*"

Garrett held up his left hand. "Engaged."

Wyatt copied the move. "Married."

"Hell," Luna spat.

Garrett couldn't help it any longer. He looked at his watch with a grunt. "We're at ninety minutes and climbing, Z. Tick fucking tock."

Luna scrunched her lips at him. "What's his issue?"

"I'm afraid it's one I share," Z offered in a slightly more diplomatic tone. "I need to talk to you."

Luna tossed her hair over both shoulders. "Fine. Talk."

"Inside."

"No. Here."

Z rose up over her, looming like a damn grizzly about to bite her head off. "*Inside,* damn it!"

The woman's reaction was definitely a surprise plot twist. Garrett watched the intrepid, leg-flinging Luna transform into a weak-kneed kitten during the four syllables of Z's fearsome growl. Her eyelids drooped, her lips parted, and her tongue swept out between them before she rushed out a breathy, "Yes, Sir." She turned like a dancer in a daydream, leading the three of them inside the building.

As Garrett had hoped, the warehouse's interior looked like a typical artist's studio. Canvases both finished and blank were stacked along the textured plaster walls. Several easels, lots of tarps and racks of paints cluttered the rest of the area. A loft overhead was shielded by gauzy curtains, but he discerned a big bed and kitchen area through them. And curled up in a puddle of the curtains? A sleeping white cat.

There were two elements in the scene that fit the circle-

what-doesn't-belong-here option. Suspended from a heavy
chain directly over Luna's workspace was a pair of thick
leather suspension handcuffs. Even Garrett could tell the
bondage gear had gotten some enthusiastic use. But that
delightful discovery was secondary to the jackpot they all spied
at the other end of the room. Garrett's breath whooshed out
before he joined Zeke in running over to it.

The machine wasn't an ordinary printer. It resembled a
space-age weaving loom, though it was twice the size of its
medieval ancestor. It measured a little over four feet long and
was about as high. A sheet of clean plastic film was pre-loaded
into it—but just beyond the machine, still littered across the
expanse of empty floor in front of a rolling garage door, were
slivers of the vinyl that had been part of the previous print job.
Every single one of them was pink or lavender.

"Thank fuck," Garrett muttered.

"Not yet," Zeke retorted. The back ends of the guy's
jaw turned to gritted granite again. He pitched his voice back to
a bellow at the woman giving them a pout from across the
room. "Luna!"
She sashayed closer. "Yes, dear?"

Z pointed at the vinyl confetti. "Who were they?"

"Who were who?"

"You didn't pay for this printer yourself, honey.
Somebody brought it here so they could take advantage of your
talent and your work space. They had you design a custom
wrap for a van today."

Luna tilted her head up at Z with a soft smile that made
her face even more stunning. Holy shit, this space queen was
dangerous. Garrett was just glad that Zeke knew it.

"You…think I have talent?"

"As I've told you a thousand times," Z responded
patiently. He took a deep breath as Luna pressed herself to
him, purring in what was supposed to be gratitude. "Luna, let
me be clear. We don't have time. I need those names. *Now.*"

She threw him another bratty pout. "Who says I even
knew who they were?"

That was it. The latch on Garrett's tolerance broke off.

"Goddamnit." He rushed forward. "Listen, Morticia Addams, the lives of three women are at stake here. Maybe *that* makes a difference to you?"

Luna glared. "Damn. You need to get laid."

"Hawk," Z interjected. "Just chill."

Garrett pinned a glower into his friend. "You want to get Rayna off that express boat for Bangkok or not?"

Zeke's face instantly fell. Garrett realized, too late, that his galloping temper had pulled out one too many stones in Morticia's castle walls. Luna's snap at Z confirmed it.

"Who's Rayna?"

Z's lips flattened. "Just a woman I've been watching over for work. Don't ask me anything more, Luna. You know I can't talk about my job."

She nodded fast. The line clearly wasn't new to her, and neither was the pained glimmer in her eyes because of it. "And now this 'just a woman' is in trouble, thanks to the van I wrapped today."

"Yes." Zeke brought his hands up and wrapped them around hers. Just that motion seemed to push some button in Luna. The woman gazed up at his friend like CNN just informed the planet that the universe revolved around Zeke Hayes. Z reacted by stepping closer to her, his posture filled with determination. Garrett released a quiet but admiring breath. Z just earned a shitload of check marks on the steel balls rating sheet. To endure that crazy stalker glint in Luna's eyes in hopes she spilled a couple of scumbags' names to him…that took fucking fortitude. It also served as crystal clear proof of what Rayna had started to mean to the man.

Unfortunately, Garrett wasn't the only one to recognize that.

"You like her." Luna's words were smoky rasps, burned at the edges with accusation. "Don't you, Z? You like her a lot."

Zeke weighed the question for a long moment. Though the canyons of his face changed little, storm clouds of conflict raced across them.

At last, he replied, "Yeah, baby girl. I do."

Luna nodded again. Her move lacked confidence this time. She shifted on her high-heeled boots, making Garrett marvel for a second. How she didn't fall on her face in those things was beyond his mental scope. Another surprise: how the hell she managed to get her hands stuffed into her back pockets after pulling them from Z's grasp. The leggings looked like another custom cling vinyl job.

"Is he being straight up?" She nodded in Garrett's direction. "Is her life really at stake?"

"If that boat they've got her on leaves American waters, then yes." He watched Z's shoulders slump from that. He couldn't remember ever seeing his friend so vulnerable. "She won't be dead, but she'll wish she was."

Luna absorbed that with an impassive expression. But she kept up that balance-changing thing, which made Garrett as nervous as watching a tightrope walker. If she fell and split her head, they'd be way the hell up Shit Creek. It was reassuring to see Wyatt eyeing her with the same trepidation.

He planted his feet and shoved down his anxiety. The faster Morticia processed this, the better. He saw that deep inside the gothic pain slut exterior, Luna seemed to have a heart. The trouble was, it clearly yearned for Zeke's in return.

At last, Luna snapped her chin at Z. The new look on her face made Garrett want to grab his friend and yank him back, just in case the woman was secretly packing a blade or another pair of those handcuffs. Likely both. Was it possible for a woman to simultaneously want a guy's heart on a plate and his dick between her thighs?

Her lips twisted with determination. "If I give you the names, I want something in return."

Zeke responded to that with a soft laugh, though there wasn't a thread of humor in the sound. After another moment, he nodded slowly back at her. "I bet you do."

One side of her generous mouth curled up. "So we have a deal?"

Zeke faced off to the woman, staring at her like a convicted man in front of an electric chair. "Yeah, baby girl. We have a deal."

Luna lifted the other end of her mouth just before wrapping her arms around Z's neck and pulling him down for a long, lingering lip-lock. "You want to use whips or floggers?"

"Doesn't matter." Zeke's voice matched the brutal jerks he used to get away from her. "You know I'm going to open you up with either."

She ran both hands up her thighs, as if to spread out the heat from her delighted shiver. "Yes, Sir!"

"The names, Luna. *Now.*"

Five minutes later, the three of them threw their asses back into Garrett's truck. Wyatt had barely closed his door before Garrett peeled away from the curb. Z was already on the line to Franzen, requesting every shred of information on the tampon van boys that the Feds could get their hands on.

"Cut a right ahead," Z ordered him. "I have a buddy down the street who'll let us use his place until we spin up a plan for catching up with those cocksuckers."

"Check," Garrett said before whipping the truck onto Harrison. After setting the course straight, he glanced over at his friend. "Did you just agree to what I think you did?"

"Yes," Z snapped. "And if you mention it again, I'll turn your balls into shark chum." The guy checked his phone for an update from Franz. His punch against the dashboard relayed the negative result. "Let's just get our shit together and find our women before it's too fucking late."

Angel Payne

Chapter Sixteen

"Eat!"

Sage looked up at the guy who spat the order at her and slipped him a curious stare. The kid needed a haircut and a shave. Hell, he needed to be out enjoying his summer break, or flipping burgers so he could take his girl out this weekend. What the crap was he doing with a SIG P238 shoved in her face, wearing a glower that belonged on an asshole three times his age? And more importantly, why did she care?

Because her mind, now as drained as her body, was finally giving in to anguish.

Yeah, the pom poms were unraveling. Her desperate efforts to keep them glued together were failing with every passing minute. She felt her spirit paying the price, standing in a pile of torn hopes, shattered courage, and the stabbing shards of one undeniable truth.

The night had come. The guys hadn't. The morning had come. The guys still hadn't.

Now, this goon-in-training was trying to tell her that refusing a roast beef sandwich was going to earn her a bullet in the skull. Seriously?

"Sage." Josie's voice came at her ear, still not wavering from its plane of reassuring calm. The woman had either popped a bottle of Quaaludes yesterday in place of tasting wine with them or she had nerves molded of steel. "You need to eat, sweetie. You didn't have any breakfast."

Sage stared back up at the gun. The hollow hole might as well have been a mirror. She felt just as black and empty. Fate had finally gotten her home, finally with Garrett again, and she'd wasted every second of the blessing. She'd spent the time playing head games with him, being so impatient to "fix" him, that she'd missed the most important part of finding him again…of being a real submissive to him.

She'd never just loved him.

"Sage." Josie's prompt was more urgent in her ear.

185

"Come on. A few bites. Keep up your strength. It's actually not bad. Look, they even included dessert."

"That's not dessert." Rayna grimaced into her chocolate pudding.

"Eat it!" The kid jabbed the SIG at her again.

Josie grabbed her wrist and squeezed. "*Sage.*"

She turned her weary smile at the woman. Josie's optimism was amusing. And heartbreaking. "He's not going to shoot me, Jo. He's not going to shoot anyone. They just want us healthy and rosy when we get to Bangkok." She dipped her gaze back to her feet. "Bony slaves don't sell as well as plump ones."

She felt Josie's head-to-toe tremor. But the woman spat, stronger than ever, "That's *not* going to happen."

Sage looked away, feeling her soul split down the middle. One side yearned to keep riding the rah-rah bandwagon with Josie, refusing to believe that every passing minute dragged them closer to the fate none of them would speak about. The other half screamed at her to get a clue, to wake up and smell the whole kettle of coffee before dumping its scalding truth over her head. Maybe then, the burns would sink in. The pain became part of her again. It was less torture once you got used to it. She had to believe that. She *had* believed that, back in those days when sorrow was normal and hope a luxury. It had only been a couple of weeks since she'd left that darkness behind. Surely it couldn't be that hard to acclimate to it all again.

Who the hell was she kidding?

She closed her eyes, wondering if she could dare remembering Heaven one more time. But there was no way she couldn't. As soon as the word bloomed in her mind, Garrett did, too.

My heart. She felt the warmth of his murmur down her neck, and rejoiced in the wings that opened in her heart in answer.

My hero. She heard the whisper as if she gave it to him once more, and watched those sensual angles of his lips spread into a brilliant smile. His gaze ignited with that blue fire that adored her, desired her, claimed her. Hers. He was forever hers in their warm, wonderful paradise…

Until reality smashed a boot to her backside again.

Her gaze was jolted open to the view of Junior as he lowered his foot, his face fixed in a vicious leer. He maintained his proximity, so his crotch consumed her view. "Eat your lunch, slut, or I'll give your mouth something else to do."

Before she could help herself, she rolled her eyes. She bought in to that threat less than she believed the twerp would shoot her. The crew had clearly been given orders to keep her, Josie, and Rayna in well-fed, pristine condition for their new overseas owners.

But who had given those orders? The blank behind that question mark remained strangely vacant, though Sage knew it wouldn't stay that way. King's stateside partner was definitely on his *A* game, which meant that sooner or later, the slimy shit would slither out from under his rock to flaunt his triumph in orchestrating their recapture. When he did, she'd tell the bastard to find some men for his dirty work, and not the last rejects from the Seattle boy band auditions.

With that thought as encouragement, she dug a toe under the plate in front of her and upended the whole thing at Junior. The guy yelled then used the *f* word in at least four different ways as a slab of roast beef dropped off his crotch, leaving behind a streak of bright yellow as a souvenir.

Josie and Rayna broke into giggles. Their mirth turned to horror when the goon advanced on Sage, swinging his pistol into a wide backhand. Sage clenched her jaw and squared her shoulders, swearing she wouldn't show this punk even a flinch of fear. She was the Hawk's woman. Proving it right now became the sole object of her will and desire in her heart.

Nevertheless…this was going to hurt.

With a resounding *thwack,* a hand wrapped around Junior's wrist. The fingers of that hand were long, elegant, and shaded like coffee with a bunch of cream.

"Temper, temper."

Like the hand, the intervening voice was smooth yet lethal. The words were spoken with unalterable command—

and an accent where street boss collided with jungle dictator.

A whole tub of ice dumped into Sage's chest. Her heart leapt from the freezing floe and begged her throat for sanctuary. But there would be no refuge from the fear now. No safety. No more hope. The fire Garrett had given her a minute ago was now doused as thoroughly as the memory that had brought it, wiped by the monster in front of them now. A yellowed smile parted his slick lips. Cavalier confidence defined his posture.

"Well, well, well," the man drawled. "Hello again, bitches."

No matter how deeply she wanted to pass out or how savagely she wanted to shiver, Sage's first concern was for Rayna. Her friend saw something extra in King that was always beyond Sage's scope, like an extra layer of evil only certain people could view. Since the scum sucker made *her* skin feel invaded by maggots, she had no idea what persecution it must be for Rayna. Like the cold predator he was, King picked up on every drop of her terror, and never ceased to exploit it. Sage was certain that was why Rayna got picked for the "special" piercing back in Thailand.

It was why the asshole paced over to her now.

"My pretty kitty." King cupped her chin with two fingers, using the hold to jerk up her head. "You are as lovely as I remember, Rayna. And I am not the only one who thinks so anymore, am I? Oh, no. I have listened to him talking to you, your big brave soldier boy." He grinned wider and chuckled. "The glorious Zeke Hayes!" Rayna groaned and tried to wrench her face away, but King held fast. "Ohhh, little Ray-Ray, what is this? Tears for your Zekie? I am not complaining. Those tears are very sexy." He pulled her closer in order to lick his way up one side of her face. "And delicious."

Josie's Quaaludes picked a shitty time to wear off. The woman surged at King, a snarl turning her pixie features into demonic rage. "Leave her alone."

King pivoted to Junior and grabbed the kid's pistol. He swiveled the gun so the butt protruded from his fist, right before he slammed it into Jo's jaw. Sage and Rayna cried out as Josie's head whipped over and her body curled in pain. But the woman herself didn't emit a sound. Sage gulped in silent admiration.

King handed the gun back to his minion. "Do not make me regret we invited you to the party, bitch."

A slew of retorts begged to be let out, regarding the nature of Josie's "invite" and King's demented idea of a "party." Sage pressed them down, more concerned about Josie herself. With a little turn, she was able to get a visual on the woman. Jo's face was contorted with pain, but she was conscious. She had both her hands wrapped around her middle, straining outward as much as the zip ties would allow. As Sage watched, her own gut somersaulted. She blinked to re-set her objectivity, but when she accessed the woman again, the flip did an encore. Josie's movement, so fervent and protective, combined with the remembrance of yesterday, when she'd refused all the wine samples...

Oh, hell.

As if Jo could hear that silent outburst, she raised her gaze. A flash of understanding passed between them. Sage returned Josie's desperate stare by looking to her belly and back up to her eyes, giving her a steady nod of promise. She'd do everything in her power to keep Garrett's unborn cousin safe.

"King."

She barked it at the asshole like an order. Though Junior's stare widened with shock, King rotated toward her with an expression of mild amusement. It wasn't the first time she'd dared to speak to him like this. It also wasn't the first time she expected to pay the consequences. She just prayed the penalty would be fast and brutal, not one of King's leisurely mental torments. The bastard knew her weaknesses as thoroughly as he knew Rayna's, which meant that when he really wanted to inflict damage, he bypassed the needles and the pistol whippings in favor of drilling a straight into her psyche. And damn it, King's gaze glittered with the eager excitement that he was ready to do just that.

"My darling Sage." He loomed over her, reaching to

189

stroke the top of her head. "I have so missed our little discussions. What do you wish to talk about today? The weather? The yummy wine you drank yesterday?" His hand stilled. "The fact that your fiancé will likely kill himself searching for you?"

Sage jerked her head away. Well, tried. King had anticipated the move, and still gripped enough of her hair that her action tore a small chunk out of her scalp. A pained snarl ripped free but she clamped it short. "Actually, I'm wondering how your ass is feeling, buddy."

His snicker punched the air over her head. "Oh? And why is that?"

She smirked. "Couldn't have been comfortable, buying your freedom by letting every prison guard in Bangkok screw you twice."

To her bewilderment, King didn't tear out more of her hair. He actually stepped away as his body rocked back on a chortle. "Ah ha! I understand now!"

Sage glared up through her hair. "That you're a cock-loving coward who can't make a living at anything but selling people?"

The delighted expression never left King's face. He cocked his head playfully at her. "Ohhh, you really are in the dark, my sweet." He clucked his tongue. "Poor little women. Your soldier boys certainly like keeping secrets, don't they?"

Sage's gaze flew to Rayna before she could stop it. Her friend's face was covered in confusion, and she was certain she returned the mirror treatment on that.

She lashed her stare back to King. "What the hell are you talking about?"

King rocked on his heels like a kid who held all the candy. "I hate to smash your fantasy about my ass in a Bangkok jail…" He touched a finger to his chin. "Well, maybe I don't."

Sage scowled. "What?"

"They still call it extradition here, do they not?"

She felt her forehead scrunch harder. "You were extradited to the States? You were extradited *here*?"

"Mmmm…in a sense, yes."

"Oh, for the love of—yes or no, King?"

He preceded his reply with that maddening chuckle again. "To your government and to your sweet soldier boys, the answer to that would be yes."

Sage supplied the conclusion he never gave. "But…?"

King straightened his gaze. A strange benevolence entered his regard of her, almost a gentle pity. It terrified Sage more than any look the man had ever wielded. She pressed herself deeper into the pillows as he went on, "Lord Byron said it best, I believe. 'Happiness was born a twin.' And you know, my sweets, that happiness is doubled when the hospital misfiles a twin's birth certificate. Do you know what happens then? You get to grow up as one person. You only have to attend half the school, deal with half the beatings of your drunk mother, half the murder attempts from the crack addict who calls himself your stepfather." The moment of compassion passed. The man's face twisted back into its sadistic leer. "And yet, you can get into twice the trouble, and make twice the money from it."

Sage didn't cower in the pillows for long. Her spine straightened as blocks of comprehension stacked up her spine. Every one of them was made of a special concrete called horror. "Are you…saying…"

His lips twitched. "Come on, come on. You almost have it, don't you?"

She was too amazed to bother with getting riled. "Are you saying that you have an identical twin…and *he's* now sitting in prison instead of you?"

King shrugged with such ease, he earned an approving grin from Junior. "It was my turn for the detention spa last time. Besides, Mua knows that his little vacation will be over in…" – he glanced at his watch – "about twelve hours." He swept his smile back across the bed. "Until then, my special bitches, we have a busy afternoon ahead. Are you ready for your fun?"

Josie lifted her head. Her jaw looked like a face painting job splashed in rain, dark reds and fuchsias smeared

191

across her skin. "Sorry. I don't think my bruises match my cruise wardrobe."

King walked over and pushed a couple of fingers into the darkest part of the woman's injury. When Josie whimpered, he smiled. "The colors are quite lovely, my dear. I am certain we shall find something nice for you to wear with them. And do not worry your pretty head about appropriate cruise wear. We shall be on land for your festivities this evening."

From the corner of her eye, Sage caught Rayna's head jerking back up. She copied the move. "What do you mean?"

King gave them a silken smile. "You, my sweetlingss, have caught the eye of some domestic buyers. They are in town tonight, and have cleared their schedules for a sampling party." He spread his hands, nearly celebratory about it. "It is exciting, yes? My more extreme clientele are usually the kind who enjoy the feel and taste of foreign pussy for their romps, but these collectors are more interested in domestic fare. Their timing could not be more perfect."

Sage got off a snarky glower. "Because you've got a bad boys leather party on the calendar for tomorrow night?"

King shook his head and chuckled. "Because your sweet soldier boys will be on planes bound for Bangkok tonight, rattling their swords and screaming about saving you, though all the while, you are disappearing from right under their feet." He laughed again, but the expression faded as he issued his next words. "You know what they say about karma, bitches. And now your oh-so-special soldiers will reap everything they have sown of it with the King."

The bastard finished that off by turning his back on them. Rayna and Josie joined Sage in her glowering silence, but she could feel their silent, terrified, helpless screams as loud as the din in her own soul. The only relief for the torment was fantasizing that her palms could shoot fire, and she incinerated the monster before he took another step. Certainly before he called back his parting instruction to Junior.

"The stylists will be here to prep them soon. Cut those clothes off all three of them. Make sure that they shower."

If King threw a winning lottery ticket back down the

stairs, the kid wouldn't have grinned wider. "Yes, sir!" As soon as King closed the hatch, Junior leaned over and yanked out a dagger that was strapped to his calf. He grinned wide as he paced straight to Sage. "Might as well start with my favorite slut."

As the kid started slashing apart her clothes, Josie gave her fingers a squeeze. "Stay strong. We're right here with you, Sage. We're right here."

Sage jammed her eyes shut, struggling to hold back the reply she longed to blurt at the woman.

But why can't I be anywhere but here?

* * * * *

The question refused to leave her mind. Like a sloppy-drunk party guest who kept hitting the replay button on a bad breakup song, the words were a reminder of where she really was, of the tunnel into which her life was headed. Even after she'd seen her clothes in a torn puddle on the floor, even after the stylists had coated her in makeup then pushed her into a corset and panties, even after she'd been piled into a limousine with Josie, Rayna, and three bodyguards, the words echoed in a haunting refrain.

Why…why…why…

Anywhere but here…anywhere, please.

During the drive, she fixed her gaze on the black glass of the limo's tinted window, trying to conjure where Garrett and Zeke were by now. They would have called Franzen, and likely been able to convince the CO that King was involved with this shit. Maybe after that, the guy had approved a team and they were loaded into a Chinook, halfway to Bangkok by now.

The black pane made it so easy to conjure the contrast of Garrett's rugged, golden handsomeness as the team flew through the night. The wind lifting his tawny hair off his strong forehead. The smoky determination in his long-lashed blues. His long nose, leading the eye down to the angles of his mouth, which was undoubtedly tilted up at one end as he contemplated slitting open King's throat this time around.

The image went fuzzy after that. Tears had a way of

doing that, even to fantasies.

Sage tilted back her head and forced back the sting, sniffing determinedly. These assholes weren't going to get the extra brass ring of her sorrow. Like always, it stayed inside. *Deep* inside. Pushed to a place where they couldn't touch it or her. They could pound their bodies as deep into hers as they wanted, but from the moment she stepped out of this limousine, they'd never claim her as a person. Sage Weston would cease to exist—and now it was by her choice, not theirs.

All too soon, that moment arrived.

Sage's instincts, along with the feel of the road, told her they'd gone over the 520 Bridge and into Medina: the land of Bill Gates, Jeff Bezos, Charles Simonyi, and other people who sucked different air than what the rest of humanity breathed. Sure enough, the driver slowed the car up to a pair of massive, stylized steel gates that glistened in the misty night. When they slid back, they rolled up a driveway that likely doubled as the landing strip for the owner's private jet. A diamond-shaped reflecting pool in front of the house had a lighted fountain that looked like a giant steel cheese curl.

When the limo stopped, the henchmen got out first. During the two seconds they were alone inside the car, Rayna let out a harsh, heavy sob. "Fuck! Sage, I don't know if I can do this!"

"Of course you can." Josie ripped the words into her. They weren't a surprise. From the moment King had gone battering ram on her face with the SIG, the woman had changed from nurturing mama hen into savage mama tiger. "You'll do this, Rayna, and anything else it takes to stay alive. Look, I know you've both had it with having to tow this line, but you don't have a choice. I won't give you one. If we have any chance of finding a way out of this, we need to work together. We have to keep our senses keen and our eyes open. Agreed?"

Sage joined her friend in returning the woman's tough love with a fast nod. Senses keen. Eyes open. She could do this. She could—

Shit.

"Eyes open" was deleted from the options list pretty fast. .

One moment, she was tottering on the stone driveway in her mile-high heels. The next, Junior the Henchman was leaning over her, fitting a soft leather blindfold over her eyes and the bridge of her nose.

Sage's equilibrium swam. She felt herself falling over but had no idea if she was about to crack open the front or back end of her skull. Lanky arms caught her, and she picked up on Junior's distinct scent of chicken wings and sweaty T-shirt. She had no choice about having to inhale the stuff for a few minutes more. Not if she intended to keep at least half her promise to Josie now.

Senses keen. Senses keen. Senses keen.

With the mantra embedded in her instinct, she tried to stay upright in the damn heelss while listening, smelling, or hearing any element of their surroundings that could help their chances at breaking for an escape. As she suspected, the mansion was on the water. Lake Washington was more placid than the depths of Elliott Bay, but she still heard boats rubbing against a dock and ducks honking at each other. Before they got to the front door of the big house, Junior pulled her off to the left, around a corner, down a slight incline. The wind hit her with more force, filled with more mist. They were being led closer to the water, which could be a good thing or a bad thing, depending on where the boat keys were kept.

Junior finally pulled her to a stop. Heavier footsteps approached behind them. The spicy smell of a clove cigarette swirled with the mist. Cologne joined that combination. It was smooth, *not* an in-your-face American scent.

The new arrivals to the party were definitely foreign. And definitely staring at her. The weight of their rearview inspection pressed on her bare shoulders and upper back, but Sage straightened her spine and forced her head to stay high. She wouldn't bend for these animals. Not unless they made her, damn it.

A door opened, and King's distinct laughter danced out into the night. "Gentlemen! Welcome! I trust you had no trouble with the directions?"

"They were flawless." A refined baritone voice gave the words, though its slight European accent brought out every note of wickedness in the follow-up. "Everything so far is impeccable."

Sage barely resisted the urge to jab him in the leg, or worse, with one of her stilt heels. At the moment, her balance was more important to keep intact.

"I am so glad you think so," King replied. "Please come in. I think you will be pleased with these facilities. We have made certain they provide all the equipment for you to exercise your special tastes."

A few feet to her right, a choked gasp cut the air. Rayna was letting the fear get to her. Her outburst was followed by a sharp smack. Rayna cried out louder. "Knock it off, bitch!" her henchman commanded.

This exchange took place as the Europeans filed inside the building. King apparently traded places with them, because his was the next voice to slice the air. The bastard wasn't happy.

"You twit! What did I say about hitting them?"

Rayna's guard fumed aloud. If Sage was a mind reader, she'd likely find the guy debating about how to point out that King had personally violated that rule already, and the evidence was plastered across the left side of Josie's face.

The henchman finally protested, "She was about to scream."

"Then let's handle the challenge, shall we?" King shifted as if taking something from each of the guards. No. Wrong perception. Sage found out just how wrong in the next second. The asshole had been giving them all something. "Fasten the bits well. If any of them slip, I'll have your balls for it."

Before Sage had a second to process what he'd said, her lips were being shoved apart by a long leather tube, fitted horizontally between her teeth like a horse's bit. Though the contraption was much cleaner than a wad of dirty rags, the fuck-you on her fear threshold was the same. The black void of her vision rushed the nightmare along. In an instant, she was back in that sweltering jungle. Back in that Quonset hut. Back in that moment where accepting the defeat was easier than fighting it.

Senses keen? Why? There was no way out of this. Nowhere to run, nowhere to be, nobody to become except the pawn into which King had transformed her. Garrett was going to touch down soon in a land where he'd spend weeks searching for her, when she would actually be in some Bavarian dungeon, helpless to escape, concentrating on nothing but taking her next breath.

"Move." Junior jabbed his gun into her back. The feel of the barrel was different. They'd likely let the henchmen play with bigger toys for this part of their little adventure. She guessed he now had a semiautomatic of some sort.

They were led inside, where it was blessedly warmer. That didn't soften the cold impact of the wood floor when Sage was pushed down to her knees. She smelled savory hot food and rich red wine, making her empty stomach growl, until the other essences in the room snuck into her awareness. More leather. The tang of heavy chains. The musk of recent sex.

Oh, God.

She wasn't hungry any more.

One breath after the other. One breath after the other.

Leather couches crunched as people sat. Glassware clinked on tables. King chatted with the men as if they were at a casual cocktail party. Comments were traded about the wine and the weather, all as if they didn't stand there with three bound, bit-gagged, half-naked women kneeling on the floor nearby. Their insouciance started to piss her off. She tried to contain the feeling, logically tracing it back to her terror, which turned the confusion of her mind into sheer chaos.

By the time the men approached them again, she literally thought she'd burst from her skin.

King let out a long, anticipatory sigh. "So, my friends…you have had some time to look at our fresh flowers. As you know, the first two are young, healthy, and very strong. The third is older, but in magnificent condition…and might

197

bring an experienced flair to certain services."

One of the men reacted to that with a heavy cough, before he said on a chuckle, "Indeed."

Another man echoed the mirth. "Gustav is a bit...errmm...anal about some things."

King laughed heartily. "Well, then! Perhaps she is the perfect fit. Or can be stretched to be!" After the men rewarded him with jokes that sounded like verbal slabs of grease, he offered, "Would you like to have a try at her, my friend? We can fasten her down on any of the benches for you."

A deep grunt came from Gustav's direction. "Perhaps later. Klaus has bigger wood to saw than me tonight, and less time to get to it. There is that saying, yah? Age before beauty?"

King laughed again, punching the sound full of even more fake hilarity than before. "All right, then! Klaus leads the fun tonight!"

"As I do *every* night."

The voice behind those words had been the quietest one of the trio—which made its owner the one Sage feared the most. The measured control of it was roughened in certain places by vocal gravel that tugged weirdly at her gut. She didn't want him to touch her, yet every time he spoke, that was all she could think about.

"Well then, Klaus my friend, which one of our young flowers would you like to smell deeper?"

Sage didn't want to hear the bastard's answer. If he picked Rayna, she'd be in agony. If he picked her, she'd be in Purgatory.

A leg pressed against her back. Another slid in front of her, and pressed a hard boot to her kneecaps. A large hand, full of steel-fingered command, descended on her head.

"The blond has a certain sass about her, yes?"

Sage tried to swallow. Only trouble was, her mouth had gone bone dry.

"Ah!" King exclaimed. "Very good choice! Where would you like her to be placed? The stockade? The fucking swing? The whipping bench?"

"I place my own sluts."

The man's voice took on an edge of anger with the statement. Sage's chest vibrated in reaction, struggling to get air into her freezing, shaking body. Klaus hoisted her up, but her legs weren't into cooperating with his control *or* hers, dangling beneath her like numb rags. Klaus supported her with one hand twisted in her corset strings and the other now wound into her hair.

"Somebody take off those silly shoes," the man barked. "And you, boy—hand me your knife." Sage trembled harder at that, and whimpered against the gag. "Be still." Klaus gave her the order on a growl. His hand left her hair, shifting to her bound wrists instead. With a single swipe, he cut loose the zip tie.

Adrenaline shot into Sage. She didn't stop to ponder why he'd done something so stupid, choosing instead to just capitalize on it. Though her hands barely worked, she formed them into claws and aimed straight for his face. Just a moment of distraction was all she needed. Once she could see again, she could run. And once she could run—

Her wrists were instantly bound again. Klaus slammed one of his hands around both of them. He twisted his grip with the force of an iron winch, trapping her so tight, she yearned for the zip ties again. Before she could stop it, an enraged yowl tore past the gag. Gustav and King chuckled, but from Klaus, there was nothing but a deep and hard growl.

"Try that again and I'll break them, little sassy." He jerked her arms down, rearranging her hands behind her back. "And if I must buy broken merchandise, that makes me want to smash it up more."

With her wrists throbbing and her spirit reeling, Sage gave the asshole a reluctant nod. She wouldn't be any use to Rayna and Josie if this bastard decided to start breaking bones.

Without another word, Klaus hooked a finger into the front of her corset and hauled her across the room. She gulped, shoving aside a mental comparison to a state fair cow being led to the auction block.

He stopped and made her do the same. She felt the man shift to stand right in front of her. With two more fast *thwicks,* he cut away the tiny panties that matched her corset. Sage corkscrewed her hands together to keep from covering her sex, now exposed to the man's long, silent gaze.

"Beautiful," he murmured.

She kept reminding herself to breathe. From the blackness behind her mask and the void into which her voice had been banished, every passing minute felt more surreal, less like it was her body doing this. Her heart and soul? They were nowhere to be found any more. She moved like an automaton, taking orders like a robot no matter how her body reacted biologically to this hell.

Klaus turned her a little. He slid up behind her, his very large body pressed to her back. "Up onto the cross now, my sassy," he commanded into her ear, just before pushing her a few steps forward.

Sage struggled to swallow again. To feel anything other than pure fear. To gain back even a shred of composure to the arms and legs that shivered as if Klaus helped her step onto a bondage cross made of ice instead of steel. Nothing worked. He was stripping her, pulling off the corset and tossing it aside. He was spreading her, closing leather bonds around her wrists and ankles so her body aligned with the big X now. He was turning her into a mass of dread, of grief…and most horridly, of shame.

Because her heart wasn't the only thing weeping through this ordeal.

The tissues at her core betrayed that truth with pulsing, rushing clarity. Her pussy knew exactly what was about to happen, and readied itself with clenching, wet anticipation.

She dug her teeth into the gag, and sobbed in self-disgust.

The man behind her worsened the moment. Klaus pressed himself against her, sliding one arm around her waist then wrapping the other up to caress one of her breasts. His mouth closed in against her ear, roughening her skin with his thick beard, and he spoke in a grate so low, only she could hear it.

Only…the European inflection was gone.

In its place was a perfect, dulcet lilt that zapped everything inside her back to life. It was an accent she dreamed about. Lived for. Even joked about. She liked to call it "Iowa farm stud." And Garrett always glowered at her for it.

"I know we both dreamed of something like this happening differently, sugar…but if we can get through it, I'm gonna get you out of here. I absolutely promise it, my heart."

Angel Payne

Chapter Seventeen

Her long, sweet moan was one of the most beautiful things Garrett had ever heard. In it, he heard everything she couldn't tell him in words. Her shock. Her joy. And her complete, open surrender. She was bypassing her fear, her independence and this outright shitty circumstance to give herself to him. To lay her body and her life completely in his hands.

She moved him. Amazed him. Made him love her more deeply than he ever had.

And made him yearn to reclaim her, even if he had to do it in front of an audience of animals.

He walked behind the St. Andrews Cross on the pretense of double-checking the cinches in the bonds, but instead used the moment to get his face in front of hers. "Sugar, we had to present ourselves to this ass munch as sadistic pricks with money. I can't give your sweet ass much of a warm-up on this, and I'm sorry. If it's unbearable, give me your Girl Scouts promise, okay? Right hand, three fingers up. Moan for me if you understand."

Sage lifted her head and let out a long, convincing keen for him. Her motion threw her face into the beams of the dungeon lights, and he saw the sheen of tears on them. An inferno burned through his chest, and he had to envision steel ropes around his wrists to keep from reaching up to her shimmery cheeks. He took a deep breath and prayed at least a few of the drops were from happiness.

After he walked back in front of the cross, he turned to the well-stocked supplies area. King must have raided every BDSM stockpile within five miles. A wooden pole sprouted about twenty floggers. Next to that, a whip rack was stocked just as fully. There was also a large cabinet with lighted shelves that were organized by toy type: dildos, clamps, inserts, electrosex devices, canes, crops, paddles…

There were more, but Garrett stopped at the paddles.

Knowing King watched his every move, he bypassed the leather and fur-covered beginner versions, going for stricter devices such as a Scottish tawse and a long suede dragon's tail.

He tested each implement on his forearm, as Zeke had instructed him. The action made it possible for him to throw a fast glance over at his friend. Z was ready with a reassuring nod, though that did nothing to help the guy from looking like a Hell's Angels reject in his fake beard and nose. Wyatt's ensemble was no better, with dark glasses and a false paunch that put him far into Bad Santa territory. But the three of them had long since passed the minutes of ribbing each other about their disguises. They were deep in the lion's den now, and though Garrett had prayed the events wouldn't come to this, the only way out was distracting the beasts long enough so Z and Wyatt could quietly let Josie and Rayna in on their identities, along with the main goals here.

They'd conduct a clean deal to "purchase" the girls from King. All the evidence would be monitored live, captured from Z's necktie cam. As soon as they left, the Feds would take over, arresting King *again,* hauling his ass back off to FDC Sea-Tac. There would be a special treat waiting for him when he arrived: a cellmate. The goons with the tampon box van had easily spilled about King's twin brother. The pair would be watched day and night until their arraignment, now being rushed to priority status thanks to the dozen or more charges this whole stunt added to their crimes.

"Ahhh, the dragon's tail. Excellent choice."

Speak of the fucking devil. King murmured the approving words with a matching smile, speaking like Garrett was simply checking out fishing rods. Garrett had to consciously tell his lips to give an answering smirk, instead of grabbing one of the whips and saving FDC a shitload of money, effort, and paperwork by just strangling the bastard right now.

"You think so?" He forced civility to the reply.

King nodded. "It gives better control than a whip, yet yields just as much…fun."

"Hmm." Garrett had to navigate his brain past not only

his fury, but the need that stung every inch of his cock since the second he'd gotten Sage naked. Damn it, the cramped quarters inside this fancy suit weren't helping matters one bit.

In an impatient heat, he shucked the jacket. After folding it into a lump, he stuffed it against King's chest. "Well then, my friend, why don't you take care of this for me, have yourself a seat, and let me proceed to the 'fun.'" He jabbed his head at a plush chair in a corner to the right. The selection wasn't by accident. King would be across the room from all the guards, who were rapidly dropping into the zero effectiveness zone anyhow, thanks to their fixation on his nude fiancé.

It would be a miracle if he got out of here tonight without killing someone.

He needed to focus on Sage. On getting *her* out of here, away from this cocksucker's clutches, forever.

King complied with his directive like an unthinking puppy. Thank fuck that even the thought of a few Benjamins turned the asshole's mind to applesauce. The relief allowed Garrett to take a measured breath, knowing it would be the last of its kind for a while. Once he turned back to Sage, all bets would be off on his lungs cooperating with his brain. He had a feeling the command center between his ears was going to be busy controlling other things. Well, trying to.

Hell.

The speculation was more accurate than he estimated.

Though he was the one who'd locked her to the cross that way, beholding her anew was a jolt that stopped his feet, burned his veins, and swelled his cock with aching heat. No wonder all the guards were standing there like lusting gorillas. With her body opened in this position, one could admire every nuance of her figure. She'd always been glorious, but with the muted lighting of the room playing across her stretched naked limbs, she became a siren of sensuality, a vessel of surrender, waiting for a commander to harness her, tame her, possess her.

Eat shit, you motherfuckers. I'm that commander.

He made sure every step he took communicated that message, making the little crowd of perverts back up as he paced out a semi-circle in front of the cross. As he moved closer to Sage, her shoulders went taut and her ass cheeks clenched. That sight alone made his erection surge against his pants. Christ, she was magnificent, all naked sinew, dewy skin, and writhing anticipation. Tiny tremors raced along her body, confirming a fact that hit him like a lightning bolt: every sensation she was going to feel, every bite of pain and drop of arousal, was now under his control. The power was so intoxicating, he was damn glad he'd only sipped at the wine King had offered earlier. He was well on his way to the best high of his life, pumped on this heady exhilaration, this rush of power, this gift of complete trust.

Holy hell, why had he denied this for so long?

And why the fuck did he pick the shittiest times to arrive at major life epiphanies?

He dropped his head, the only reasonable method he could manage to clear it. Continuing to fill his stare with Sage was *not* the key there. He'd damn-near blown his cover a minute ago just by gazing too long, which had almost turned into the catastrophe of going over to her again, of touching her. He would've run his hands everywhere too…anywhere. Up her beautiful arms. Down her tapered legs. Across her belly…then lower. He would've dipped into the crevice of her moist, pouting sex, and lingered there for a long while. He would've awakened her skin and stirred her senses, coaxing her body to prepare itself for the impacts to come…

But he'd gotten an invite to this soiree by pretending to be a hardcore sadist. The kind of guy who didn't get off on fun warm-ups or gentle lead-ins. The kind of guy who took a quality dragon's tail and made sure his submissive knew how he'd be using it.

His fingers tightened around the wrapped leather handle. Every second he hesitated meant a tiny slip of credibility. He'd briefed Sage on what was to come. She was expecting this. And maybe, judging by the peeks he got at the shiny, wet layers between her thighs, she was even looking forward to it. And damn, *damn,* how he'd love to see her perfect, round buttocks marked by a stroke he'd given her…a brand he alone had burned into her…

Thwack.

He let out a heavy breath, hardly believing he'd done it.

Hardly believing it had felt so incredible.

Hardly believing that Sage's long moan would double the pressure in his balls—and the lust that claimed everything south of his beltline.

Thwack.

He curled the tapered suede around again, marking her a little lower and a little harder. This time, a brilliant red streak rose along her skin. The next instant, he gave the welt an identical twin, aiming for the spot where her darling heart of an ass started tapering into her waist. With every measured lash, he made sure to watch for the safety sign from her right hand, but the fingers there were nowhere near a scout's oath. Sage had the digits folded around the edge of her wrist cuff, kneading the leather in time to the breaths that came in giant swooshes through her nose. Her left hand did the same to its own bond.

He ran a fast visual on the edges of all her beautiful fingers. They all had good color and were ambulating fine. Thank Christ, because he sure as hell didn't want to stop. To see what he did to her, turning her into this writhing, surrendering creature he was preparing for his pleasure alone, pulled out a mate from the most primitive parts of his own soul, his own body, the very beat of his heart and throbs in his cock.

He elbowed the sweat off his face, sucked in a couple of breaths, and let the animal step out a few steps more.

Smack. Smack. Smack.

Sage screamed past the gag this time, the succession of blows meaning a higher concentration of pain to process. His little audience actually looked ready to clap in approval, until he stopped the morons with a glare. In the opposite corner, King emitted a hum of approval. Garrett forced back his frustration. He hated that he and Sage had to do this here, now. He hated that they hadn't had a fucking word of foreplay or negotiation, that this crucial, beautiful new step for them was being used as a distraction tactic for a goddamn rescue mission,

207

and—

The words halted his little morosity session.

Rescue Mission.

If he didn't do this, he wasn't walking out of here with her.

He had to phase King and his shitheads out, and tie his concentration to one person alone. The only person in this room who mattered. The only person in his *world* who mattered.

That meant laying into her with another trio of lashes.

Sage let out another high keen, bucking against her bondage. Garrett was sure he'd be sending up a thousand prayers for redemption, because the sight made him harder than a stallion on steroids. His pulse pounded with lust, and his cock wept with pre-cum. The swells of his woman's ass were crisscrossed with red ribbons, like a present he longed to rip open. He had just the right tool with which to do that...

No. Not yet.

As deeply as he longed to throw down the slapper, step to her, then unzip and aim for nirvana, Garrett still felt the weight of King's assessment. He was supposed to be a moneybags pervert who got off on pain as much as sex. He had to push the act one step harder.

Forcing himself to flick a cocky grin at King, he slid the dragon tail back onto its shelf before pulling out a new pair of play toys. The first, a mini slapper with diamond-shaped holes, got tucked into his pocket. The second was a leather mitt that fit snug around his big hand. He lifted it into the light, watching the entire front surface of the mitt twinkle thanks to the tiny steel tacks embedded into the leather. King let out another commending hum, but Garrett ignored the ass this time, afraid he'd ram the thing into the man's ugly face.

All that mattered was Sage. Who had, unbelievably, gotten five times more gorgeous in the last thirty seconds.

He had no idea how he was going to keep his cock confined for another second, let alone the long minutes it would take to complete this long act of pleasure and pain. The damn thing was now painful cargo between his thighs, and got worse with every step he took back to where Sage waited in trembling silence, her body so golden, her ass so red, her surrender so beautiful.

There was no way he could keep his mouth off her—but a gentle kiss on the nape wasn't going to fly in the believability department. Sweet and soft wasn't where his instinct yearned to be, anyhow. He gave in to the primal roar that commanded him instead, sweeping her hair off one shoulder in order to sink his teeth into it. Sage gave him a shuddering groan in return, a sound he felt as much as heard. It spurred him to give her another bite, higher on her shoulder and harder into her skin, in the moment before he dragged the tack-lined glove down the middle of her back.

She started to unravel.

And was fucking spectacular as she did.

After another long groan from deep in her throat, she arched her head back, making her body smash against the cross. Her shoulders heaved as she pulled in air by raw, desperate spurts. Her arms coiled, twisting the wrist bonds one way and the next. Her profile was awash in bittersweet tension, her eyes closed and her lips wrapped around the bit, soaking the leather as she worked to keep herself halfway composed for him.

Garrett barely held back from crushing his lips on her again. He yearned to taste her, suckle on her, murmur his deep and adoring praise to her. Amazement rode that same tidal wave of reaction. How could it be that here, now, in the deepest throes of her submission, she'd never been more breathtaking to him…or claimed his love with more powerful force? He didn't bother figuring it out. He was too busy fighting the longing to hold her, enfold her, bury himself inside her until they both couldn't see straight or talk right…

Damn it, he had to stay focused.

He had to remember what the fuck he was doing here. Why the fuck he was doing it.

He had to play the sadist with her, in order to save her.

Give me just a few minutes more of courage, sugar, and I'll make it all worth it…I promise.

209

With a determined sweep of movement, he shifted to stand behind her again. He rotated his hand, assuring that the mitt would cover more skin, before dragging the spikes up the length of Sage's spine.

The guards *ooh'ed* and *ahh'ed* in approval. Sage hissed and twisted, but when there were no raised fingers from her right hand, he pressed in a little harder, and stroked the mitt back down. The furrows on Sage's back began to bloom bright red. He hadn't broken the skin, but had come hideously close—though that wasn't the factor causing Garrett the most perplexity here. It was the woman beneath the marks. Where Sage had seemed to just tolerate the lashes with the dragon's tail, this treatment clearly tripped a different switch in her. She didn't just moan. She keened and begged with need. She didn't just shiver. She damn-near thrashed against her tethers, her body like a stripped electric wire searching for a puddle to plunge into. For a second, Garrett even thought she—

No.

She didn't really enjoy this, did she?

He tested the theory by plowing some fresh welts from her waist to nape.

Sage didn't let out a shriek of reaction.

She sighed.

Garrett was damn glad he'd had a few years of experience at containing shit like sudden shock. He wrestled with a massive wash of the stuff now, especially because she joined that sound with a subtle buck of her hips that bypassed all the crap of this situation, and spoke to him alone. Oh hell, how he loved that motion. It usually came on nights where she'd had a little to drink, a lot of foreplay, and was at the point where her body overrode her discretion. She became something different on those nights, a creature of raw need, begging him to fill her, fuck her.

But this was more than that. He saw now that the pain he'd dealt her had acted like a key in a lock, throwing open doors she'd had to keep shut for so long. And now the portals were unbolted, setting free a creature he could have never imagined, wild and aching and…needing. Yes, she actually needed him now. Her circuit was tripped, but not complete. She'd been opened, but not detonated.

She needed more.

Garrett started the next stroke of the mitt between her shoulder blades. He didn't end it until he'd gotten to the bottom of her ass, and had raked the tacks right across her suede whip tracks too.

This time, Sage screamed.

He didn't give her more than a moment to process the sensations.

He let the mitt slip from his hand before he kicked it out of the way on his surge to press against her. With primal need, he bracketed her hips with his. He was finished with not touching her, not connecting to her. He needed to feel her heartbeat, taste her sweat, smell her arousal, absorb her ultimate explosion of power.

That meant taking her over the edge.

He was damn glad he'd brought along the mini slapper.

The five-inch paddle, made of leather that had little diamond cutouts, had been more of an afterthought to play into the charade for King. But right now, even the ruse was secondary to giving this brave, bold, amazing woman what she needed the most: a release from herself. A release into him. *Because* of him.

Oh, hell. He was really starting to understand why Z loved this shit so much.

He was on fire now, blazing with the need to rocket them both higher. His thighs coiled with it. His cock throbbed with it. He knew Sage felt it too. She tilted her head back against him, her neck arched in sensual splendor. Little rivers of her saliva dripped from the edges of her mouth, and he burned her skin with the false beard as he leaned in, licking the liquid off her chin.

"You taste so fucking good," he growled. "And you're gonna feel even better, aren't you, with your body wrapped around my cock?" He punctuated that by sliding his hand over the curls of her moist mound. "You're going to take me deep, little girl. You're going to take every inch I give you, every inch I fuck you with. But first," –he brought the slapper around and positioned it over that wet, open apex— "you're going to take this."

Smack.

He brought the paddle down with unwavering force.

Sage crashed her hips back against his, and let out a long moan.

Garrett dipped his other hand between her thighs, plunging two fingers into her slick, sweet cunt. He locked them there as he lowered the slapper to her clit. He did it again. Her tunnel convulsed around him, heaving and kneading, sucking at his digits. The answering instinct in his senses flared hotter, and he filled her ear with the rough breaths of that awakening beast. All the while, he didn't let his fingers slip from inside her. With a determined twist of his hand, he spread her more, letting her know just where he planned to go when he replaced his fingers with his dick.

She quivered around him, and gasped again.

He raised the paddle, and dealt her two more smacks. With only a half beat in between, he gave her two more. Then a pair that were harder.

The only sound he got in return was his woman's harsh, heaving breaths. But there wasn't a single moan or mewl between the gasps. Beneath him, Sage was limp and pliant, completely abandoned to him, open and ready. Her vagina continued to stroke his fingers as if worshipping them, pulsing in the cadence of a sexual prayer chant. *Please fuck me...please fuck me...please fuck me...*

Yes. Oh damn, yes.

He hurled the slapper away. After pulling his fingers out of her pussy, he frantically loosened his belt and fly. Inside seconds, his cock had freedom at last. No, wait. In the seconds after *that,* it had freedom. Every inch he parted her folds and sank into her was another cloud his senses hit on the way to bliss. He could finally give it all back to her...the strength, the courage, the agony, the ecstasy. *Everything.* He soared as he finally pounded it all into her, fucking her with every inch of his sex, every drop of his sweat, every piece of his heart. That was just the beginning. He swore not to stop until his soul crashed the gates of hers, and she knew he planned to stay there forever.

"Deeper." He drilled it at her as he dug his fingers into her hips. "All the way, little girl. Take every inch of it."

Behind him, there was a drone of conversation. Maybe it was more, as if the guards and even King himself were giving out verbal high-fives. Garrett's senses were too far gone to care. The surface of the lake outside could have gone up in flames and not rivaled the amazing bonfire of his body.

He pumped even harder when the flames turned to lava that pooled in his balls. He flattened his chest to Sage's spine, allowing nothing between her and the cross except his hand, sliding to find the erect nub of her hottest desire. Her clit was hard and hot between his fingers. Amazing. She felt so fucking amazing.

Her whole body shook as he relentlessly rubbed that sensitive ridge. He didn't stop until she started screaming again, her torment so shrill, insane, exquisite.

"Do it." He gave the order into her ear as he tugged at her clit. He flicked just the tip with his thumb. "Do it now. *Now!*"

Her orgasm was so intense, her scream ceased to make noise. That was just fine by him. The tension translated all the way through her cunt, squeezing her walls down on him, making it impossible to resist the fiery flood of his own eruption. The cum raced up his cock, bursting from him with violent, radiant intensity. His ass clenched. His thighs quivered. A massive bellow tore off his lips.

"Fuck!"

The chit-chat in the room totally stopped. Or maybe his blood thundered so loud, it drowned every other decibel in the place. Whatever the explanation, Garrett descended back to reality on a parachute of comfort that took its time catching full air, especially when he looked to the guards—and their collective gapes still fixed on his woman. And why the hell not? She was a wild, kinky dream incarnate, with her body marked, her pussy aglow, and her limbs still spread and bound…

He was seriously going to kill someone tonight. Maybe a whole handful of the maggots, if they didn't get back to their goddamn posts.

One of the goons laughed, like he'd heard that thought and couldn't wait to disprove it. He was just a kid really, if it wasn't for the totally depraved glint in his eyes. He handed his gun to the asshole next to him as he reached for his fly. "The slut is mine next."

After two wide steps, Garrett had the fucker's collar in his fist. "The merchandise is *mine,* period." He barely remembered to keep up the fake moneybags accent. "Put the little wiener away, *drecksau,* and do your fucking job."

King reacted to all of this with a placating laugh. The greedy jackoff would chuckle at his own mother's funeral if somebody paid him for it. "Such a show, Klaus my friend! So I assume that you are…satisfied with your sample?"

He didn't spare a glimpse at the dickwad. "Yes." Instead, he concentrated on getting Sage ungagged, blindfold-free, and off the cross. After getting all the bindings off her head and face, he unfastened the four cuffs. She stayed plastered to the wood, unable to move on her own. Carefully, he peeled her sweat-soaked body away, turning her enough to gather her in his arms. "We have a deal, Mr. King. Now get me a damn blanket. I don't want the slut damaged by the cold."

One of the guards handed over a flannel blanket. Garrett wrapped it around Sage before pacing back to the little living room area. As he bundled her close, he settled into the corner of a couch that was close as possible to the bar area. Tucked behind the wide wood counter was a service door. He, Z, and Wyatt had spotted the portal the second they'd entered and exchanged glances to identify it as their best escape route—*if* they needed it. They conjectured, based on the exterior floor plan they'd memorized from the drone shots Franzen had ordered, that the door led to a service portico from the kitchen. From there, they'd have the option of making a break for the Escalade they'd driven here or signaling to the SOC-R boat waiting for them out on the lake, manned with a team who were ready to speed in for a water extraction.

But only if they needed it.

Zeke and Wyatt had used the distraction of the last half hour to get Josie and Rayna nearer the door too. All looked good for their contingency plan, but a seamless mission was always much better than Plan B. As King settled into a chair opposite them, looking relaxed as Pluto gazing on the River Styx, Garrett could practically taste their hitch-free ending to this nightmare. All they had to do was pay this asshole off. They'd be out the door with the girls. The FBI would take over for their part of taking King down.

Z stepped over and sat next to him on the couch. In one hand, he carried a sizable leather briefcase. Inside was the king's ransom they'd be turning over to this gutter shit, along with the dozen tracking beacons that had been molded into the "rubber bands" around the bills inside. Even if King decided to split up the load, they'd be able to follow his money trails. Thank fuck for micro technology.

King spent more than a lingering stare on the case. Garrett wouldn't be surprised if the ass wipe started drooling next. "It is all there, my friend," he assured. "Twenty-five thousand for each of the women and your finder's fee of fifteen thousand."

King spread his hands. "I have no doubt of that, my friend. I am simply perplexed we are discussing payment now." He flicked his gaze to Zeke. "Surely you and Gustav are interested in having your own test sessions?"

Z cocked one brow with well-practiced ease. "Will the other two do what she just did?"

King flashed a dirty grin. "Absolutely."

"Then take the money. I have plans for my new acquisition that do not involve putting my dick on public spectacle."

Garrett was tempted to chuckle. He was damn glad they'd gotten a recording of that. Cover identity or not, he was pretty sure that was the first and last time he'd hear Zeke turn down an offer to play with a subbie for an audience. For a long second, King scrutinized Z as if he didn't believe it either. But

215

he'd seen Zeke maintain his cool in situations like this—hell, worse than this—for close to five years now. King wasn't the first leech they'd had to pry off humanity's ass. He wouldn't be the last. Garrett just wished he could make it hurt a little worse for the bastard, like demanding he hand over both ball sacs along with the girls.

Z unlocked the case by pushing on a remote fob that hung on a chain around his neck. When the lock buttons pulsed green, he pushed the case to King. Garrett half expected the asshole to cackle with glee, and King's smirk hinted that way, but the Bastard kept his cool while popping the case latches.

Reverently, King lifted back the lid.

Whoa. Seventy-five thousand dollars looked nice when it was all pretty, lined up and bundled. But the only thing Garrett saw was he and Zeke in the hallway outside Franz's office, waiting to have their asses tossed into slings if King really got away with that money. But this was part of the process. One more step to cross off on the glitch-free list. He forced back an impatient sigh, but it pushed in his throat again when Sage started stirring in his arms. The endorphins she'd been swimming in were starting to evaporate. Her back and her ass would start stinging soon. God*damn*, how much longer?

Apparently, *much* longer. With the speed of a turtle in the sun, King took out a map magnifier. He perused several hundred-dollar notes from the top of the stacks. After verifying the authenticity of the money, the guy looked back up and smiled again. "It is an immense pleasure doing business with you, gentlemen." He pointed at Z's chest. "And I shall take that little toy of yours now too."

Zeke closed his fist over the fob. "You get the toy when we leave with the merchandise."

King pouted. "Come now. Is that any way to treat a new friend? I have shown I can be trusted, have I not? Tit for tat is in order, gentlemen, if you desire to earn the same from me. Or perhaps you do *not* desire to earn the same?"

The bastard's gaze narrowed. The expression had "glitch" written all over it. Instinctively, Garrett pulled Sage in tighter. He felt a matching degree of tension roll off Zeke. His friend emitted a growl. "You have seventy-five thousand reasons to trust us, *friend*."

King backpedaled fast. With a nervous laugh, he spread his hands once again. "But of course. I wasn't implying—"

"Mmmm."

Sage's groan, while loud, wasn't what yanked King to a stunned stop. It was the hand she slinked up around Garrett's neck, trying to pull him down for a fierce kiss. Garrett acted on sheer instinct in complying with her behest, hoping their long, tongue-tangling embrace swirled enough happy subbie mental mist back into her that she dropped into blissful silence again.

He should have known better.

The strength of her grip, the passion of her mouth, the undulation of her body...they all should have blasted one massive warning sign in his senses. *Massive Glitch Ahead.*

It happened as soon as he tried to clear the hair from her face. Her eyes, still glassy and lost, focused on him like some cravat-necked lord from one of her costume romance movies. Her lips, shiny and swollen, lifted in a dreamy smile.

"Garrett." Her breathy inflection didn't prevent the word from reverberating throughout the room like cannon fire. "Oh Garrett, thank you, baby."

One second of total silence passed.

In the next, the air crackled from at least a dozen rounds getting chambered into rifles, along with the clicks of three hand guns. His, Zeke's, and King's.

"Shit," Garrett muttered.

"Sounds about right," Z returned.

Angel Payne

Chapter Eighteen

Shit, shit, shit!

Sage dragged a hand through her hair as Garrett swung her next to him and whipped out a gun from under his pant leg. Thirty seconds. She couldn't believe it. That was all the time it had taken for her senses to tumble from their cloud of satiation and endorphins into an ocean of pure dread, lined on the bottom by rocks of raw remorse.

I'm sorry. So sorry!

It was an apology Garrett would never hear aloud. He couldn't afford the time, and he sure as hell couldn't afford the distraction, now that he and King glared down their gun barrels at each other. There was just one huge discrepancy in that. King and his .45 caliber were backed up by at least ten semi-automatic rifles, brandished by guards who imagined this all as some grand adventure instead of a very real, very dangerous stand-off. Sage gulped as she watched their untrained bodies twitching, and their trigger fingers behaving worse.

Shit, shit, shit.

"Listen to me, King." Garrett's assertion pounded the air with shockingly calm command. "This changes nothing about the deal."

He grabbed her and tucked her tighter behind him, but not before Sage got a longer look at his profile. Between the ruthless granite of his gaze, the rugged set of his mouth, and the maturity added by the false facial hair, he really had been transformed into a different person. Yes, she realized that was the whole idea of undercover work, but this makeover was different. Some parts of him weren't simply makeup and costume glue. Some parts were wholly the man he'd become— the man who, crazily enough, had to be in disguise for her to see clearly for the first time. Gone was the reckless soldier boy who'd battled bar drunks for her. This was Garrett the man, who sat in front of a madman's gun for her. Who might still take a bullet from that gun for her.

The man she loved deeply and desperately, now more than ever.

King's hyena laugh sliced her thoughts apart. The man poked his gun harder at Garrett in emphasis. "This changes nothing?" he barked. "Is that so? On what fucking planet does it change *nothing* for you, Sergeant Hawkins?"

Garrett's composure stayed resolute as the heights of Rainier. He nodded at the briefcase. "You have your money. We have what we came here for. This doesn't have to get messy. Take your pay-off and go."

Sage expected another of the man's wild chortles. When King's response was a glowering silence instead, she admitted a jolt of bafflement—and terror. She didn't like being wrong *or* scared about a monster like him.

"Is that what you think?" the bastard. "You *truly* deem that I got what I came here for?"
"He's on the straight-up, asshat." The intrusion came from Zeke, who also looked five times more menacing despite a beard and nose that must've been stolen from an Abraham Lincoln costume set. "The money's all there. And it's all real."

"Oh ho, no doubt it is!" King rebutted. "Just as it is all marked, no doubt, by the—how did you put it—asshats who supplied it to you."

"Guess I should take that as a compliment." Wyatt spoke up, likely as a calculated move to swing King's head around to where he still stood between Josie and Rayna. "The wrapping job is mine. Took a long time too, when we got all that flow from the bank after selling off Garrett's condo."

Sage's heartbeat seized again on the stunned setting. Garrett sold the condo to do this? He loved the condo even more than she did. Stupid, sacrificing, amazing man. She would've battered him raw, if he wasn't sitting there with nearly ten guns aimed at his beautiful heart.

Damn it, she had to help fix this! But how? She was sitting here, literally a sitting duck, trapped naked in nothing but a flannel blanket, and—
Wait.
Naked. Blanket.

She pressed her lips together to keep from smiling. She had more than what she needed, didn't she?

King's distraction with Wyatt gave her the ideal opportunity to start repositioning herself, inch by inch. Garrett felt her shifting, and tried to grab her ankle in the guise of soothing her, but she dug her heel into his fingers with rebellious resolve.

"So should I now call you the rubber band man?" King cracked at Garrett's uncle. "Surely you don't still prefer Gustav? Or maybe you'll just tell me who the fuck you really are."

"No need to get testy. The name's Wyatt Hawkins. You won't mind if I continue to call *you* Mr. Cocksucker, right?"

"Hawkins," drawled King. "So big daddy bear has come to save the wee one?"

"I'm his uncle. And he hasn't needed saving since the days I was balls-deep in your mama, ass face. I came for her." He cut Josie out of her blindfold and cuffs then did the same to Rayna. "And her." He nodded toward Sage. "And her. And needless to say, my trigger finger gets awfully twitchy when it's covered in rubber band burns. So if you don't mind, we'll be toodle-loo'ing now."

King responded to that by raising a hand. As Sage expected, all the guards jumped to high alert. Three of them lurched toward Wyatt, Josie and Rayna. There were two dedicated to Garrett alone. The rest lurched into the same raised hackle mode, covering both doors, ready to shoot an ant on the wall if it moved.

None of them was paying attention to the naked girl in the blanket.

Which made it completely easy to sneak along the back of the couch. And surprisingly effortless to take a stance on the armrest as she peeled the blanket loose, spreading it outward, exposing her nudity in full glory. And outright fun to watch at least three of the soldiers turn to her with worshipful gapes.

And completely awesome to leap forward on a wild yell as she tossed the thing onto the assholes.

She jumped down to advance on the other guards, who

struggled to comprehend that bare tits, ass and other accessories were coming after them like a banshee on a vendetta. That was fine by her. She *was* a banshee on a vendetta.

She veered to the left, back into the dungeon area where Garrett had taken her to the moon and back. The whip rack lay just two steps in. She grabbed a couple of the shorter single tails before turning back to face the three goons who followed her.

"Who wants a crack at me first, gentlemen?" She braced her legs and snapped the poppers on the floor, splitting the air with a pair of frightening cracks. "Huh. That was pretty cool, huh? Must've been beginner's luck. You know, these things take practice. I've only played around with one, years ago. I'm not very good at all. God only knows what I'll hit in my current delirium." She flicked the leather lengths again. The soldiers scampered backward.

"Sage. Holy fuck!" The bellow came from Garrett, but she didn't take her sights off the three henchmen in front of her.

"Do not listen to the bitch!" King screamed. "Take her down, damn you. Take her down!"

"The only things going down are your weapons, assholes." She took a second to pray before cutting one of the whips at the closest guard. The lash came nowhere near her intended target, the guy's gun hand, but it actually did flick into his crotch, making him fall to the floor in groaning agony. His gun slid away as he grabbed his balls and sobbed. Her heartbeat roaring, the heat of her terror burning behind her eyes, she bared her teeth at the remaining pair of goons. "Who's next?"

The guards vacillated. They looked to King, only to discover that Zeke had used her antics as the ideal distraction. Their boss's glare had a distinct new accessory: the butt of Z's pistol. "That's such a pretty forty-five, cocksucker," Zeke murmured. "I think my buddy would dig getting a closer look at it." He dipped a glance at Wyatt. "Why don't you set it down on the floor now. Yep, right there is fine. Do me a favor and slide it over to him."

When King obeyed the first part of the demand, but defiantly kicked the pistol in the opposite direction from Wyatt, Z let out a chuckle. "Ooohhh, you're so cute, King. I love how you make me giggle in girlish delight."

The guards in front of Sage huffed in frustration. "Screw this," one of them blurted. He bolted from the building. The other three, including the guy she'd just whipped in the balls, rushed out after him. King roared in rage when the sound of a started car came from the open door. The engine purred, likely that of a Jag, BMW, or high-end Mercedes. Obviously, the goons had chosen King's personal car for their escape.

If a human could breathe fire, Sage was certain King would spit full explosions at Zeke. The man glared like a caged dragon, lips twisting, skin mottling. "This shit is *not* done!"

Zeke barked in laughter. "Oh yeah, fuck nugget, it's done." With his free hand, he pulled out a pair of fast plastic cuffs and folded them out. Before he moved again, he looked around at King's remaining minions. A couple of them still wrestled with the blanket, though Wyatt had already fished out their guns, and now stood with the pile stacked between his spread legs. "I'm gonna put these on your boss man now, okay?" Zeke stated. "You know that if any of you try to stop me, my friends will put a bullet in your chest." He nodded Sage's direction. "Whip girl will probably be happy to cut your crotch open for good measure too."

Garrett glowered at his friend. "Are you encouraging her?" He stomped over and jabbed a finger at the corner where he'd left her skimpy outfit. "Put your damn clothes on, Sage. Now!"

Zeke chuckled again, leaning over to King with the cuffs. Sage was about to give a sarcastic "Yes, Sir" to her fiancé, when she witnessed the same crazy incident that everyone else did.

King greeted Zeke with a hug.

No. *Oh God, no.*

King didn't give Z a hug. It was a knife. A big one. That he drove right into Z's gut.

"It's *not* over," the monster said with a gritted smile. "Nooooo!"

Rayna's scream filled the room. Garrett lunged, slamming King away before the bastard could pull the knife free and make Z bleed out. Sage dashed over, trying to help Garrett pin King down, but the asshole got a solid backhand in on her cheek and she fell away. Seconds later, King scrambled clear from Garrett too. He stumbled to his feet, wrenched open the door—

Then crumpled against the jam, and slid down it.

A streak of blood followed his descent, flowing from the bullet wound in his forehead. There was a nick in the wood, clearly made by another bullet that had missed.

Sage tried to get in air past her shocked gasps. She hadn't even heard the shots. What the hell?

She stared back across the room. A shocked exhalation left her.

She'd set herself up to behold Wyatt to be standing there with the smoking gun.

The weapon was braced in Rayna's trembling hands.

"You want *over,* asshole?" Her friend's voice wobbled past lips that glistened with tears, and teeth that were bared in rage. "*Now* it's over."

Chapter Nineteen

"God, I'm glad you didn't really sell this place."

Sage's husky murmur resonated against Garrett's chest as the last rays of the sunset disappeared over the lake. They left behind a sky that looked like a watercolor, too good to be real. Whipped cream clouds danced with shades of lavender, orange and amber over the silhouetted trees, and were reflected in the calm ripples along the water outside.

Inside the condo, where they nestled on the couch with each other, Garrett chuckled quietly while twirling a strand of her hair around his fingers. He'd never get tired of ending their days like this. Though the last week had been an insane whirl of debriefs at the base, another round of media for Sage, and checking in at the hospital with Z at least once a day, they'd made sure to slot this time together at or near sunset.

Okay, so most nights, the couch cuddle hadn't been exactly the "end" of their day. It led to ways that formed an even better conclusion for them both. *Way* better. Garrett and his new alter ego, who'd fast earned the title "Sir G" from Sage, were becoming fast comrades in the quest of bringing their woman a world of submissive pleasure. The stockpile in the nightstand now included a couple of mini floggers, nipple clamps, a remote-operated vibrator, several anal insertables, and lots of scented lube. And he wanted more. Much more.

He only hoped she could handle more—because tonight, she was going to get it.

Just the thought of his little surprise made Garrett shift a little, concertedly commanding the rocket jet between his legs to hold on to its fucking fuse. Sage pulled away from him a bit, crunching her brow in a frown. "I'm sorry, baby. I walked in here and instantly started talking about my visit with Ray at the hospital. I spaced on dinner. You're probably hungry, right?"

"Nope." Garrett smiled softly at her. "Not hungry. I grabbed something late this afternoon. Figured you'd be eating with Rayna. How's she doing?"

Sage gave a little shrug. "She's talking to the counselors every day. She's in the business of saving lives, not shooting people, no matter how much she hated King. It's a lot for her to deal with right now. But focusing on Z is helping her, for sure."

"That's good. Real good. And how is Sergeant Hayes himself coming along, besides grouchy as fuck?"

Sage laughed. "He's still grouchy as fuck. He'll probably be out tomorrow, in time to wreak hell on Rayna's weekend."

The affectionate tone of her voice actually shifted him into a serious mien. "Z doesn't say too much to me about her, you know."

"About Rayna?" When Garrett nodded, she pressed, "So what does that mean?"

"That he's ass-over-elbows nuts about her."

"Oh." She flashed an adorably girlish grin. "Awesome!" The smile dropped when he didn't deviate his gaze from her. He could keep up the cover on a mission for days if he had to, but keeping this surprise from her tonight was damn-near killing him. Maybe it was because his cock had been invested in the fun since about three this afternoon. "Are you sure you aren't hungry?" she insisted. "You look really hungry."

Garrett answered with a small, wolfish grin. He tangled his fingers deeper into her hair, using the hold to dip her head back, exposing her neck to him. He leaned and gently scored her skin with his top teeth. "Oh, I *am* hungry."

"Mmmmm." She brought her hands up to his head too. "I think I can help out with that craving, Sir G."

Garrett shook his head. He pulled up so he could gaze into her brilliant green eyes again. "Uh-uh. No Sir G tonight, sugar."

Sage stuck out her lower lip. "What? Why not?"

"Because I want you to call me something else."

"All right. Ummm…what?"

He shook his head again, intentionally slow and wicked about it. "You don't get to find out until you go upstairs."

Her answering huff was a tantalizing tease of its own.

226

"Garrett!" she protested. "Not even a hint?"

He twisted his hold harder in her hair. "Every second you sit here sassing me, sugar, is another second of discipline I get to take from you later."

That caused her eyebrows to jump. "Dih—dih—discipline?"

Garrett forced back his smile this time. He set her free before rising to his feet and folding his arms. "You're still wasting time on sass."

Sage popped up from the couch. "All right; okay. I get it!"

"Bedroom," he called as she sprang for the stairs. "Follow *every* instruction on the note I left for you."

"Yes, Sir!"

He finally bared the smile as he walked down the hall to the guest bedroom. During the trip, he cracked open a door in his mind, enough to let Sir G slip into the fray. Hell, this was going to be fun.

Chapter Twenty

Sage stood at the door of the guest bedroom, shifting a little on her bare feet, nervous as hell.

"This is ridiculous," she groused beneath her breath. "You're being stupid, Weston. It's just Garrett. You know him. You love him. You're getting married. In June. You have a date and a church already, and—"

She stopped herself on a rickety moan. Oh God. She was surely going to hell. Had she actually just talked about walking into a church to get married, when she stood here dressed in nothing but a barely-there black leather bra and a pair of matching panties that covered even less? And did the tissues between her thighs actually quiver and get creamier with arousal, as she looked again at the note in her hand? Granted, the words were now a little smeared because she'd picked it up and read it about a hundred times since finding it on their bed...

> *Use the fresh razor in the shower. Shave yourself*
> *everywhere. Put your hair up.*
> *When you're done, come to me in the guest bedroom.*
> *Wear only what I've placed here.*
> *Master*

She ran a finger over that last word in open amazement...and growing, heated arousal. "Master," she whispered.

Shit on a gigantic platter. She had to be dreaming this, right? She was going to wake up on the couch, having fallen asleep on Garrett's chest, and embarrassed because she'd drooled all over him. This couldn't really be happening. This was surreal, insane; a manifestation of her deepest sexual fantasies...

Nope. Wrong.

He was a manifestation of those fantasies.

229

He was leaning in the doorway to the guest bathroom, waiting for her in sensual silence. Oh, who was she kidding? "Sensual" was the world's hugest understatement for the creature who stood before her now, with smoke in his eyes, half a smile on his lips, and soft black leather sheathing his huge, chiseled legs. From the waist up, he was sinfully bare, every striation of his golden muscles gleaming in the light of what seemed a thousand candles.

Candles.

After noticing how their light danced on Garrett's body, Sage noticed the votives themselves. Indeed there seemed to be thousands, all lighted and placed on frosted glass shelves that had been mounted at various heights along the perimeter of the room. Shit, the room! Even it had been transformed. The guest bed was still here, though she barely recognized the thing. In place of its demure art deco comforter, the mattress was now fitted with a tight cover in a shade of royal blue, in what looked like a leather texture. A steel truss system rose up around the bed, with several attachments already in place...including leather cuffs that seemed to wave at her in welcome. She swung her stare over to take in even more. In the corner opposite the bed, there was a big X-shaped cross just like the one she and Garrett had used at King's Medina kink mansion, along with another piece of equipment that appeared kind of like a prayer bench, lined in dark purple velvet.

Wow. Wow. *Wow.*

Okay, maybe she already was in church. Or Heaven. Or a wild, glorious combination of the two.

"Damn," she finally got out. "Garrett...sweetheart...this is—"

"Just the beginning." He cut her off as he pushed away from the door and stepped over, his strides given a more menacing air by the heavy motorcycling boots he wore. "That is, if tonight goes well."

She laughed, trying to make light of the fact that his boots alone had just made her more wet than the Puget Sound in January. "Oh, I definitely think it—"

He snatched her words from her again, along with the

very breath behind them, by grabbing her chin with his palm and hitching her face up. His stare sent a long lick of blue fire straight to the deepest parts of her pussy. "You're not in here to think, S." His murmur smoldered hotter than his stare, descending deeper as he addressed the confusion that must have risen in her eyes. "Do you have any questions about that?"

She managed to get enough moisture into her mouth to speak. "Are—are you saying you want to go further with this, Sir?"

He smoothed his fingers across her face. His gaze consumed her with its fierce possession, and its pure adoration. "Oh yes, sugar."

She swallowed hard. "H-how much further?"

"That's a journey we'll take together. It'll be in steps. But listen to me, and hear my promise to you. My need to dominate you will *never* quell my need to make you happy, to make you soar." He pressed a soft kiss on her lips. "To keep you safe."

Sage smiled. "I know." She raised her hand, meshing her fingers with his. "So…what happens now?"

Garrett let their hands fall apart. Gone was the cameo appearance from his gentle Dom. The hard-hewn conqueror was back, standing before her with an agenda in his eyes. An agenda that didn't involve a lot of couch cuddling anymore.

Shit. *Shit.*

"Kneel for me, Sage."

Yes. *Yes.*

That simple act pulled her mind and body into deeper focus on him. She heard his quiet rumble of satisfaction, and rejoiced. She felt him step to her again, and melted. As his long fingers descended atop her head, a long sigh left her trembling lips.

"From now on, when you choose to come in here with me, you are no longer Sage. You will be only S. And I will be simply Master. Do you understand?"

"Yes," she whispered. "Yes, Master."

"We'll certainly discuss things that Sage has done,

perhaps to address how she'll be disciplined for them, but Sage herself belongs to that world, out there. She belongs to the place where you have to worry, to think, to care. S does none of those things. In her, Master does the worrying. S is here merely to be a receptacle of things on Sage's behalf." His hand spread harder against her scalp. "Do you still understand?"

She lifted her face. Dear sweet God, if this man was stunning as Garrett, he was resplendent as Master. Every inch of his gaze exuded power, strength, control. He was huge and mighty and confident, yet every molecule of air he breathed on her, every inch of his touch on her, was composed of his loving care, his fervent protectiveness. She was terrified of him like this, yet her body, her senses, her very blood and breath never wanted him more.

"Yes." She gave it to him on a raw rasp. "I still understand, Master."

"And…do you still want this? With me? Even after everything I've told you?"

"Oh, yes!" Hoping he excused her for the burst of beginner's zeal, she grabbed his other hand and pressed a kiss on his upturned palm. Garrett used that hand to guide her back to her feet. She was greeted by a beautiful warmth, pouring from his deep cyan eyes.

"That pleases me," he told her, "but I want you to be sure." He nodded toward the bed. "You see this equipment and you know what it means, right? That when I say you'll be a receptacle for Sage, I mean for rewards *and* punishments. You will always have safe words. You'll always be able to slow me down or stop me if you need to, then we'll take it outside and talk." His fingers alighted on the column of her neck, trailing possessively along both sides of her wind pipe. "But when you're in here, S…when you're in my realm…you're mine. *All* of you belongs to me."

By the time Sage remembered she had a voice, let alone how to use it, he'd trailed his touch down, coming to the black bra clasp between her breasts. "I still want this," she insisted. "I still understand, Master. Ohhh, Master…oh…ummm…"

She interrupted herself as he played with the fastening.

His voice alone had turned her nipples into nubs of sheer need. Now, she literally couldn't talk from the intense need. Over the last week, he'd been fond of learning what her breasts could endure. Because of those test runs, both those peaks were hypersensitive to the tiniest brush of arousal, especially if that brush was in his hands.

But the real challenge here was…Garrett knew that too. A stolen glance up at his face confirmed that fact with crystal clarity. He was like a bronze container of serenity and composure. She, on the other hand, could think of nothing else but letting his long, magical fingers roam all over her aching breasts.

"Did you need to finish that, S?"

"Y-yes." She forced her voice into compliance, even though he teased at the clasp in maddening experimentation, making her bend toward him in a wanton grovel. "Yes Master, I did need to…to…"

"Focus," he murmured. "Lock your hands behind your waist and concentrate. I'm right here, and I'm listening. Now continue."

"I'll—I'll try. Oh! Ohhhh…"

Continue? He expected her to continue, to concentrate at all, when he opened the bra and pushed it down her arms but did nothing with her exposed swells except run his knuckles along their undersides?

"Yes?" he prompted. "I'm right here. I'm listening, sugar."

"I know!" she finally snapped. "I know, okay? But damn it, Gar—Master—please!"

He simply kept up the maddening teasing. His fingers traced heat into the flesh of her breasts, but he went nowhere near the tight-puckered circles that tingled in their centers, squeezing and hurting for his touch.

"I'm gonna let that outburst slide, because you followed it up so sweetly," he stated. "Do *not* unlock those hands, S. Use the stance to help yourself focus, to give me the words. Tell me what you're feeling, my heart. Say it."

"Are you kidding me?" She couldn't help it. The

pressure was loaded so damn high, pushing at her nipples with tormenting need, and it was *his* doing. "God, Garrett, can't you tell? Frustrated. I'm frustrated, okay? I feel trapped, and helpless, and—and you won't do what I want you to. What I need you to!"

She averted her eyes, now getting to pile awkward and embarrassed onto that heap of adjectives. Exasperated and enraged joined the list when Garrett moved his hands back in, framing her face completely with them, forcing her stare back up to his.

"Now you're getting a glimpse of how I felt when Sage took on King's guards all by herself."

She dropped her jaw. *That's* what this was all about? "I—I was trying to save our asses!"

"We're not discussing you. We're discussing Sage. Who was naked and unarmed."

"Not for very long."

"A pair of whips doesn't count as armed, damn it."

"It worked, didn't it?"

His fingers curled into her scalp again, and he growled. It wasn't his usual mountain lion growl, either. This sound belonged to Bigfoot, or something worse. Scratch that; it *was* worse. The rumble didn't just resonate with a big dose of angry. It vibrated with pain. And yes, fear. He was battling to hide that part from her, but she saw it flashing through the smokescreen in his gaze too. She'd terrified him that night with her daredevil move. Yes, it was the step that swung the advantage their direction, but it very well could've been the stunt that got her killed.

Her gut twisted, followed soon by her heart. He really had been a knuckle-dragging, overbearing beast since they'd gotten back, but he'd had damn good reasons for all that chest beating. He was a different creature now, and she had to learn his different sides all over again—just like he had to learn hers. And, quite possibly, just like he'd have to corral in some parts of her beastie side from time to time.

They were learning together. Growing together. And this room was going to give them some of the most fun and sexy ways to do that.

With that conclusion at the forefront of her mind, she dipped her head, and gave her Master a resigned nod. "You're right. It might have worked, but that didn't make it the most sane action plan."

Garrett inched closer. He kissed the top of her head. "Thank you. I accept that, as well as the sweet sincerity with which you gave it. Now," –he lowered both hands to her breasts again, though this time, he thumbed both nipples with enough pressure to make her sob— "you're going to accept my discipline for it too."

She thought about protesting. Part of her wanted to. Her heart had seriously been in the right place. The trouble was, her head hadn't been. One more factor led to the second soft nod she gave him, with her head still lowered. She wanted this. Needed it. Had craved it since the first swat Garrett gave her pussy back in Thailand. She'd spent so damn long making all the decisions, doing all the governing, worrying about her very survival. For a while, she longed to be a little reckless and have someone *else* call her shit about it—which meant that for a while, they were probably going to be in this room a lot.

She tried not to smile about that.

Just like she tried not to let a few drops of fear sneak into the dutiful response she whispered to Garrett. "Yes, Master. Of course."

Another low rumble rolled out of him, but this time it was laced with an undertone of anticipation. "Very nice. But you'll look nicer with those panties off, kneeling naked in the middle of the bed for me."

Sage moved to obey. With every step she took over to the bed, her mind seemed to ambulate as well, shifting into a zone not reality or fantasy, but a surreal place in between. The fog of the headspace was only thickened by the ethereal music Garrett had plugged into the sound system speakers, a dreamy melody backed by a throbbing, blatantly sexual dance beat. Almost instantly, the depths of her body responded to it, coiling on themselves to squeeze out more drops of anticipation into her tight channel, her pouting pussy lips.

"Are you ready, S?"

She let out a soft laugh, hoping he didn't take it the wrong way. "Hell yes, Master."

"What's your safe word, S?"

She laughed louder, unable to help it. "Cauliflower, Master."

"Is something funny, S?"

Her nervousness spiraled into a moment of punchy stupidity. "I don't know, Master. *Is* something funny?"

Hell. She was going to regret that. He confirmed that for her the next second, grabbing her hair and twisting it hard. She whimpered as he yanked her head back, positioning her for his plunging, devouring, tongue-tangling kiss. When he finally let her go, he kept her jaw captive for a moment longer, letting her fast gasps twine with his heavy breaths. Sage pushed toward him again, yearning for another kiss, but he yanked his hand away in order to grab one of her wrists, pulling it directly over her head.

Trepidation did a fast trample on her desire as he secured a leather cuff around her wrist, then hooked the restraint in place with a distinct *clink* of a caribiner hook. He climbed onto the bed behind her before doing the same thing to her other wrist.

She was strung up for him now, pretty literally. With her arms locked over her head and her legs curled at the knee and pressed against him, she wouldn't be scrambling out of this anytime soon.

Her heart pounded against her ribs in time to the fuck-friendly music.

But as she listened to Garrett readying numerous toys behind them, she had a feeling that a little of her Dom's fun was coming before the fucking.

She closed her eyes and sucked in a deep breath. Another.

He stole the calming effect of both gulps when he fitted his mouth against her ear, and his hands circled around to tug hard at her nipples once more. "So, S's tits are begging for a little attention tonight, yeah?"

She licked her lips and replied, "Yes, Master."

"That's damn fortunate, because I was thinking that S's nipples need to share Sage's punishment tonight. After all, they were pretty naughty during that escapade in Medina, too."

"Uh…yes, Master."

She was happy she got that out, because her voice said a scared-shitless *sayonara* again in the next second. Garrett had dropped his finger teases on her nipples for a moment, only to bring his hands back bearing new toys for them. Okay, the clover clamps weren't exactly "new." He'd brought them home a few nights ago, excited about the possibilities of controlling how much tension he could deliver to her nipples with a simple tug of the string attached to each clamp. Sage had barely made it through one tiny pull on each string before pleading with Garrett to take the clamps off. These things were tight. Repeat that: *tight.*

With a pleasant little hum, Garrett stretched out her left nipple. The pleasure of his fingers on her skin almost outweighed the dread of knowing what was about to come.

"Ready?" he asked.

Oh, shit.

"Yes, Mas—owwww!"

He didn't let her prepare for the right clamp. It didn't matter anyway. Her breasts were turned into a pair of squeezed, stinging pinpoints, dominating every breath she took as Garrett turned and readied other playthings in the space she couldn't see, directly behind them. Sage winced. Oh, yay for her. *More* toys.

"Breathe through it, sugar," he finally said. "They're going to be on for a while."

"Crap!" she snapped. "Why?"

Her reply for that was a hard pair of spanks, one on each ass cheek. She let out a high yelp as her ass flared with fire and the clamps swung on her nipples, pulling on the flesh in tormenting new ways.

"What part of 'punishment' didn't you comprehend, S?"

She hissed through her teeth, but bit back the extremely

237

creative oath that sat at the tip of her tongue. "All right. I know. I'm sorry."

"Really?"

His question was sincere. She wanted to answer it that way too, but all of this was overwhelming to process. Being helpless had been a lot more glamorous to think about, maybe because it never came in the combo package with having to be responsible for an apology at the same time. "Yes! Fine. I'm really sorry. Damn it, Garrett!"

She knew what was coming before he delivered it, and she squeezed her buttocks to ready herself for the spanks. The preparation still didn't save her skin. He'd gone for an upgrade. Instead of his bare palm, a hard paddle was wielded on her ass. Sage screamed from the shock as much as the pain, especially when he didn't stop with just one blow. Five whacks later, he threw the paddle away. He had the gall to press his body against her instead, caressing her ass cheeks with long steady sweeps, grazing her neck with hot nips of his teeth and tongue.

"You have some nerve!" She was seething, despite how good those rough kisses felt. "You know that, you fucker? You have—"

He sucked out the air she needed for the rest of that by pushing himself even tighter against her. Hell. He was damn-near wrapped around her, with his hands ramming her hips back into the cradle of his. Gone was the Dom who'd been patiently explaining his moves to her, even the torturous clover clamps. Returned was her prince of blatant carnality. His muscles pulsed against her and his lungs heaved against her back. His breath was like a wild firestorm in her ear.

He pulled her tighter to him by hooking his hands into the valleys that joined her thighs to her torso. "Who are you in here?" he snarled.

His voice was so low, so vehement, so primal, Sage hesitated to answer.

"*Answer me!*"

Ohhhh, God. His demand was bestial now, stirring the darkest, deepest caves of her sexual instincts. Sage shivered and gasped, her muscles dissolving, her sex blossoming, her heartbeat thudding like the downed prey of a ravenous lion. *Yes. Consume me. Take it all. Please!*

"Who. Are. You?"

A long breath escaped her. Sage listened to every second of it departing her body, flowing past her lips…knowing that she'd just let go of a lot more than a sigh.

"I am…S."

He didn't let up an inch of his proximity. "And who am I?"

"You are Master."

"And who do you belong to…when you're here with me?"

"You."

"Completely?"

"Yes, Master. Completely."

The words did something bewildering to her. And magical. This was even better than the fog that had infiltrated her mind earlier. She was released, floating, carried away from…well, everything. From King, from captivity, from the media wanting her to relive it for them, even from her own memory, which would never fully let it go. It was all gone, and now she was so light and free, even the feel of the claws on her breasts changed, radiating heat into her skin instead of pain. And her Master gave her wings to soar even farther. With gentle precision, his fingers slipped inward to find the center of her sex, sliding and kneading, finally pressing at the exquisitely sensitive button that waited, trembling and tight, for his contact.

"Ohhh! Master! Yes!"

"You're a good girl, S." The words themselves praised, but his tone, rough and determined, turned them into a dictate. Sage reveled in it, instantly giving him a little nod in response.

"I—I want to be, Master."

"I know, sugar." With his fingers still fondling her clit, he slid his other hand around to the aperture at her backside. Sage moaned in greater delight. He'd been experimenting on her ass hole all week with different toys, and had even gotten a sizable dildo inside her last night. Each experience had been filled with everything she wanted most from the evolving stages of their Dominant/submissive journey: pain mixed with pleasure, surrender mixed with sin, her body stretched to take Garrett into heights of fulfillment he'd never had before. But he hadn't breached her ass with his own body. She knew he craved to. Maybe, she mused, he'd been saving it for a special occasion.

Maybe tonight, that time had come.

Her heartbeat kicked in both anticipation and trepidation. The feeling intensified when she heard the flip of a plastic lid and a distinct liquid spurt. Her pulse raced into triple time when one of his fingers, now slicked with cool lube, slid into her tight entrance.

More wet squirts. Another finger in her ass. He gently pumped the digits, earning him deeper access. He released his hand from her pussy to help spread her back cheeks. Sage didn't mind. He was opening her in a new, dirty, decadent way, and it coaxed out an answering animal in her, loving the coarse rumbles from his chest, the growing tension in his muscles, the lust that radiated from him like fireballs off the sun. Her breath started spilling from her in high, pleading sighs.

"Oh, fuck me, S." Garrett practically grunted it as he twisted a third finger and a hell of a lot more lube inside her. "This rosette of yours is so damn tight and perfect."

"Thank you, Master." She worked her knees a little farther apart, hoping it gave him a better view. It sure made everything feel even more incredible. Her ass was so wide. So vulnerable. So enlivened and sensitive. She felt her hips undulating, driven by the growing heat between her legs. She needed him inside her. She needed him everywhere.

"I'm going to claim it tonight, S." The distinct rasp of his zipper cut into the air, followed by the creak of the leather as he worked to set his cock free. "You know that, don't you?"

"Yes," she whispered. "I know."

He emitted a low groan, and there was the sound of lube being slurped along skin. "And you still want to be a good girl for me? Even if that means having my cock in your ass?"

"More than anything, Master."

"Then I am a very lucky Master."

The scent of more fresh lube filled the air. The music changed to a new track, lifting into a sensual crescendo. Garrett fitted himself tight and close behind her.

He pushed the bulb of his penis into her back hole.

Sage grimaced. His erection was as sizable as he was, and he was stuffed into every crevice her body could accommodate. The tissues were tested to their hilt with this gigantic invasion, and it was a tight, tense fit. But her Master was steady and slow, no matter how violently his body shook with the effort of holding himself back.

"You can do this, S." He rolled his hips a little, getting his cock another fraction into her aperture. "*We* can do this. God*damn*, you take my breath away."

"It's...tight."

"It won't always be."

"I know."

He stroked her hair. "You okay?"

After she nodded, he coaxed, "Push against me, like we practiced. Work to accept it. Work to feel me. I'm so fucking deep, sugar. Do you know what this does to the head of my cock? It's like a torch, blazing and burning, because of you. Nobody else does this to me, S. Nobody ever will."

The sultry, naughty cadence of his words started to have an accompaniment. As his cock contacted the depths of her ass, it rubbed against that magic juncture inside her, where the eyes-into-the-back-of-her-head orgasms lived. Sage recognized the pressure as soon as it intensified, and she moaned in surprise.

"Mmmm," Garrett affirmed at her shoulder. "Somebody's G-spot just got woken up." With a husky laugh, he trailed his hand back into the vortex of her thighs, from the front now. "That means it's time to rouse S's hot little cunt again too."

"Uh—that's okay, Master—we don't really need to—" How the hell could she tactfully tell him that his wicked lip service, along with the illicit invasion in her ass and the increasingly hard knocks on her G-spot, were working plenty

fine for a lead-up to her *Very Happy Camper* stamp for
tonight? If he added his sinfully long fingers back into the mix,
playing with her pussy like he had been—

She let out a shriek of both agony and ecstasy.
Everything, *everything,* was alive from the tip of her engorged
clit to the nerves around her back opening. She'd never felt
such an insane mix of throbbing pain and utter stimulation
before. With every moment that passed, she thought she was
going to shatter. And incredibly, the pleasure intensified. She
needed it to stop. She never wanted it to end.

"Tell me." The voice of her Master echoed in her head,
demanding she listen and obey. "Tell me what you desire now,
S."

She struggled to make him happy. She really did. But
thoughts alone were impossible, let alone converting them to
words. "I—I—"

He bit her ear lobe in primal possession. "Do you still
want my fingers teasing your hard little clit?"

"Oh." It was more gasp than voice. "Y-yes."

"Do you still want my huge cock in your tiny ass?"

"Yes. Oh, yes!"

"Do you want me to drive it into you until I come?
Until my hot white milk drenches everything inside you?"

He damn-near spiraled her into oblivion. She was a
shuddering, needing mess. Heat, pain, arousal, absolution,
completion…every moment brought them all and more. Her
world had become this, a string of utterly perfect, utterly
sublime moments, each one better than the last. Dear God, she
was going to explode. Dear God, she *hoped* to explode.

"Aggghhh," she finally choked. "Y-yes. Yes, Master!"

His huge body tightened against her. Crap on a freaking
stick! How did he still function at all, let alone like his muscles
had morphed into cast iron, when she felt like a runny egg?

"Yes what?" he prompted, nibbling her ear again.

She gulped and forced the words to form. "Yes, I want
your cock deep inside me."

"And what else?"

"I want your cum deep inside me too."

"That's beautiful, sugar. Now say it again."

"I want your cum inside me, Master." The plea came more easily this time. Saying the filthy words for herself unlocked even more delicious lust in every cell of her sex, in every corner of her mind. She gave it all to him with eager abandon. It was what he demanded. It was what she needed. "Please...come deep in my ass."

He answered her with a long, pleased groan. "Sweet sugar, that's thoroughly what I intend."

His breath got hotter and heavier along her neck. He fingered her clit more feverishly while wrapping his other arm around her waist. He ripped the breath from her lungs as he drove even deeper into her backside, now filling her to the hilt with his bulging cock. Sage tried to relax, to give him extra room, but he was too big, too hard, too consuming. He took the space he needed, eclipsing everything but the power of his cock in her body and the pressure he was building in her pussy. Thought ceased to matter. Even feelings ceased to matter. She only craved the detonation. It was coming. It was coming...

"I'm gonna spill it, sugar." His voice came on hard chuffs of breath. "And you're going over with me." His fingers jerked her throbbing nub to a painful, beautiful precipice. Just as she felt her body hurling over that edge, he did one more thing. With his other hand, he tugged both the strings on the nipple clamps. As he did, he yelled a single command. "Now, S! We're coming now!"

Torment and release. The fire of pure pain, the rain of pure ecstasy. A scream of unthinking agony—and glory. It all collided in her conscious, washed together by the flood that Garrett gave her, drenching her in his seed, surrounding her with his body, drowning her in his domination. It was an orgasm unlike any she'd had before. Hell, it was unlike *a lot* of things she'd felt before. It rolled over her again and again, even after he set her hands free from the cuffs, letting her fall forward across the bed. Sage used the freedom to get more leverage, rocking her body back against his. "More," she begged. "Don't stop. Please!"

Garrett laughed softly. "I think that can be arranged, my

love."

"Thank you." She pressed her head against the mattress, and wasn't surprised when the tears started to flow. She let them come this time. All of them. The massive freedom he'd given her body had also emancipated a huge chunk of the pressure in her soul, and now it poured from her in a catharsis that could've never been possible otherwise. It was magic, a miracle, one of the most precious gifts Garrett had ever given her.

Garrett. Her hero. Her love. And now, her incredible Master.

S couldn't have been happier.

Chapter Twenty-One

Garrett pulled her tighter in his lap as a cool night breeze soughed through the cedars and pines before sweeping across the lake in a soft *shoosh*. The summer sky stretched above like cobalt silk woven with silver and lavender thread.

None of it was more breathtaking than the woman in his arms.

He bent his head to watch the light from the fire pit flicker on her face. Sage had always stopped the air in his chest with those spring green eyes, the classic slant of her nose, those full lips so perfectly made for his…but tonight, her beauty arrested him in a million new ways. He'd seen her face etched in agony then set free by it. He'd seen her lips open in the heights of ecstasy, the depths of torment, the unbound glory of being torn apart by a climax from the inside out. He'd seen her sweet body open for him in the same way she'd opened her heart to exploring this with him, with the unbound joy of a perfect submissive.

When he'd slipped the diamond on her finger last year, he'd never thought he could love her more.

The Sage who'd come back to him from the dead had proved him so fucking wrong about that.

She broke into his thoughts with her soft giggle against his chest.

"What?" he asked, stroking her hair.

"I was just thinking about the phone call I had with Josie today. We were talking about she and Wyatt coming back out for a visit before the baby gets here. I was thinking of what they might think about the renovation to the guest room."

Garrett added his chuckle to hers. "I don't think they'll mind staying in the new guest room at all."

"Me neither." She gave him a cute little bite on her bottom lip before leaning up to kiss him. "Thank you," she whispered, "for working so hard."

"Well, it's not done yet," he protested. "There's room

for a few more things. And once I find where we can rig things—"

Sage kissed him into silence. "I didn't mean the play room." Her gaze glittered up at him, rivaling the sky in for spectral conviction. "I meant the work you did on *you*. Coming to the place where you could accept this in yourself, embracing it, translating it into what was good for us…" She chewed her lip again, though this time he watched her use it to fight back tears. In the end, she lost the fight. "I know how hard it must have been," she whispered. "The courage it must have taken." She slipped the tips of her fingers to his jaw. "You've given me such a gift."

He shook his head. No. She had it wrong, and he had to set her straight. *He'd* given *her* a gift? Where the hell did she get that from?

"Sage. No. Don't you see? You—"

She slid her fingers to his lips. "I see things just fine. I see *you* perfectly." Her mouth took the place of her fingers, spreading the warmth of her adoration into him with slow, sweeping circles. When she finally pulled away, a smile of pure love lingered on her lips. "My hero."

Hell. He felt traitorous stings behind his own eyes now. "My heart."

"I love you, Master."

"I love *you,* my little S."

"Thank you for saving me."

"No, my sweet submissive. Thank you…for saving me."

Made in the USA
Middletown, DE
13 May 2015